W9-BLM-373

RARITAN PUBLIC LIBRARY
54 E. SOMERSET STREET
RARITAN, NEW JERSEY 08869
908-725-0413

2/19

The Red Address Book

The Red Address Book

SOFIA LUNDBERG

Translated by

ALICE MENZIES

Houghton Mifflin Harcourt
Boston   New York   2019

First U.S. edition

Copyright © 2017 by Sofia Lundberg
English translation copyright © 2019 by Alice Menzies

All rights reserved

For information about permission to reproduce selections from this book, write
to trade.permissions@hmhco.com or to Permissions, Houghton Mifflin Harcourt
Publishing Company, 3 Park Avenue, 19th Floor, New York, New York 10016.

hmhco.com

First published in Sweden in 2017 as *Den röda adressboken* by Forum
Published by agreement with Salomonsson Agency

Library of Congress Cataloging-in-Publication Data
Names: Lundberg, Sofia, 1974–author. | Menzies, Alice translator.
Title: The red address book / Sofia Lundberg ;
translated by Alice Menzies. Other titles: den röda adressboken.
English Description: First U.S. edition. |
Boston : Houghton Mifflin Harcourt, 2019.
Identifiers: LCCN 2018001420| ISBN 9781328473011 (hardcover) |
ISBN 9781328473516 (ebook)
Subjects: LCSH: Older women — Fiction. | Reminiscing in old age — Fiction.
Classification: LCC PT9877.22.U535 R6313 2019 | DDC 839.73/8 — DC23
LC record available at https://lccn.loc.gov/2018001420

Book design by Greta D. Sibley

Printed in the United States of America
DOC 10 9 8 7 6 5 4 3 2 1

For Doris, heaven's most beautiful angel
You gave me air to breathe and wings to fly.

And for Oskar, my most precious treasure

The Red Address Book

1

The saltshaker. The pillbox. The bowl of lozenges. The blood-pressure monitor in its oval plastic case. The magnifying glass and its red bobbin-lace strap, taken from a Christmas curtain, tied in three fat knots. The phone with the extra-large numbers. The old red-leather address book, its bent corners revealing the yellowed paper within. She arranges everything carefully, in the middle of the kitchen table. They have to be lined up just so. No creases on the neatly ironed baby-blue linen tablecloth.

A moment of calm as she looks out at the street and the dreary weather. People rushing by, with and without umbrellas. The bare trees. The gravelly slush on the asphalt, water trickling through it.

A squirrel darts along a branch, and a flash of happiness twinkles in her eyes. She leans forward, following the blurry little creature's movements carefully. Its bushy tail swings from side to side as it moves lithely between branches. Then it jumps down to the road and quickly disappears, heading off to new adventures.

It must almost be time to eat, she thinks, stroking her stomach. She picks up the magnifying glass and with a shaking hand raises it to her gold wristwatch. The numbers are still too small, and she has no choice but to give up. She clasps her hands calmly in her lap and closes her eyes for a moment, awaiting the familiar sound at the front door.

"Did you nod off, Doris?"

An excessively loud voice abruptly wakes her. She feels a hand on her shoulder, and sleepily tries to smile and nod at the young caregiver who is bending over her.

"I must have." The words stick, and she clears her throat.

"Here, have some water." The caregiver is quick to hold out a glass, and Doris takes a few sips.

"Thank you . . . Sorry, but I've forgotten your name." It's a new girl again. The old one left; she was going back to her studies.

"It's me, Doris. Ulrika. How are you today?" she asks, but she doesn't stop to listen to the answer.

Not that Doris gives one.

She quietly watches Ulrika's hurried movements in the kitchen. Sees her take out the pepper and put the saltshaker back in the pantry. In her wake she leaves creases in the tablecloth.

"No extra salt, I've told you," Ulrika says, with the tub of food in her hand. She gives Doris a stern look. Doris nods and sighs as Ulrika peels back the plastic wrap. Sauce, potatoes, fish, and peas, all mixed together, are tipped out onto a brown ceramic plate. Ulrika puts the plate in the microwave and turns the dial to two minutes. The machine starts up with a faint whirr, and the scent of fish slowly begins to drift through the apartment. While she waits, Ulrika starts to move Doris's things: she stacks the newspapers and mail in a messy pile, takes the dishes out of the dishwasher.

"Is it cold out?" Doris turns back to the heavy drizzle. She can't remember when she last set foot outside her door. It was summer. Or maybe spring.

"Yeah, ugh, winter'll soon be here. The raindrops almost felt like tiny lumps of ice today. I'm glad I've got the car so I don't have to walk. I found a space on your street, right outside the door. The parking's actually much better in the suburbs, where I live. It's hopeless here in town, but sometimes you get lucky." The words stream from Ulrika's mouth, then her voice becomes a faint hum. A pop song; Doris recognizes it from the radio. Ulrika whirls away. Dusts the bedroom. Doris can hear her clattering around and hopes she doesn't knock over the vase, the hand-painted one she's so fond of.

When Ulrika returns, she is carrying a dress over one arm. It's burgundy, wool, the one with bobbled arms and a thread hanging from the hem. Doris had tried to pull it loose the last time she wore the dress, but the pain in her back made it impossible to reach below her knees. She holds out a hand to catch it now, but grasps at thin air when Ulrika suddenly turns and drapes the dress over a chair. The caregiver comes back and starts to loosen Doris's dressing gown. She gently pulls the arms free and Doris whimpers quietly, her bad back sending a wave of pain into her shoulders. It's always there, day and night. A reminder of her age.

"I need you to stand up now. I'll lift you on the count of three, OK?" Ulrika places an arm around her, helps her to her feet, and pulls the dressing gown away. Doris is left standing there, in the kitchen, in the cold light of day, naked but for her underwear. That needs changing too. She covers herself with one arm as her bra is unhooked. Her breasts fall loosely toward her stomach.

"Oh, you poor thing, you're freezing! Come on, let's get you to the bathroom."

Ulrika takes her hand and Doris follows her with cautious, hesitant steps. She feels her breasts swing, clasps one arm tight against them. The bathroom is warmer, thanks to the under-floor heating beneath the tiles, and she kicks off her slippers and enjoys the warmth beneath the soles of her feet.

"Right, let's get this dress on you. Lift your arms."

She does as she is told, but she can raise her arms only to chest height. Ulrika struggles with the fabric and manages to pull the dress over Doris's head. When Doris glances up at her, Ulrika smiles.

"Peekaboo! What a nice color, it suits you. Would you like some lipstick as well? Maybe a bit of blusher on your cheeks?"

The makeup is set out on a little table by the sink. Ulrika holds up the lipstick, but Doris shakes her head and turns away.

"How long will the food be?" she asks on her way back to the kitchen.

"The food! Ah! What an idiot I am, I forgot all about it. I'll have to heat it up again."

Ulrika hurries to the microwave, opens the door and slams it shut again, turns the dial to one minute, and presses start. She pours some lingonberry juice into a glass and places the plate on the table. Doris wrinkles her nose when she sees the sludge, but hunger makes her lift the fork to her mouth.

Ulrika sits down across from her, with a cup in her hand. The hand-painted one, with the pink roses. The one Doris herself never uses, for fear of breaking it.

"Coffee, it's liquid gold, it is," Ulrika remarks. "Right?"

Doris nods, her eyes fixed on the cup.

Don't drop it.

"Are you full?" Ulrika asks after they have been sitting in silence for some time. Doris nods and Ulrika gets up to clear away the plate. She comes back with steaming coffee in yet another cup. A dark blue one, from Höganäs.

"There you go. Now we can catch our breath for a moment, hmm?"

Ulrika smiles and sits down again.

"This weather, nothing but rain, rain, rain. It feels like it's never ending."

Doris is just about to reply, but Ulrika continues:

"I wonder if I sent any extra socks to the nursery. The little ones will probably get soaked today. Oh well, there must be spares they can borrow. Otherwise I'll be picking up a grumpy sockless kid. Always this worrying about the kids. But I suppose you know what it's like. How many children do you have?"

Doris shakes her head.

"Oh, none at all? You poor thing, so you never get any visitors? Have you never been married?"

The caregiver's pushiness surprises Doris. These young women don't usually ask this kind of question, at least not so bluntly, anyway.

"But you must have friends? Who come over occasionally? That looks thick enough, anyway." She points to the address book on the table.

Doris doesn't answer. She glances at the photo of Jenny. It's in the hallway, but the caregiver has never even noticed it. Jenny, who is so far away and yet always so close in her thoughts.

"Well, listen," Ulrika continues. "I've got to rush off. We can talk more next time."

Ulrika loads the cups into the dishwasher, even the hand-painted one. Then she turns the machine on, gives the counter one last wipe with the dishcloth, and before Doris knows it, she's out the door. Through the window, she watches Ulrika pull on her coat as she walks, and then climb into a little red car with the agency's logo on the door. With shuffling steps, Doris makes her way to the dishwasher and pauses the wash. She pulls out the hand-painted cup, carefully rinses it, and then hides it at the very back of the cupboard, behind the deep dessert bowls. She checks from every angle. It's no longer visible. Pleased, she sits back down at the kitchen table and smooths the tablecloth with her hands. Arranges everything carefully. The pillbox, the lozenges, the plastic case, the magnifying glass, and the phone are all back in their rightful places. When she reaches for the address book, her hand pauses, and she allows it to rest there. She hasn't opened it in a long time, but now she lifts the cover and is met by a list of names on the first page. Most have been crossed out. In the margin, she has written it several times. One word. *Dead.*

The Red Address Book
A. ALM, ERIC

So many names pass by us in a lifetime. Have you ever thought about that, Jenny? All the names that come and go. That rip our hearts to pieces and make us shed tears. That become lovers or enemies. I leaf through my address book sometimes. It has become something like a map of my life, and I want to tell you a bit about it. So that you, who'll be the only one who remembers me, will also remember my life. A kind of testament. I'll give you my memories. They're the most beautiful thing I have.

It was 1928. It was my birthday, and I had just turned ten. The minute I saw the parcel, I knew it contained something special. I could tell from the twinkle in Pappa's eyes. Those dark eyes of his, usually so preoccupied, were eagerly awaiting my reaction. The present was wrapped in thin, beautiful tissue paper. I followed its texture with my fingertips. The delicate surface, the fibers coming together in a jumble of patterns. And then the ribbon: a thick red-silk ribbon. It was the most beautiful parcel I had ever seen.

"Open, open!" Agnes, my two-year-old sister, leaned eagerly over the dining table with both arms on the tablecloth, and received a mild scolding from our mother.

"Yes, open it now!" Even my father seemed impatient.

I stroked the ribbon with my thumb before pulling both ends and untying the bow. Inside was an address book, bound in shiny red leather, which smelled sharply of dye.

"You can collect all your friends in it." Pappa smiled. "Everyone you meet during your life. In all the exciting places you'll visit. So you don't forget."

He took the book from my hand and opened it. Beneath *A,* he had already written his own name. *Eric Alm.* Plus the address and phone number for his workshop. The number, which had recently been connected, the one he was so proud of. We still didn't have a telephone at home.

He was a big man, my father. I don't mean physically. Not at all. But at home there never seemed to be enough room for his thoughts. He seemed to be constantly floating out over the wider world, to unknown places. I often had the feeling that he didn't really want to be at home with us. He didn't enjoy the little things of everyday life. He was thirsty for knowledge, and he filled our home with books. I don't remember him talking much, not even with my mother. He just sat there with his books. Sometimes I would crawl into his lap in the armchair. He never protested, just pushed me to the side so I didn't get in the way of the letters and images that had caught his interest. He smelled sweet, like wood, and his hair was always covered with a thin layer of sawdust, which made it look gray. His hands were rough and cracked. Every night, he would smear them with Vaseline and wear thin cotton gloves as he slept.

My hands. I held them around his neck in a cautious embrace. We sat there in our own little world. I followed his mental journey as he turned the page. He read about different countries and cultures, stuck pins into a huge map of the world that he had nailed on the wall. As though they were places he had visited. One day, he said, one day he would head out into the world. And then he added numbers to the pins. Ones, twos, and threes. He was ordering the various locations, prioritizing them. Maybe he was suited to life as an explorer?

If it hadn't been for his father's workshop. An inheritance to look after. A duty to fulfill. He obediently went to the workshop every morning, even after Farfar died, to stand next to an apprentice in that drab space, with stacks of boards along each wall, surrounded by the sharp scent of turpentine and mineral spirits. My sister and I were usually allowed to watch only from the doorway. Outside, white roses climbed the dark-brown wooden walls. As their petals fell to the ground, we and the neighborhood children would collect them and place them in bowls of water; we made our own perfume to splash on our necks.

I remember stacks of half-finished tables and chairs, sawdust and wood chippings everywhere. Tools on hooks on the wall; chisels, jigsaws, carpentry knives, hammers. Everything had its rightful place. And from his position behind the woodworking bench, my father, with a pencil tucked behind one ear and a thick apron of cracked brown leather, had a view over it all. He always worked until dark, whether it was summer or winter. Then he came home. Home to his armchair.

Pappa. His soul is still here, inside me, beside me. Beneath the pile of newspapers on the chair he made, with the rush seat my mother wove. All he wanted was to venture out into the world. And all he did was leave an impression within the four walls of his home. The highly crafted statuettes, the rocking chair he made for Mamma, with its elegantly ornate details. The wooden decorations he painstakingly carved by hand. The bookshelf where some of his books still stand. My father.

2

Even the smallest movements require mental and physical exertion. She moves her legs forward a few millimeters and then pauses. Places her hands on the armrests. One at a time. Pause. She digs in her heels. Grips the armrest with one hand and places the other on the dining table. Sways her upper body back and forth to get some momentum. Her chair has a high, soft back support, and the legs rest in plastic cups, which raise it a few centimeters. Still, it takes her a long time to get to her feet. On the third attempt she manages it. After that, she has to stand still for another second or two, with her head bowed and both hands on the table, waiting for the dizziness to pass.

Her daily exercise. The stroll around her small apartment. Down the hallway from the kitchen, around the sofa in the living room, pausing to pick any withered leaves from the red begonia in the window. Then on to her bedroom, and her writing corner. To the laptop computer, which has become so important to her. She gingerly sits down, in yet another chair resting on plastic supports. They make the chair so high, she can barely fit her thighs beneath the desk. She lifts the lid of the computer and hears the faint, familiar whirr of the hard drive waking up. She clicks the Internet Explorer icon on the desktop, and the online version of her newspaper greets her. Every day, she is amazed by the fact that the entire world exists inside this tiny little computer. That she, a lonely woman in Stockholm, could keep in touch with people all over the world, if she wanted to. Technology fills her days. It makes waiting for death a little more bearable. She sits here every afternoon, occasionally even in the early morning or late at night, when sleep refuses to co-operate. It was her last caregiver, Maria, who taught her how it all worked. Skype, Facebook, email. Maria had said that no one was too old to learn something new. Doris agreed, and said that no one was too old to realize her dreams. Shortly after that, Maria handed in her notice so that she could resume her studies.

Ulrika doesn't seem so interested. She has never mentioned the computer or asked what Doris is up to. She just dusts it in passing as she sweeps through the room, ticking off task after task on her to-do list. Maybe she's on Facebook, though? Most people seem to be. Even Doris has an account, the one Maria set up for her. She also has three friends. Maria is one. Then there's her great-niece, Jenny, in San Francisco, plus Jenny's older son, Jack. Doris checks in with their lives every now and then, follows images and events from another world. Sometimes she even studies their friends' lives. Those with a public profile.

Her fingers still work. They're a little slower than they used to be, and sometimes they start to ache, forcing her to rest. She writes to gather her memories. To get an overview of the life she has lived. She hopes it will be Jenny who finds everything later, once Doris herself is dead. That it will be Jenny who reads and smiles at the pictures. Who inherits all of her beautiful things: the furniture, the paintings, the hand-painted cup. They won't just be thrown out, will they? She shudders at the thought, brings her fingers to the keys, and starts to write, in order to clear her thoughts. *Outside, white roses climbed the*

dark-brown wooden walls, she writes today. One sentence. Then a
sense of calm as she navigates through a sea of memories.

The Red Address Book
A. ~~ALM, ERIC~~ DEAD

Have you ever heard a real roar of despair, Jenny? A cry born of desperation? A scream from the very bottom of the heart, which digs
its way into every last atom, which leaves no one untouched? I have
heard several, but each has reminded me of the very first, and most
terrible.

It came from the inner yard. There he stood. Pappa. His cry
echoed from the stone walls, and blood pulsed from his hand, stain-
ing red the layer of frost covering the grass. There had been an accident in his workshop, and a piece of metal was wedged in his wrist.
His cry ebbed, and he sank to the ground. We ran down the steps
and into the yard, toward him; there were many of us. Mamma tied
her apron around his wrist and held his arm in the air. Her cry was
as loud as his when she shouted for help. Pappa's face was worry-
ingly pale, his lips a shade of bluish-purple. Everything that happened next is a haze. The men carrying him to the street. The car
that picked him up and drove him away. The solitary dry white rose
growing on the bush by the wall, and the frost embracing it. Once
everyone had gone, I stayed where I was in the yard and stared at it.
That rose was a survivor. I prayed to God that my pappa would find
the same strength.

Weeks of anxious waiting followed. Every day, we would see
Mamma pack up the remains of breakfast — the porridge, milk, and
bread — and head off to the hospital. She would often come home
with the food parcel unopened.

One day, she came home with Pappa's clothes draped over the

basket, which was still full of food. Her eyes were swollen and red from crying. As red as Pappa's poisoned blood.

Everything stopped. Life came to an end. Not just for Pappa, but for all of us. His desperate cry that frosty November morning was a brutal end to my childhood.

The Red Address Book
S. SERAFIN, DOMINIQUE

The tears at night weren't mine, but they were so constant that sometimes I would wake and think they were. Mamma started sitting in the rocking chair in the kitchen once Agnes and I had gone to bed, and I got used to falling asleep to the accompaniment of her sobs. She sewed and she cried; the sound came in waves, through the room, across the ceiling, to us children. She thought we were sleeping. We weren't. I could hear her sniffing and swallowing, trying to clear her nose. I felt her despair at having been left alone, no longer able to live securely in Pappa's shadow.

I missed him too. He would never sit in his armchair again, deeply absorbed in a book. I would never be able to crawl into his lap and follow him out into the world. The only hugs I remember from my childhood are the ones Pappa gave me.

Those were difficult months. The porridge we ate for breakfast and dinner became more and more watery. The berries, which we had picked in the forest and then dried, started to run out. One day, Mamma shot a pigeon with Pappa's gun. It was enough for a stew, and it was the first time since he had died that we were all full, the first time the food had made our cheeks flush, the first time we had laughed. But that laughter would soon die out.

"You're the oldest, you'll have to look after yourself now," she said, pressing a scrap of paper into my hand. I saw the tears brimming in her green eyes before she turned away and, with a wet cloth, began frantically rubbing at the plates we had just eaten from. The kitchen we stood in at the time, so long ago, has become a kind of museum of childhood memory for me. I remember everything in detail. The skirt she was busy sewing, the blue one, draped over the stool. The potato stew and the foam that had run over during cooking, drying down the side of the pot. The lone candle, which bathed the room in a dim glow. My mother's movements between the sink and the table. Her dress, which swung between her legs when she moved.

"What do you mean?" I managed to ask.

She paused but didn't turn to look at me.

I continued. "Are you kicking me out?"

No reply.

"Say something! Are you kicking me out?"

She looked down at the sink.

"You're a big girl now, Doris. You have to understand. It's a good job I've found for you. And as you can see, the address isn't too far away. We'll still be able to see each other."

"But what about school?"

Mamma looked up and stared straight ahead.

"Pappa would never have let you take me out of school. Not now! I'm not ready!" I shouted at her. Agnes whimpered anxiously in her chair.

I slumped down at the table and burst into tears. Mamma came to sit next to me and placed her palm on my forehead. It was still cold and damp from the dishwater.

"Please don't cry, my love," she whispered, pressing her head to mine. It was so quiet that I could almost hear the heavy tears rolling down her cheeks, mixing with my own.

"You can come home every Sunday, that's your day off."

Her comforting whisper became a faint murmur in my ears. Eventually, I fell asleep in her arms.

I woke the next morning to the brutal and undeniable truth that I was being forced to leave my home and my security for an unfamiliar address. Without protesting, I took the bag of clothes that Mamma held out to me, but I couldn't look her in the eye as we said goodbye. I hugged my little sister and then left without a word. I carried the bag in one hand, and three of Pappa's books, tied together with a thick piece of string, in the other. There was a name on the scrap of paper in my coat pocket, written in Mamma's ornate script: *Dominique Serafin.* That was followed by a couple of strict instructions: *Curtsy nicely. Speak properly.* I wandered slowly through the streets of Södermalm toward the address below the name: *Bastugatan 5.* That was where I would find my new home.

When I arrived, I paused for quite some time outside the modern building. Red window frames surrounding big, beautiful windows. The façade was made of stone, and there was an even walkway leading into the yard. It was a long way from the simple, weathered wooden house that had been my home until now.

A woman came out through the door. She was wearing glossy leather shoes and a shiny white dress without a defined waist. She had a beige cloche hat pulled down over her ears, and a small leather bag in the same shade hung from her arm. Ashamed, I ran my hands over my own worn, knee-length wool skirt, and wondered who would open the door when I knocked. Whether Dominique was a man or a woman. I couldn't know; I had never heard such a name before.

I walked slowly, my feet pausing on each step of the polished marble staircase. Two floors up. The double doors, made from dark oak, were taller than any doors I had ever seen. I took a step forward and lifted the knocker, a lion's head. The sound echoed faintly, and I stared straight into the lion's eyes. A woman dressed in black opened the door and curtsied. I began to unfold the note for her, but another woman appeared before I had time to finish. The woman in black moved to one side and stood with a straight back against the wall.

The second woman had reddish-brown hair, which she wore in two long braids wound into a thick bun at the nape of her neck. Around her neck hung several strings of white pearls, slightly varied in size and shape. Her three-quarter-length dress, with a pleated skirt, was made of shiny emerald-green silk, which rustled when she moved. She was wealthy; I knew that immediately. She looked me up and down, took a drag on the cigarette that she held in a long black holder, and then blew the smoke toward the ceiling.

"Well, what do have we here?" She had a strong French accent, and her voice was hoarse from smoking. "Such a pretty girl. You can stay. Come, come inside now."

With that, she turned and disappeared into the apartment. I remained where I was on the doormat, my bag in front of me. The woman in black nodded for me to follow her inside. She took me through the kitchen to the adjoining maids' bedroom, where the slender bed that would be mine stood alongside two others. I placed my bag on the bed. Without being told to, I picked up the dress lying there and pulled it over my head. I didn't know it at the time, but I would be the youngest of the three servants, left with the jobs the others didn't want.

I sat on the edge of the bed and waited, my feet pressed firmly together and my hands tightly clutched on my lap. I can still remember the feeling of loneliness that enveloped me in that little room; I didn't know where I was or what awaited me. The walls were bare and the wallpaper yellowed. There was a small bedside table next to each bed, with a single candle in a holder. Two half-burned down, one new, its wick still waxy.

It wasn't long before I heard loud footsteps on the tiles and the rustle of my new mistress's skirt. My heart was racing. She paused in the doorway, and I didn't dare meet her gaze.

"Stand up when I come into the room. There. Back straight."

I got up, and she immediately reached for my hair. Her slim, cool fingers moved all over me; she craned her neck and came closer, inspecting every millimeter of my skin.

"Nice and clean. That's good. You don't have lice, do you, girl?"

I shook my head. She continued to inspect me, lifting wisp after wisp of hair. Her fingers moved behind my ear; I felt her long nails scraping my skin.

"This is where they usually live, behind the ear. I hate creepy-crawlies," she mumbled, a shiver passing through her body. A ray of sunshine had found its way in through the window, highlighting the fine, downy hairs on her face, which rose above a layer of light powder.

The apartment was big and full of paintings, sculpture, and beautiful furniture in dark wood. It smelled of smoke and something else, something I couldn't quite place. It was always calm and peaceful during the day. Life had been kind to my employer, and she never had to work; she was well-off enough. I don't know where her money came from, but sometimes I fantasized about her husband. About her keeping him locked up in the attic somewhere.

Guests often came over in the evening. Women in beautiful dresses and diamonds. Men in suits and hats. They entered, wearing their shoes indoors — a practice I find odd even to this day — and strolled around the drawing room as though it was a restaurant. The air filled with smoke and conversations in English, French, and Swedish.

My nights in the apartment introduced me to ideas I had never heard of before. Equal pay for women, the right to education. Philosophy, art, and literature. And new behaviors. Loud laughter, furious arguments, and couples kissing openly in the bay windows and corners. It was quite a change.

I would crouch down when I crossed the room to collect glasses and mop up spilled wine. High heels moved unsteadily between the rooms; sequins and peacock feathers floated to the floor and became wedged between the hallway's broad wooden tiles. I would have to lie there until the early hours, using a small kitchen knife to remove every last trace of the festivities. When Madame woke, everything had to be perfect again. We worked hard. She expected freshly ironed table runners every morning. The furniture had to be shiny, the glasses free of flecks. Madame always slept until late morning, but when she eventually left her bedroom, she would walk through the apartment, inspecting it one room at a time. If she found anything noteworthy, it was always me, the youngest, who got the blame. I quickly learned what she might spot, and would do one last loop through the apartment before she woke, righting the things the other maids had done wrong.

The few hours of sleep I got on the hard horsehair mattress were never enough. The seams of my black uniform irritated my skin, and I was constantly tired from the long days. And from the hierarchy and the slaps. And from the men who laid their hands on my body.

The Red Address Book
N. NILSSON, GÖSTA

I was used to people occasionally falling asleep after having too much to drink. It was my job to wake them and send them on their way. But this man wasn't asleep. He was staring straight ahead. The tears ran slowly down his cheeks, one by one, as his eyes focused on an armchair where another man — young, with a halo of golden-brown curls — was sleeping. The young man's white shirt was unbuttoned, revealing a yellowed undershirt. On the tan skin of his chest, I could see a tattoo of an anchor, unsteady lines in greenish-black ink.

The man noticed me.

"You're upset, sorry, I . . ." I hurried to leave.

The man turned his head, lowering his shoulder to the leather armrest so that he was now half-lying across the chair.

"Love is impossible," he slurred, nodding toward the other armchair.

I tried to make my voice sound firm. "You're drunk. Please, sir, get up; you need to leave before Madame wakes." His hand gripped mine as I struggled to pull him to his feet.

"Don't you see, miss?"

"Don't I see what?"

"That I'm suffering!"

"Yes, I can see that. Go home and sleep it off, and your suffering will feel a little lighter."

"Just let me sit here and look at this perfection. Let me enjoy this perilous electricity."

His words became tangled as he attempted to capture his mood. I shook my head.

It was my first meeting with this delicate man, but it certainly wouldn't be the last. Often, as the apartment emptied and the new day dawned over the rooftops of Södermalm, he lingered, lost in thought. His name was Gösta. Gösta Nilsson. He lived farther down the street, at Bastugatan 25.

"One can think so clearly at night, young Doris," he would say whenever I asked him to leave. Then, with drooping shoulders and a bowed head, he would stagger off into the night. His cap was never straight, and the tattered old jacket he wore was too big; it hung slightly lower on one side, as though his back was crooked. He was handsome. Often tan, his face had classical features — a straight nose and thin lips. There was plenty of goodness in his eyes, but he was usually sad. His spark had gone out.

Only after several months did I realize that he was the artist whom Madame worshiped. His paintings hung in her bedroom, huge canvases featuring brightly colored squares and triangles. No theme to speak of, just explosions of color and shape. Almost as if a child had been let loose with a brush. I didn't like them. Not at all. But Madame bought and bought. Because Sweden's Prince Eugen did the same. And because surrealist modernity had a particular power that most people couldn't understand. She appreciated the fact that Gösta, like her, was an outsider.

It was Madame who taught me that people come in many different shapes. That others' expectations of us are not always right. That there are many routes to choose from on the journey we are all making toward death. That we might find ourselves at difficult junctions, yet the road may still straighten. And that the curves aren't dangerous.

Gösta always asked a lot of questions.

"Do you prefer red or blue?"

"To which country would you travel if you could go anywhere at all on earth?"

"How many one-öre sweets can you buy with one krona?"

After that last question, he always tossed me a krona. He flicked it into the air with his index finger and, with a smile, I caught it.

"Spend it on something sweet, promise me that."

He could see that I was young. That I was still a child. He never reached to touch my body the way the other men did. He never made comments about my lips or budding breasts. Sometimes he even helped me in secret: picking up glasses and taking them to the corridor between the dining room and kitchen. Whenever Madame noticed, she would slap me afterward. Her thick gold rings left red marks on my cheeks. I covered them with a pinch of flour.

3

"Hi, Auntie Doris!"

The small child grins and waves frantically, so close to the computer screen that only his fingertips and eyes are visible.

"Hi, David!" She waves back and then raises her hand to her mouth to blow him a kiss. At that very moment, the camera swings to one side, and her kiss lands on the mother. She smiles when she hears Jenny's laugh. It's infectious.

"Doris! How are you? How are things this week?" Jenny cocks her head and moves so close to the camera, only her eyes are visible. Doris laughs.

"I'm OK, don't worry about me." She shakes her head. "The girls come over every day to check on me. But enough about this old dame. What have you been up to? How are the kids? Have you been finding time to write?"

"Ah no, not this week. It's hard, with the kids. But maybe someday I'll start finding more time, when they're a bit older."

"Jenny, if you keep putting it off, someday might never come. You've always wanted to write. You can't fool me. Try to find the time."

"Yeah, maybe one day. But right now, the kids are most important. Look, let me show you something. Tyra took her first steps yesterday, look how cute she is."

Jenny turns the computer toward her young daughter, who is on the floor, chewing the corner of a magazine. She whimpers when Jenny lifts her. Refuses to stand on her own, slumps back down as soon as her feet touch the floor.

"Come on, Tyra, walk, please. Show Auntie Doris." Jenny tries again, speaking in Swedish this time: "Stand up now, show her what you can do."

"Just leave her be. When you're one, magazines are much more exciting than an old lady on the other side of the world."

Jenny sighs. Moves into the kitchen, with the computer in her arms.

"Have you redecorated?"

"Yeah, didn't I tell you? It looks good, right?" Jenny spins around with the computer, making the furniture blur into nothing but lines. Doris follows the room with her eyes.

"Very nice. You have an eye for interiors, you always did."

"Oh, I don't know about that. Willie thinks it's too green."

"And you think . . . ?"

"I like it. I love light green. It's the same color Mom had in her kitchen, do you remember? In that little apartment in New York."

"It wasn't in New York, was it?"

"Yeah, the brick building, do you remember? The one with the plum tree in the tiny little garden."

"In Brooklyn, you mean? Yes, I remember. With the big dining table that didn't quite fit."

"Yeah, exactly! I'd completely forgotten about that. Mom refused to give it up when she divorced that lawyer, so they had to saw it in two to get it into the room. It was so close to the wall that I had to suck my stomach in to sit on one side of it."

"Oh yes, life was certainly never boring in that house." Doris smiles at the memory.

"I wish you could come for Christmas."

"Yes, me too. It's been so long. But my back is too bad. And my heart. My traveling days are probably over."

"I'll keep hoping anyway. I miss you."

Jenny turns the computer toward the counter and stands with her back to Doris.

"Sorry, but I just need to make Tyra a quick snack." She takes out bread and butter, lifts her whining daughter onto one hip.

Doris waits patiently while Jenny butters the bread.

When she returns to the screen, Doris asks, "You seem tired, Jenny. Is Willie helping you out enough?" Tyra presses the bread to her face, sitting on Jenny's lap now. The butter smears across Tyra's cheeks, and she pokes out her tongue to reach it. Jenny is holding her with one arm, and she uses the other to pick up a glass of water and take a big sip.

"He does his best. He's got a lot going on at work, you know? He doesn't have time."

"What about the two of you, do you have time for each other?"

Jenny shrugs.

"Almost never. But it's getting better. We just need to make it through this, the baby years. He's good, he struggles a lot too. It's not easy supporting an entire family."

"Ask him for help. So you can get some rest."

Jenny nods. Kisses Tyra on the head. Changes the subject.

"I really don't want you to be alone over Christmas. Isn't there anyone you can celebrate with?" Jenny smiles at Doris.

"Don't worry about me, I've spent plenty of Christmases alone. You've got enough to think about as it is. Just make sure the children have a good Christmas and I'll be happy. It's a children's holiday, after all. Let me see, I've said hello to David and Tyra, but where's Jack?"

"Jack!" Jenny shouts loudly, but there's no answer. She swings around, and Tyra's bread drops to the floor. The little girl starts to cry.

"JACK!" Jenny's face is red. She shakes her head and picks up the bread from the floor. Blows gently on it and hands it back to Tyra.

"He's hopeless. He's upstairs, but he . . . I just don't understand him. JACK!"

"He's growing up. Like when you were a teenager yourself, do you remember?"

"Do I remember? No, not at all." Jenny laughs and covers her eyes with her hands.

"Oh yes, you were a wild child, you were. But look how well you turned out. Jack will be fine too."

"I hope you're right. Sometimes being a parent is such a thankless task."

"It goes with the territory, Jenny. It's meant to be that way."

Jenny straightens her white shirt, notices a lick of butter, and tries to rub it off.

"Ugh, my only clean shirt. What am I going to wear now?"

"You can't even see it. That shirt suits you. You always look so pretty!"

"I never have time to get dressed up these days. I don't know how the neighbors do it. They've got kids too, but they still look perfect. Lipstick, curled hair, heels. If I did all that, I'd look like a cheap hooker by the end of the day."

"Jenny! You've got the wrong idea. When I look at you, I see a natural beauty. You get it from your mother. And she got it from my sister."

"You're the one who was a real beauty in her day."

"At one point in time, maybe. We should probably both be happy, don't you think?"

"Next time I fly over, you'll have to show me the pictures again. I never get tired of seeing you and Grandma when you were young."

"If I live that long."

"No, stop it! You're not going to die. You have to be here, my darling Doris, you have to . . ."

"You're big enough to realize that we're all going to die one day, aren't you, my love? It's the one thing we can be completely sure of."

"Ugh. Please stop that. I have to go now, Jack has football practice. If you hang on, you can talk to him when he comes down. Speak again next week. Take care."

Jenny moves the computer to a stool in the hallway and shouts for Jack again. This time, he appears. He's wearing his football uniform, his shoulders as wide as a doorway. He runs down the stairs two at a time, his eyes fixed on the floor.

"Say hi to Auntie Doris." Jenny's voice is firm. Jack looks up and nods toward the small screen and Doris's curious face. She waves.

"Hi, Jack, how are you?"

"*Ja,* I'm fine," he says, replying in a mixture of Swedish and English. "Gotta go now. *Hej då,* Doris!"

She raises her hand to her mouth to blow him a kiss, but Jenny has disconnected her.

The bright San Francisco afternoon, full of chatter and children and laughter and shrieking, is replaced by darkness and loneliness.

And silence.

Doris shuts down the computer. She squints up at the clock above the sofa, the pendulum swinging back and forth, with its hollow ticking. In time with the pendulum, she rocks back and forth in her seat. She doesn't manage to get up, remains where she is to gather her strength. She places both hands on the edge of the table and gets ready for another attempt. This time, her legs obey her, and she takes a couple of steps. Right then, she hears the front door opening.

"Ah, Doris, are you getting some exercise? That's nice to see. But it's so dark in here!"

The caregiver hurries into the apartment. Turns on all of the lights, picks things up, clatters around, talks. Doris shuffles into the kitchen and sits down on the chair closest to the window. Slowly organizes her things. Moves them around so that the saltshaker ends up behind the phone.

The Red Address Book
N. NILSSON, GÖSTA

Gösta was a man of many contradictions. At night, and in the early hours of the morning, he was fragile, full of tears and doubts. But in the evenings preceding those moments, he was desperate for attention. He lived off it. Needed to be at the center of the discussion. Climbed onto the table and broke into song. Laughed more loudly than anyone else. Shouted when political opinions differed. He was happy to talk about unemployment and female suffrage. But most of all, he spoke about art. About the divine in the act of creation. What the fake artists would never understand. I once asked him how he could be so sure he was a genuine artist himself. How did he know it wasn't the other way around? He pinched me hard in the side and subjected me to a long tirade about cubism and futurism and expressionism. The blank look on my face was like fuel. It ignited his laughter.

"You'll understand one day, young lady. Form, line, color. It's so fantastic that, with their help, you can capture the divine principle behind all life."

I think that he enjoyed my lack of understanding. That he was relieved when I didn't take him as seriously as the others did. It was like sharing a secret. We could be walking side by side through the apartment; he would hang back, then jump forward, from time to time, to resume our pace. "Soon I'll say that the young lady has the greenest eyes and the most wonderful smile that I've ever seen," he would whisper, and my face would always flush, the same shade of red. He wanted to make me happy. In that alien environment, he became my comfort. A replacement for the mother and father I missed so dearly. He always sought my eye when he arrived, as if to check that I was OK. And he asked questions. It's odd; certain people feel particularly drawn to each other. That was how it was with Gösta and me. After just a few meetings, he felt like a friend, and I always looked forward to his visits. It seemed he could hear what I was thinking.

Occasionally, he would bring company when he came over. It was almost always some young, tan, muscular man, far removed, in both style and demeanor, from the cultural elite who generally frequented Madame's parties. These young men usually sat quietly in a chair, waiting while Gösta emptied glass after glass of deep red wine. They always listened intently to the conversation, but never joined in.

I saw more than that, once. It was late at night, and I had stepped into Madame's room to fluff up her pillows before she went to bed. Gösta's arm was around a young man's hip. He let go, as though he had burned himself. They were standing close together, face to face, in front of two of Gösta's paintings, which were propped against the bed. Neither said anything, but Gösta looked me straight in the eye and held a finger to his mouth. I plumped the pillows with one hand and left the room. Gösta's friend disappeared into the hallway and out the front door. He never came back.

They say that madness and creativity go hand in hand. That the most creative among us are those who stand closest to gloominess, sadness, and obsessional neuroses. At the time, no one thought like that. Back then, feeling unhappy was considered ugly. It wasn't something people talked about. Everyone had to be happy all of the time. Madame with her impeccable makeup, her smooth hair and glittering jewels. No one heard her anguished weeping at night, once the apartment had fallen silent and she was left alone with her thoughts. She probably threw her parties to keep those thoughts at bay.

Gösta attended for the same reason. Loneliness drove him from his apartment, where his many unsold canvases were stacked against the walls, a constant reminder of his poverty. He was often marked by the sober melancholy I had noticed when we first met. When in that state, he would remain seated until I forced him out. He always wanted to return to his Paris. To the good life he had loved so dearly. To the friends, the art, the inspiration. But he never had the money. Madame provided him with the dose of Frenchness he needed to survive. One short moment at a time.

"I can't paint anymore," he sighed one evening.

"Why do you say that?" I never knew how to respond to his gloominess.

"It amounts to nothing. I don't see pictures anymore. I don't see life in clear colors. Not like before."

"I don't understand any of that." I forced a smile. Rubbed his shoulder with one hand.

What did I know? A girl of thirteen. Nothing. I knew nothing about the world. Nothing about art. To me, a beautiful painting was one that depicted reality as I understood it. Not by means of distorted, colorful squares forming equally distorted figures. I thought it was probably a stroke of luck that Gösta could no longer produce those terrible paintings that Madame stacked in her wardrobe in order to put food on his table. But later, I would find myself pausing, feather duster in hand, in front of his work. The confusion of colors and brushstrokes occasionally managed to catch my imagination, letting it run wild. I saw something new. With time, I learned to love that feeling.

The Red Address Book
S. SERAFIN, DOMINIQUE

She was restless. I'd heard that from the other girls. The parties kept her removed from everyday life; the moves kept her removed from boredom. Her upheavals were always sudden, unpredictable, yet there was always a reason for them. She had found a new apartment that was bigger, better, in an area with a higher status.

Almost one year to the day after our first meeting, she came into the kitchen. Stood with her hip and shoulder against the brickwork beside the wood stove. With one hand, she played with the brim of her hat, the strap beneath her chin, her necklace, her rings. Nervously, as though she was the maid and we were the masters. As though she was a child about to ask an adult for permission to take a cookie. Madame, who otherwise stood so straight, with her head held high. We curtsied and probably all thought the exact same thing: we were about to lose our jobs. Poverty scared us. With Madame, we had an abundance of food, and despite the tough working days, our lives were good. We stood in silence, our hands clasped in front of our aprons, stealing furtive glances at her.

She hesitated. Her eyes wandered among us, as though she faced a decision she didn't want to make.

"Paris!" she eventually exclaimed, flinging her arms wide. A small vase on the mantelpiece fell victim to her sudden euphoria. The small fragments of china scattered between our feet. I immediately bent down.

Silence descended over the room. I felt her eyes on me and looked up.

"Doris. Pack your bag, we're leaving tomorrow morning. The rest of you can go home, I don't need you anymore."

She waited for a reaction. Saw the tears welling up in the others' eyes. Caught the anxiety in mine. No one said a word, so she turned, paused for a moment, and then quickly left the room. From the corridor, she shouted:

"We're taking the train at seven. You're free until then!"

And so, the next morning, I found myself in a shaky third-class carriage en route to the southern tip of Sweden. All around me, strangers twisted and turned on the hard wooden benches; those worn seats gave my backside splinters. The carriage smelled musty, like sweat and thick, damp wool, and it was full of people clearing their throat and blowing their nose. At every station, someone would leave and someone new would board. Every now and then, a person transporting a cage of hens or ducks between parishes would appear. The birds' droppings smelled pungent, and their piercing squawks filled the carriage.

Few times in my life have I felt as lonely as I did on that train. I was on my way toward my father's dream, which he had shown me in books, back when my childhood was still secure. But during that ride, the dream felt more like a nightmare. Just a few hours earlier, I had run along Södermalm's streets as fast as my legs would carry me, desperate to get to my mother's apartment in time to hug her and say goodbye. She smiled, the way mothers do, swallowed her sadness, and held me tight. I felt her heart pounding hard and fast. Her hands and forehead were damp with sweat. She must have been crying earlier, because her nose was blocked and I didn't recognize her voice.

"I wish you enough," she whispered in my ear. "Enough sun to light up your days, enough rain that you appreciate the sun. Enough joy to strengthen your soul, enough pain that you can appreciate life's small moments of happiness. And enough friends that you can manage a farewell now and then."

She fought her way through these words, which she so wanted

to say, but then she could no longer hold back the tears. Eventually she let go of me and went back inside. I heard her mumbling, but I didn't know whether the words were directed at me or at her.

"Be strong, be strong, be strong," she repeated.

"I wish you enough too, Mamma!" I shouted after her.

Agnes lingered in the yard. She clung to me when I tried to leave. I asked her to let go, but she refused. Eventually, I had to pry her chubby little fingers off my arms and run as fast as I could, so she couldn't catch up with me. I remember the dirt beneath her fingernails and her gray wool hat, dotted with small red embroidered flowers. She cried loudly as I left, but soon fell silent. Probably because my mother had gone outside to fetch her. Even now, I regret not turning around. Regret not taking the opportunity to wave goodbye to them.

My mother's words became a guiding light in my life, and just thinking of them has always given me strength. Enough strength to make it through the hardships to come.

The Red Address Book
S. SERAFIN, DOMINIQUE

I remember the moon, a thin sliver against a pale-blue backdrop, and the rooftops beneath it, the laundry hanging on the balconies. The smell of coal smoke from the hundreds of chimneys. The train's rhythmic pounding had become a part of my body over the long journey. Day had just started to dawn as we finally approached Gare du Nord after many long hours and several changes. I got up and leaned out of the third-class window. Breathed in the scent of spring and waved to the street children running barefoot along the tracks, their hands outstretched. Someone tossed them a coin, which halted them abruptly. They flocked around the small piece of treasure and started to fight over who would get to keep it.

I kept a tight hold on my money. I held it in a small, flat leather purse, knotted to the waistband of my skirt with a white ribbon. At regular intervals I reached down to check that it was still there. Ran my hand over the soft corners I could feel beneath the fabric. My mother had slipped the purse into my hand just before I left, and it contained all the money she had been saving, money she used only in special circumstances. Perhaps she loved me after all? I was so angry with her, often thought that I never wanted to see her again. But at the same time, I missed her so unfathomably much. Not a day went by without my thinking about her and Agnes.

That purse was my one source of comfort as I rolled toward my new life. Its weight against my stomach kept me calm. Then the wheels screeched loudly as the brakes were applied. I clasped my hands to my ears, making the man across from me smile. I didn't smile back, just hurried to leave the train.

A porter was lifting Madame's luggage onto a black iron trolley. I waited next to that growing mountain, my own bag wedged between my feet. The young porter ran back and forth. His face was glistening with sweat, and when he used his shirtsleeve to wipe his brow, it turned brown with dirt. Bags, trunks, round hatboxes, chairs, and paintings were stacked on top of one another on the soon-overloaded trolley.

People were pushing past us. The long, dirty skirts of the poorer passengers swept by the glossy shoes and neatly pressed trousers of the upper-class men. But the elegant ladies waited on board, in the first-class car. Only when the platform was empty, and the second- and third-class passengers had disappeared, did they slowly, in their high heels, descend the three iron steps.

Madame's face broke into a smile when she saw me waiting. The first words to leave her mouth weren't, however, a greeting. She sighed about the long journey and her boring travel companions. About her aching back and the uncomfortable heat. She mixed French and Swedish, and I quickly got lost, though she didn't seem bothered by my lack of responses. She turned on her heel and started walking toward the station building. The porter and I followed her. He pushed the trolley ahead, using his hip to manage the weight. I grabbed the metal pole at the front and pulled, to help him. I carried my small suitcase in my other hand. My dress was damp with sweat and I caught its musty, sharp odor with every step I took.

The arrivals hall, with its elegant green cast-iron pillars, was full of people moving in every direction across the stone floor. The sound of their footsteps echoed loudly. A small boy in a light-blue shirt and black shorts started following us, waving a pink rose in the air. His lank bangs hung limp over a pair of bright blue eyes, which stared at me, pleading. I shook my head, but he was stubborn, holding out the flower and nodding. His hand begged for money. Behind him was a girl with two thick brown braids. She was selling bread, and her brown dress, much too big for her, was dotted with flour. She held out a piece to me and waved it back and forth, so that

I would catch its freshly baked scent. I shook my head again and sped up, but the two children did the same. A man in a suit blew a huge cloud of smoke into the air ahead of me. I coughed loudly, which made Madame laugh.

"Are you shocked, my dear?"

She stopped.

"It's nothing like Stockholm. Oh, Paris, how I have missed you!" she continued, smiling broadly before launching into a long tirade in French. She turned to the children and said something in a firm voice. They looked at her, the girl curtsied and the boy bowed, and they ran away, footsteps pattering.

Outside the station building, a chauffeur was waiting for us. He held open the back-seat door of a high black car. It was my first-ever car ride. The seats were made of the softest leather, and when I sat down, the scent of it rose, and I breathed it in deeply. It reminded me of my father.

The floor of the car was covered in small Persian rugs; red, black, and white. I made sure to place my feet on either side of them, so as not to get them dirty.

Gösta had told me about the streets, about the music and the smells. The ramshackle buildings of Montmartre. I stared aimlessly out the window and saw the beautifully ornate white façades rushing by. There, in the exclusive neighborhoods, Madame would have fit in, like all the other elegant ladies. Pretty dresses and expensive jewelry. But that wasn't where we stopped. She didn't want to fit in. She wanted to stand out in contrast to her surroundings. To be someone who caused others to react. For her, the unusual was normal. That was why she collected artists, authors, and philosophers.

And it was precisely to Montmartre that she took me. We slowly climbed its steep slopes and eventually pulled up at a small building with peeling plasterwork and a red wooden door. Madame was delighted, her laughter filling the car. As she eagerly waved me in, to the stale, musty rooms, she radiated energy. The few pieces of furniture were covered in sheets, and Madame moved from one room to the next, pulling them back. Revealing colorful fabrics and dark woodwork. The style of the house reminded me strongly of her apartment in Södermalm. Here too were paintings, many paintings, hung in double rows on the walls. A muddle of themes, a variety of styles. A glorious mishmash of modern and classical. And there were books everywhere. In the living room alone, she had three tall bookshelves built into the wall, holding row upon row of beautiful leather-bound books. Beside one of them stood a ladder on runners, which made it possible to reach the volumes at the very top.

Once Madame had left the room, I stood by the shelves, scanning the names of famous authors. Jonathan Swift, Rousseau, Goethe, Voltaire, Dostoyevsky, Arthur Conan Doyle. I had only heard people speak of these names; now their books were all here. Full of ideas I had heard of, but not understood. I took a volume from the shelf, only to discover it was in French. They were all in French. Exhausted, I slumped into an armchair and mumbled the few words I knew. *Bonjour, au revoir, pardon, oui.* I was tired from the journey and everything I had seen. I couldn't keep my eyes open.

When I woke, I found that Madame had draped a crocheted blanket over me. I pulled it tight around my body. The wind was blowing in through one of the windows, and I got up to close it. Then I sat down to write a letter to Gösta, something I had promised myself I would do as soon as I arrived. I gathered all my first impressions and jotted them down as well as I could, with the meager language of a thirteen-year-old. The sound of the train platform beneath my feet as I crossed it, the smells surrounding me, the two children with the bread and the flower, the street musicians I heard from the car, Montmartre. Everything.

I knew he would want to hear it all.

4

"You'll be seeing a new girl next week. A temp." Ulrika articulates every word, a touch too loudly. "I'm off to the Canary Islands."

Doris tries to shrink back, but Ulrika leans toward her and raises her voice even more.

"It's going to be so nice just to get away for a while and take it easy. Activity club for the kids, so we can relax on the beach chairs. Sun and warmth. Imagine that, Doris. All the way to the Canary Islands. You've never been, have you?"

Doris studies her. Ulrika is folding laundry, sloppily and hurriedly, crumpling the arms of Doris's tops. She stacks everything in a pile. Her words pour out as the heap grows.

"Maspalomas, that's the name of the place. Might be a bit touristy, but it's a very nice hotel. It wasn't expensive either. Only cost a thousand kronor more than one that was much worse. The kids'll be able to play in the pool all day. And on the beach. There's a nice long beach there, with huge dunes. The sand comes all the way from Africa; it blew over."

Doris turns away and looks out the window. She picks up the magnifying glass and searches for the squirrel.

"You old folks think we're crazy, jetting off all over the place constantly. My grandma always wants to know why I'm going away when we've got it so good at home. But it's fun. And it's good for the kids to see a bit of the world. Anyway, all set, Doris. The laundry's folded. Time to get you in the shower. Are you ready?"

She gives Ulrika a strained smile, lowers the magnifying glass, and places it on the table. In its exact place; she turns it slightly to get the right angle. The squirrel never turned up. She wonders where it is. What if it's been run over by a car? It's always scampering to and fro across the road. She jumps when she feels Ulrika's fingers digging into her armpits.

"One, two, and threeee!"

Ulrika quickly helps Doris to her feet and then holds her hands for a moment, until the worst of the dizziness has passed.

"Let me know when you're ready, and we'll slowly make our way over to your very own spa."

Doris nods feebly.

"Imagine if you had a real spa at home. With a jacuzzi and massages and facials. That would be something, hmm?" Ulrika laughs gently at this fantasy. "I'll buy you a face mask on vacation, and when I come back I'll give you a bit of extra care. It'll be fun."

Doris nods and smiles at Ulrika's chatter, refraining from comment.

When they reach the bathroom, Doris holds out her arms and lets Ulrika pull off her top and trousers, exposing her naked body. She takes a couple of cautious steps into the shower. Sits down on the edge of the high white stool with the perforated seat that the home-care company gave her. She holds the showerhead close to her body and lets the warm water run over her. Shuts her eyes and enjoys the feeling. Ulrika leaves her alone, goes out into the kitchen. Doris turns up the temperature and hunches her shoulders. The sound of running water has always had a calming effect on her.

The Red Address Book
S. ~~SERAFIN, DOMINIQUE~~ DEAD

I found a special place. An open square some distance from the house. La place Émile-Goudeau had a bench and a pretty fountain: four women holding a dome above their heads. The fountain radiated strength, and I loved the sound of the droplets trickling down over the figures' ankle-length dresses. It reminded me of Stockholm, of Södermalm, and its closeness to the water. Paris had only the Seine, but it was some distance from Montmartre, and the long days at Madame's house made it difficult to get down there. That was why the fountain in the square became my refuge.

I sometimes went over there in the afternoon while Madame slept, and I would write my letters to Gösta. We wrote to each other often. I gave him snapshots, glimpses of everything he was missing. The people, the food, the culture, the places, the views. His artist friends. In return, he sent me snapshots of Stockholm. Of the things I missed.

Dear Doris,

The stories you send have become the elixir of life for me. They give me the courage and strength to create. I am painting now like never before. The flowing stream of images conjured up by your words has also enabled me to see the beauty around me. The water. The buildings. The sailors on the pier. So much that I have missed until now.

You write so well, my friend. Perhaps you will become an author one day. Keep writing. If you feel the slightest of callings, never give up that feeling. We are born into art. It is a higher power, which we are given the honor to manage. I believe in you, Doris. I believe that the power to create is within you.

The rain is pouring down today, hitting the cobblestones so hard that I can hear its pounding from up here on the third floor. The skies here are so dull that I almost fear they will envelop my head if I go out. I stay in the apartment instead. Painting. Thinking. Reading. Sometimes I see a friend. But that means he has to come over here. I don't want to venture out into the bottomless depression that accompanies the late Swedish autumn. The darkness has never affected me as much as it does at this moment. I can just picture the beautiful autumn in Paris. The mild days. The bright colors.

Use your time wisely. I know you long for home. Though you never mention it, I can feel your anxiety. Enjoy the moments you find yourself in. Your mother and sister are well, so you have no cause for concern there. I shall visit them one day soon to make sure of that.

Thank you for the strength your letters give to me. Thank you, dearest Doris.

Write again soon.

I still have them, all of the letters I received. They're in a small tin box beneath my bed, and they have followed me through life. I read them sometimes. Think about how he saved me during those first few months in Paris. How he gave me courage to see the positives in that new city, which was so unlike my home. How he made me register everything that was happening around me.

I don't know what he did with my letters; perhaps he burned them in the open fire he often sat beside, but I remember what I wrote. I still recall the detailed scenes I captured for him. The yellow leaves falling on Parisian streets. The cold air finding its way in through the cracks around the windows, waking me at night. Madame and her parties, attended by artists like Léger, Archipenko, and Rosenberg. The house in Montparnasse, at 86 rue Notre Dame des Champs, where Gösta himself once lived. I sneaked in and saw what the stairwell was like, described every detail for him. Wrote which name was on each door. He loved it. He still knew many of the people who lived in the building, and he missed them. I wrote about Madame, how she wasn't throwing as many parties as she had in Stockholm, choosing to roam around the Paris night instead, looking for new artists and authors to seduce. About how she was sleeping longer and longer in the mornings, which gave me time to read.

I learned French, thanks to a dictionary and the books on her shelves. I began with the thinnest and worked up from there, novel by novel. Fantastic books that taught me so much about life and the world. Everything was there, gathered on her wooden shelves. Europe, Africa, Asia, America. The countries, the scents, the environments, the cultures. And the people. Living in such different worlds, and yet still so alike. Full of anxiety, doubt, hate, and love. Like all of us. Like Gösta. Like me.

I could have stayed there forever. My place was among the books; it was where I felt safe. But sadly that didn't last very long.

One day, on the way home from the butcher with a basket of freshly sliced charcuterie, I was stopped on the street. For one reason. Now, today, when my hunched body and wrinkled face hide every last trace of beauty, it feels good to admit it: once upon a time, I was very beautiful.

A man in a black suit rushed out of a car that had stopped dead in the heavy traffic. He took my head in his hands and stared straight into my eyes. My French was still far from perfect, and he spoke too quickly for me to understand his words. Something about how he wanted me. I was afraid, and tore myself from his grip. Ran as fast as I could, but he got back into the car, which followed me. It drove slowly, right behind me. When I reached Madame's house, I ran inside and slammed the door. Secured every lock.

The man pounded on the door. Pounded and pounded until Madame herself went to answer it. She swore at me in French.

At the very moment she opened the door, her tone changed, and she immediately invited the man inside. Glared at me and gestured for me to disappear. She stood up straight and strutted around him as if he was royalty. I didn't understand this. They vanished into the drawing room, but after just a few minutes she came rushing to me in the kitchen.

"Get washed, straighten yourself up! Take that apron off. *Mon dieu*, monsieur wants to see you."

She grabbed my cheeks between her thumb and forefinger. Nipped firmly several times to make the skin flush.

"There. Smile, my girl. Smile!" she whispered, pushing me ahead of her. I forced myself to smile at the man in the armchair, and he immediately got to his feet. Studied me from head to toe. Looked into my eyes. Ran his finger over my skin. Pinched the flesh around my slender waist. Sighed at my earlobes and flicked them with his fingers. Studied me in silence. Then he backed away and sat down again. I didn't know what I was meant to do, so I just stood there with my eyes fixed on the floor.

"*Oui!*" he eventually said, bringing both hands to his face. He got up again and spun me around.

"*Oui!*" he repeated, once I was finally standing still in front of him.

Madame tittered happily. Then something very strange happened. She invited me to sit down. On the sofa. In the drawing room. Together with them. She smiled at my wide eyes and waved firmly, as though to show that she was serious. I sat at the very edge of the seat, my knees firmly clenched together and my back straight.

I smoothed the black fabric of my maid's dress, which was crumpled where the apron had been, and listened attentively to the rapid French bouncing back and forth between the man and Madame. The few words I could understand provided no context at all. I still didn't know who was sitting in the armchair opposite me, nor why he was so important.

"This is Jean Ponsard, my girl," Madame suddenly said, in her French-tinged Swedish. As if I should know who that was. "He is a famous fashion designer, very famous. He wants you to be a live mannequin for his clothes."

I raised my eyebrows. A mannequin? Me? I barely knew what that meant.

Madame stared at me, expectation burning in those green eyes of hers. Her lips were slightly parted, as though she wanted to speak if I wouldn't.

"Don't you see? You'll be famous. This is every girl's dream. Smile!" Her irritation at my silence was so tangible that it made me shudder. She shook her head and snorted. Then she told me to pack my things.

Half an hour later, I found myself sitting in the back seat of Monsieur Ponsard's car. The bag in the trunk contained only clothes. No books. I had left those with Madame.

It was the last time I saw her. Much later, I found out that she had drunk herself to death. They had found her in the bathtub. Drowned.

5

"For she's a jolly good fellow, which nobody can deny..." Doris trails off mid-song and falls silent for a moment. "Or rather: which I cannot deny! Happy birthday, dear Jenny!" She continues singing, her eyes fixed on the screen and the smiling woman in front of her. Once she finishes, Jenny's children clap.

"Wonderful, Doris! Thank you so much! I can't believe you always remember."

"How could I forget?"

"I guess, how could you? Just think... When I came into your life, nothing was ever the same again, right?"

"No, my darling, that's when it got richer. How sweet you were! And well-behaved, laughing away in your playpen."

"I think your memories must be wrong there, Doris. I wasn't well behaved. All kids are difficult. Even me."

"Not you. You were born a little angel. You had *well-behaved* written on your forehead, I remember that with certainty." She raises her hand to her lips and blows a kiss, which Jenny pretends to catch, laughing.

"Maybe I was extra nice when you came. I needed you."

"Yes, I suppose you did. And I needed you. I'm convinced we needed each other."

"Need, I'll have you know. Can't you jump on a plane and fly over?"

"Uff, silly, of course I can't. Have you had your cake yet?"

"No, not yet. Tonight. Once all the kids are back from their activities. Half an hour before they go to bed. That's when we'll eat it." Jenny winks.

"You certainly need it. You look thin. Are you eating properly?"

"Doris, I genuinely think there might be something wrong with your eyes. Can't you see my muffin top?"

She pats her stomach and grabs a roll of fat between her fingers.

"All I see is a slim, beautiful mother of three. Don't go on a diet now, on top of everything else. You're perfect. A bit of cake every now and then won't do you any harm."

"You've always been a good liar. Do you remember when I was going to a dance at school and my dress was far too small? It was so tight that the seams split. But you found a solution straightaway, with that pretty silk scarf that you draped around my waist."

Doris's eyes glitter. "Yes, I remember it well. But you were actually a little chubby back then. It was when that dark and handsome chap . . . What was his name? Mark? Magnus?"

"Marcus. Marcus, my first great love."

"Yes, you were so sad when he broke up with you. You ate chocolate cookies for breakfast."

"For breakfast? I ate them constantly. All day long! I hid them all over my room. Like an alcoholic. *Chocoholic.* Gosh, I was so sad. And I got so fat!"

"Lucky you met Willie in the end. He got you in order."

"I don't know about order." She gestures toward the kitchen table and the piles of newspapers, dirty glasses, and toys.

"Well, at least you aren't fat," Doris says.

"No, OK, I know what you're getting at." Jenny laughs. "I'm not fat. Not like that."

"No, exactly. That sounds better. Where's Tyra? Is she sleeping?"

"Sleeping? No, that kid doesn't sleep. She's here." Jenny angles the screen so that Doris can see the little girl. The brightly colored pot that she is playing with has her undivided attention.

"Hello, Tyra," Doris coos. "What are you doing? Are you playing? What a nice pot you have there!"

The girl grins and shakes the pot in the air, making its contents rattle loudly.

"So she understands a little Swedish then?"

"Yes, of course. I speak only Swedish with her. Almost, anyway. And she watches Swedish kids' shows online."

"That's good. What about the others?"

"They're so-so. I talk to them in Swedish and they reply in English. I don't know how much Swedish they're actually picking up. I've started to forget certain words myself. It's not easy."

"You're doing the best you can, my love. Did you get my letter?"

"Yes, thank you! It arrived on time. And the money. I'll buy something nice with it."

"Something just for you."

"Yeah, or for us anyway."

"No, you know the rules. It has to be something only you want. Not the kids or Willie. You deserve a bit of luxury every now and then. A nice top. Some makeup. Or a trip to one of those spas people go to these days. Or, oh, I don't know, go out to dinner with a friend and spend the evening laughing."

"Yeah, yeah, we'll see. I'd like to take you out to dinner and laugh at old memories. We're coming next summer, I swear. The whole family. You have to . . ."

Doris frowns. "I have to what? Live until then?"

"No, that wasn't what I meant. Or yes, of course you have to live. You have to live forever!"

"Goodness me, I'm an old biddy, Jenny. I won't be able to get up on my own soon. Surely it's best to just die, no?" She studies Jenny with serious eyes, but then lights up and exclaims:

"But I'm not planning on dying before I get to squeeze that little cutie's cheeks! Isn't that right, Tyra? You and I need to meet. Don't we?"

Tyra holds up a hand and waves while Jenny blows kisses with both hands, waves goodbye, and turns off the camera. The screen, so recently full of life and love, turns black. How can silence be so overwhelming?

The Red Address Book
P. PONSARD, JEAN

It felt a bit like being sold. As though I had no other choice but to get into the back seat of that car and drive off toward the unknown. Wave goodbye to the secure life behind Madame's red painted door. She spoke my language. She had walked my streets.

Though we were sitting next to each other in the back of the car, Monsieur Ponsard didn't speak. Not for the entire journey. He just stared out the window. The car's tires bounced over the cobblestones as we drove down the hills, and I dug my fingers beneath the edge of the seat to hold on.

He was very handsome. I studied his hair, the strands of silver beautifully blended with the black. Combed to lie flat. The fabric of his suit shimmered in the light. His gloves were made of thin white leather; perfect, without a single fleck of dirt. His shoes were black, polished until they shone. I glanced down at my own dress. The black fabric looked filthy in the sunlight filtering in through the car window. I ran my hand over it. Picked off a few bits of dust, used my index finger to scrape away a spot of dried dough. That dough was probably still rising back at Madame's house.

He never asked me about myself. I don't think he even knew which country I came from. He wasn't interested in what was going on in my head. That might be one of the most degrading things you can subject someone to, not caring about their mind. The surface was all he was interested in. And he was quick to point out my flaws. My hair was too dry and too frizzy. My skin was too tan. My ears poked out when my hair was tied back. My feet were too big for a certain pair of shoes. My hips were too narrow or too wide, depending on which dress I was trying on.

My suitcase became my wardrobe. I hauled it in and out from

beneath my bed in the apartment I shared with four other live mannequins. We were all equally young, all equally lost. I never thought I would be staying there so long.

Watching over us was a matron with stern eyes and pursed lips. Her constant look of disapproval was reinforced by the wrinkles on her face. They meandered downward, from the corners of her mouth toward her chin. The sharp, deep lines on her upper lip made her look angry even when she fell asleep in her armchair in the living room. Her obvious hatred of the beautiful girls she was forced to live with manifested itself in many ways, such as her manic control of our food intake. There was to be no eating after six in the evening. Anyone arriving home later would have to go to bed hungry. She also didn't let us go out after seven. It was her job to make sure we got our beauty sleep.

She never talked to us. Whenever she had a spare moment, she would sit in a chair in the kitchen and knit tiny sweaters for a child. I always wondered who ended up wearing them. And whether she spent any time with the child. Whether it was hers.

We worked hard during the day. Long days. We put on beautiful dresses, which we showed off at department stores and occasionally in shop windows, holding our backs straight. Old ladies would nip us here and there with their fingers, feeling the fabric, studying the seams, complaining about small details to bring down the price. Sometimes we had to stand still in front of a camera hour after hour, posing. Turning the head, hands, and feet ever so slightly, to find the very best position. Standing perfectly still while the photographer pressed the button. That was what being a live mannequin involved.

With time, I learned what my face looked like from every possible camera angle. I knew that if I squinted just a little — not enough to wrinkle the skin beneath my eyes — my gaze would become more intense, even slightly mystical. I could shift the shape of my body through the mere tilt of a hip.

Monsieur Ponsard oversaw everything very closely. If we looked too pale, he would come over and pinch our cheeks himself. Always keeping his eyes fixed on something other than ours. Those thin, well-manicured fingers of his pinched firmly, and he would nod happily when he saw redness spread across our cheeks. We blinked the tears away.

6

"Are you crying?"

The temp comes over to where Doris is sitting with her elbows on the table and her head in her hands. She jumps and quickly wipes her cheeks.

"No, no," she replies, but the tremble in her voice gives her away. She pushes a couple of black-and-white pictures to one side, turns them upside-down.

"Could I have a look?"

Sara, that's her name, has been to see her a few times now. Doris shakes her head.

"They're nothing special. Just old pictures. Old friends who are no longer with us. Everyone dies. People try to live for as long as possible, but do you know what? Being the oldest is no fun. There's no point in living. Not when everyone else is dead."

"Do you want to show me? Show me a few of the people who meant something to you?"

Doris's fingers brush the stack of images. Then she pauses, her hand still.

Sara tries again. "Maybe you have a picture of your mother?"

Doris pulls a picture from the pile. Studies it for a moment.

"I didn't know her very well. Only my first thirteen years."

"What happened then? Did she die?"

"No, but it's a long story. Too long to be interesting."

"You don't need to tell me if you don't want to. Pick someone else instead."

Doris turns over a picture of a young man. He is leaning against a tree trunk, his feet crossed and one hand in his pocket. He's smiling, his white teeth lighting up his entire face. She quickly turns it upside-down again.

"Handsome. Who is he? Your husband?"

"No. Just a friend."

"Is he still alive?"

"I don't actually know. I don't think so. It's a long time since we last met. But it would be wonderful if he was." Doris smiles shrewdly and gently strokes the photograph with the tip of her index finger.

Sara puts an arm around Doris's shoulders, doesn't say anything. She is so different from Ulrika. Gentler and much kinder.

"Do you have to stop coming when Ulrika gets back? Can't you stay longer?"

"I can't, sadly. Once Ulrika is back, we're on the usual schedule again. But until then, we'll make sure we have a good time, you and I. Are you hungry?"

Doris nods. Sara takes out the foil carton and dishes the food onto a plate. She carefully separates the vegetables, meat, and mashed potato, which she smooths with a spoon. Once the food is warm, she slices a tomato and arranges the pieces in a pretty half-moon.

"There now. Looks good, doesn't it?" she exclaims happily, putting down the plate.

"Thanks, it's nice of you to dish it up like that."

Sara pauses and gives her a questioning look. "What do you mean, *like that*?"

The Red Address Book*

55

"You know, so nicely. Not all mixed together."

"Is your food usually mixed up? Doesn't sound so good." She wrinkles her nose. "We'll have to change that."

Doris smiles cautiously and takes a bite. The food really does taste better today.

"Pictures are so handy, though." Sara nods toward the pile of photographs on the table, next to two empty tin boxes. "They help us remember everything we might have forgotten otherwise."

"And everything we should have forgotten a long time ago."

"Was that why you were sad when I got here?"

She nods. Her hands are resting on the kitchen table. She brings them together, interlaces the fingers. They're dry and wrinkled, and her dark-blue veins almost seem to sit on top of the skin. She holds out a photo of a woman and a small child for Sara to look at.

"My mother and my sister," she says with a sigh, wiping away yet another tear.

Sara takes the picture, studies the two figures for a moment.

"You look like your mother; you have the same twinkle in your eye. It's the most beautiful thing when you can see the life in people's eyes."

Doris nods. "But they're all dead now. So far away. It hurts."

"Maybe you should sort them into two piles, then? One for the pictures that give you positive feelings, and one for the negative."

Sara gets up and starts rifling through the kitchen drawers.

"Here!" she shouts when she finds what she is looking for: a thick roll of tape. "We'll put all the negative pictures in one box. And then we'll wrap it in tape until there's no more left."

"You're full of ideas, you are!" Doris's eyes light up.

"Let's just do it!" Sara laughs. Once Doris is finished eating, Sara takes command of the stack of pictures. Holds them up one by one, and lets Doris point to the box where each should go. Sara doesn't ask questions, though her face reveals some curiosity about the people and places from the past who go flickering by. She calmly places the pictures in the boxes, upside-down so that Doris doesn't have to look at them. Many of the older black-and-white images end up in the negative pile. The modern color photographs, showing sweet giggling children, land in the positive. Sara studies Doris's face as she makes her decisions, gently strokes her back.

The stack is soon sorted. Sara winds the transparent tape round and round the tin box. Then she rummages through the drawer again, finds more rolls. She continues with the beige masking tape, then finishes with a few layers of silver tape. She giggles in satisfaction when she places the box in front of Doris.

"Try to get into that now!" Sara is beaming, and she raps the box with her knuckles.

The Red Address Book
N. NILSSON, GÖSTA

The sheet of paper was blank. I was tired. Had no words. Had no joy. I sat on the mattress, curled up against the wall, a cushion supporting my back. The room was green, and the color nauseated me. I wanted to get away from the wallpaper's symmetrical leaves and flowers. The flowers were big and plump, slightly lighter than the dark-green background, with stalks and leaves snaking around them. Every time I've seen similar wallpaper since, it has reminded me of my nights in that room. The idleness, the tiredness, the forced politeness among the girls. The aches in my body and the boredom in my soul.

I wanted to write to Gösta. Wanted to tell him everything he was longing to hear. But I couldn't. I couldn't manage even a few nice words about the city I had come to hate. The last golden rays of sunlight found their way in through the window, making the wallpaper even more loathsome. I slowly turned the pen so that the polished steel cast a glow on the opposite wall. A thin strip of light danced as I went over everything that had happened lately. Despairingly, I tried to transform my experiences into something positive.

My scalp ached, and I adjusted my hair, a strand hanging over my face, to lessen the pain as best I could. The hard, spiked rollers that were wound into my hair every morning left red marks, and sometimes even broke the skin. The hairdressers could be rough; they would pull and yank to achieve the perfect style. It was all about being as perfect as possible for whichever photo shoot or viewing we had ahead of us. But I was also expected to look equally beautiful the next day, and the day after that. I couldn't let holes in my scalp or skin problems get in the way, ruining the impression of a young, fresh-faced woman. The kind of woman everyone would want to be.

My appearance was my only asset, and I sacrificed everything for it. I went on diets. Squeezed my body into corsets and girdles. Applied face masks, homemade from milk and honey, in the evening. Rubbed horse liniment into my legs, to improve the circulation. Never happy, always on the hunt for more beauty.

I *was* beautiful. My eyes were big; my eyelids didn't droop. The color of my cheeks was pretty and even; this was before the sun's rays worked their way in and ruined the pigmentation. The skin around my neck was tight. But no cure in the world could improve my view of myself. We never know what we have until it's gone. That's when we miss it.

I suppose I was too caught up in my own unhappiness to write to Gösta. The environment I lived in was far removed from Gösta's idealized Paris. What would I write? That I longed to come home and cried myself to sleep at night? That I hated the noise of the traffic, the smells, the people, the language, the hustle and bustle? Everything that Gösta loved. Paris was a city where he felt free, but I was held prisoner in it. I put pen to paper and managed to scribble a few words. About the weather. I could describe that, at least. The stubborn sun that continued to shine day after day. The sticky heat on my skin. But what did he care about that? I ripped the sheet of paper to shreds and threw it away. The pieces floated down into the wastebasket to join all the other letters I'd never sent.

The buildings in the area of the department store were beautiful, ornately decorated, but the ground was all I saw. Because of the long, hard days, I could not discover and appreciate my surroundings. Most of all, I remember the smells as I walked home. Whenever I smell garbage, it reminds me of Paris. The streets were so dirty, the gutters full of rubbish. By the kitchen doors of restaurants, it wasn't unusual to see piles of fish guts, meat, and rotten vegetables.

Around the department store, everything was nice and clean, the errand boys in their tweed caps, white shirts, and vests sweeping carefully with their brooms. Gleaming cars, driven by chauffeurs in black suits, parked in a fan around the store, facing the sidewalk. I was fascinated by the elegant ladies who skipped gracefully along the streets, then in through the large doors. They became our audience. They never spoke to the live mannequins. Not a single word. They just studied us. From top to bottom, from bottom to top.

In the evening, I would often soak my feet in a bucket of ice-cold water. It stopped them from swelling after a long day in heels. The shoes I wore were often too small. Scandinavian girls tend to have big feet, but no one ever paid attention to that. The shoes had to fit everyone. They were size 37, or 38 if I was lucky. But my feet were 39s.

The weeks passed. It was the same routine over and over again. Long days, demanding hairstyles; raw, swollen feet; makeup that melted into your pores and made your skin burn. I scrubbed it off, using oil and a piece of paper. The oil got into my eyes, making my vision blur, and it was almost always with gritty eyes that I read the letters that arrived from Gösta at odd intervals.

Dear Doris,

What has happened? I feel sick with worry. Every day that passes without the postman bringing me word from you is a disappointment.

Please, let me know that you are living and doing well. Give me a sign.

Your Gösta

His anxiety became my security. I leaned against it. Played with it as though we were a pair of confused lovers with no hope of a future. I even placed a picture of him on my bedside table — a clipping

7

She rests her hand on the stack of printed sheets, slowly strokes the surface. Measures it with her finger. The pile reaches from the fingertip to the second knuckle of her index finger. What was supposed to be only a simple letter to Jenny has become so much more.

There are so many memories.

She starts to sort through the sheets and arranges them in piles by name. People who no longer exist. She opens her address book. The names are the only physical trace of those who could once laugh and cry. The dead become different in memory. She tries to picture their faces, tries to remember them as they were.

A tear falls heavily and lands at the top right-hand corner of the address book page, where, years ago, she had crossed out Gösta's name and written the word *DEAD*. The paper absorbs the liquid and the ink starts to spread. Small, swirling streams of sorrow.

A lonely home is so quiet, even the smallest sound grows loud. *Tick. Tick. Tick.* She listens to the white alarm clock with numbers as large as coins. Follows the red second hand on its way around the minute. Shakes it and picks it up to better see the numbers. It is two o'clock in the afternoon, isn't it? Not one? She holds the clock to her ear and listens; it continues to tick away. There's no doubting the eagerness of the second hand. She feels her stomach rumble; it's way past her usual lunchtime. Outside the kitchen window, the snowflakes are falling heavily. She can't see anyone out there, just a solitary car struggling up the hill. Once it disappears, the apartment falls silent again.

The clock strikes half past two. Three. Half past three. Four. Once the hour hand reaches five, Doris starts to rock gently back and forth in her chair. She hasn't eaten anything since the tasteless, plastic-wrapped cheese sandwich she had for breakfast. The one Sara left in the fridge on her last visit yesterday. She braces herself against the kitchen table and makes it onto her feet. She needs to get to the pantry. The box of chocolates Maria gave her before she left is still in there, a big, beautiful box with a picture of the crown princess and her husband. She put it there straightaway; it was too beautiful to open. But now she's far too hungry to care about that. A slight case of adult-onset diabetes also makes her sensitive to low blood sugar.

Her eyes are fixed on the door. She takes a few hesitant steps but has to stop when she starts seeing bright flashes of light. Small white stars forcing their way into her field of vision, making the room spin. She reaches out, tries to find the counter, but clutches at thin air and falls. The back of her head thuds against the wooden floor, as does her shoulder, and her hip is dealt a firm blow by the corner of a kitchen cabinet. The pain spreads quickly through her body as she lies on her back, on the hard floorboards, panting. The ceiling and walls become blurred, eventually fading into complete darkness.

When she regains consciousness, Sara is squatting next to her, a hand on her cheek. She is clutching a phone to her ear.

"She's awake now. What should I do?"

Doris struggles to keep her eyes open, but her lids droop. Her body is heavy on the floor. The uneven boards are pressing into the base of her spine.

One of her thighs is pointing to the side, and her leg seems to be twisted at an unnatural angle. Doris pats the leg gently with one hand and then groans loudly in pain.

"You poor thing, it must be broken. I've called for an ambulance, it'll be here soon."

Sara tries to hide her worry, and strokes Doris's cheek calmingly with her finger.

"What happened? Did you get dizzy? It's all my fault. The truck carrying the food crashed, and the entire delivery was late. I didn't know what to do, so I waited for it. And then there were so many other people to see. I should've come straight here, what with you having diabetes and everything... I'm so stupid! Doris, I'm so sorry!"

Doris tries to smile, but she can barely make her lips move, even less her hand to pat Sara on the cheek.

"Chocolate," she whispers quietly.

Sara looks over to the pantry.

"Chocolate, you want chocolate?"

Sara rushes over and searches among the cans and the bags of flour. At the very back of the cupboard, she finds the box of chocolates, and she tears back the thin plastic wrap and opens the lid. Carefully chooses a soft piece and holds it to Doris's mouth. Doris turns away.

"You don't want it?"

Doris sighs but doesn't manage to say anything.

"Were you trying to get to the chocolate? Was that where you were going?"

Doris tries to nod, but a wave of pain shoots down her spine, and she squeezes her eyes shut. Sara is still holding the chocolate in her hand. It's old; the surface has turned grayish-white. She breaks off a small piece and holds it out to Doris.

"Here, have a little bit in any case, to give you some energy. You must be starving."

Doris allows the chocolate to slowly melt against the roof of her mouth. When the paramedics arrive, it's still there. She closes her eyes and focuses on the sweet taste spreading through her mouth as the paramedics place their cold hands on her body. They unbutton her blouse and fasten electrodes to her chest. Link her up to machines measuring her heartbeat and blood pressure. Their voices seem to be directed at her, but she can't make out what they're saying. Doesn't have the energy to reply. Doesn't have the energy to listen. Keeps her eyes closed and dreams that she's somewhere safe. She jumps when they give her an injection for the pain. Whimpers quietly and clenches her fists when they try to straighten her leg. As they finally lift her onto the stretcher, she can't bear the pain any longer; she screams and hits the paramedic. Her tears well up and run slowly down her temple, forming a cold pool inside her ear.

8

The room is white. The sheets, the walls, the curtain around the bed, the ceiling. Not eggshell white, but blinding white. She stares up at the ceiling light in an attempt to stay awake, but her body is drowsy and just wants to sleep. She squints. The floor is the only thing that isn't white. Its dirty yellow color makes her realize that she isn't dead. Not yet. The light she is staring up at isn't heaven.

The pillow beneath her shoulders is lumpy, the small clumps of synthetic stuffing digging into her back. She slowly turns, but the movement sends a wave of pain through her pelvis, and she screws her eyes shut. She is lying in a twisted position now, and she can feel the strain from the effort in her side, but she doesn't dare move back, for fear of more pain. Her eyes and fingers are all she can safely move. She drums a slow melody with her index and middle fingers. Quietly hums the tune of a familiar song: *"The falling leaves . . . drift by my window . . ."*

"Here she is. No visitors, no family in Sweden. She's in a lot of pain."

Doris glances over to the door. She can see a nurse standing next to a man in a black suit. They're whispering, but she hears every word as though they were right next to her. They're talking about her as if she will soon be dead. The man nods and turns toward her. His white priest's collar glows against the black fabric of his suit. She squeezes her eyes shut. Wishes she wasn't so lonely, wishes Jenny was here, that she was holding her hand.

God, if you exist, make the priest go away, she thinks.

"Hello, Doris, how are you feeling?" The man pulls up a chair and sits down by her bed. Talks loudly and enunciates clearly. When she sighs, he places his hand on top of hers. It's warm and heavy against her cold skin. She looks at it. His veins loop like worms across his wrinkled skin. Just like hers. But his hand is tan and freckled. And younger. She wonders where he has been and whether he takes off his collar at the beach. She looks up at him to see whether she can make out a tan line on his neck. She can't.

"The nurse tells me you're in a lot of pain. How awful that you should fall like this."

"Yes." She whispers, but her voice still breaks with the effort. She tries to clear her throat, but she can feel the vibration in her pelvis, and she whimpers.

"It'll be fine, you'll see. I'm sure you'll be up and walking again very soon."

"I couldn't walk all that well before, either . . ."

"Well, we'll make sure you get back on your feet. Won't we? Do you need help with anything? The nurse said you hadn't had any visitors."

"My computer. I need my computer, it's back in my apartment. Can you help me with that?"

"Your computer? Yes, I can arrange that. If you just give me your keys. I heard you didn't have any family in Sweden. Is there anyone else? Anyone I can call?"

She snorts and fixes her eyes on him.

"Can't you see how old I am? My friends have all been dead a long time. You'll see, once you're my age. One by one, they all die."

"I'm sorry to hear that." The priest nods compassionately and looks her straight in the eye.

"For years, funerals were the only celebrations I went to. But now I don't even go to funerals anymore. I should probably start thinking about my own."

"We all die one day. No one can escape that."

Doris is silent.

"What are your thoughts on your funeral?"

"My thoughts? About the music, maybe. And who'll be there. If anyone will be there."

"What do you want them to play?"

"Jazz. I love jazz. I'd love it if they played some upbeat jazz. So they'll realize that the old biddy is having fun up there in heaven with all her old friends."

Her laughter turns into a cough. And yet more pain.

The priest gives her an anxious look, reaches out for her again.

"Don't worry," she manages between coughs, "I'm not afraid. If the heaven you priests always talk about really exists, it'll be great to get up there and see everyone."

"Everyone you miss?"

"And the others . . ."

"Who are you most looking forward to seeing?"

"Why do I have to choose?"

"No, of course you don't. Everyone has their importance, their own place in our hearts. It was a silly question." She can sense that he is studying her thin, feeble body.

She fights to stay awake, but the priest becomes more and more blurred, and his words blend together. Eventually, she gives up. Her head slumps gently to one side.

9

Even at night, it never gets dark in a hospital. Light from doors, windows, reading lamps, and corridors always finds its way between the eyelids, precisely when you need the darkness most. No matter how tightly she closes her eyes, it doesn't work — not that she could sleep anyway, with the effort that requires. The alarm button rests next to her right hand. She runs her thumb over it but doesn't press it. The chair the priest was sitting in earlier is now empty. She closes her eyes again. Tries to sleep, but if it isn't the light, it's the noise. The beeps when patients press their alarms. Someone in her room snoring. A door in the distance opening and closing. Feet wandering back and forth in the corridor. Some sounds are interesting, make her curious. Like the clatter of steel or the sound of someone receiving a text message. Others make her stomach turn. Old people crying out, spitting, farting, vomiting. She longs for morning, when the light and the bustle of the ward seem to absorb the very worst of the noise. Every day she forgets to ask for earplugs, but she doesn't want to bother the workers on the night shift.

Her sleeplessness makes the pain more tangible, despite the medicine. It radiates right down into her feet. In a few days, she's scheduled to have an operation. She needs a new hip joint; her own broke in the fall. She had shuddered when the nurse showed her the size of the screw, the one that will be driven into her bone, so she can get her movement back. Until then, she has to lie still, even though the hospital's physical therapist comes to see her every day, torturing her with small movements that seem impossible to carry out. It would be good if the priest came back with her computer soon. She doesn't dare hope; he's probably forgotten all about it. Her thoughts fade as she finally nods off.

When she wakes, the world outside the window is light. There is a small bird on the windowsill. It's gray, with a hint of yellow. A great tit, perhaps? Or maybe it's an ordinary house sparrow. She can't remember which of them is yellow. The bird fluffs up its feathers and plucks at its stomach with great concentration, on the hunt for irritating little insects. Her eyes follow its movements. She thinks about the squirrel back home.

The Red Address Book
P. PESTOVA, ELEONORA

Nora. So long since I last thought of her. She was straight out of a fairy tale, the most beautiful creature I'd ever met. The one everyone looked up to, wanted to be. Even me. She was strong.

I was still suffering with terrible homesickness. Not that I was alone in that, of course. At night, sporadic sobs could often be heard from the beds in the apartment on rue Poussin, but come morning, we would patiently get up, go to the ice cupboard, and get cold glass jars to hold beneath our eyes, to reduce the swelling. Then we would be made up and spend our days flashing fake smiles at rich ladies in the department store. We smiled so much that the muscles in our cheeks would sometimes ache when we got home.

Something happens to people who experience intense longing. Their eyes slowly dim, and they lose the ability to see the beauty in their surroundings, in their everyday life. The only way I could look was back. I embellished everything from my past, everything I could no longer be a part of.

Still, we endured; we were poor, and the opportunities drove us forward. We held our tongues. We put up with pins pricking our backs and hairstyles torturing our scalps.

But not Nora. She was always smiling. Perhaps it's not so strange — she was in great demand. Everyone wanted to work with her. While the rest of us posed and smiled in department stores, she was being photographed for Chanel and *Vogue*.

Eleonora Pestova — even her name was beautiful — came from Czechoslovakia. Her cropped hair was brown, and she had brilliant blue eyes. When she wore red lipstick, she looked just like Snow White. With the stiff girdle laced tight around her upper body and bottom, she embodied the boyish ideal we all strove for in the early

1930s. Back then, the dresses were straight and the skirts short, even if more feminine shapes were slowly becoming more popular. Today's newspapers write about young people being slaves to fashion, but you should have seen what it was like then!

While the rest of us walked to our bookings and had to make sure our makeup and hair stayed fresh, cars arrived to drive Nora around. We earned just enough to get by, but she made considerably more. She did buy nice bags and clothes, but luxury didn't seem to impress her. She spent her evenings curled up in bed with a book. On the bedside table that I shared with her, my picture of Gösta lived alongside her growing pile of books. Just as I had done while living with Madame, she used books to escape reality, and once she discovered that I shared her interest, she let me borrow a couple. I read them and then we sat together, night after night, curled up on the French balcony, smoking and talking about books. At least ten cigarettes per night; that was part of the diet prescribed for us. Fat girls got no work, and cigarettes — or, as they were known back then, diet cigarettes — were the miracle cure of the day. The nicotine made us giddy, so that we giggled at things that weren't even funny. Once the cigarettes stopped having an effect, we started drinking wine. We camouflaged it in large teacups, so that the matron wouldn't find out what we were up to.

Thanks to Nora and those happy evenings, Paris finally started to gain some color in my mind. I began writing to Gösta again. I no longer needed to lie; I just described what I saw all around me. I also borrowed from many of the authors I was reading, bulked up my letters with their vision of the city. On our days off, Nora and I would visit the places they wrote about. We fantasized about the nineteenth century, about the women's long, sweeping skirts; the street life, the music, the love, the romance. About life before the Depression that was now hanging over the world.

It was Nora who managed to get me my first shoot for *Vogue*.

She pretended to be ill and sent me in her place. As the car pulled up outside our door, she pushed me into it with a smile.

"Stand up straight. Smile. They won't notice any difference. They're expecting a beautiful woman, and that's what they'll get."

The car took me to a large industrial building on the outskirts of the city. There was a small metal sign on the door. Even now, I can remember the nondescript angular letters forming the photographer's name: *Claude Levi*. It was just as Nora had said. He nodded to me and pointed to a chair, where I sat to wait.

I watched as assistants carried in clothes, which they draped over wooden mannequins. Claude went to them several times, studying the clothes with the editor of *Vogue*. They picked out four dresses, all in shades of pink. The assistants brought out a number of necklaces: long ones, red ones, others made of glass beads. They turned to me. Studied me from head to toe.

"She looks different."

"Wasn't she brunette?"

"She's pretty; it'll be better with a blonde," the editor said, with an approving nod. Then they turned away from me again. As though I, a living and breathing person, wasn't there in the room. As though I was just one of the wooden mannequins.

I sat there until someone came to move me to another chair. There, my nails were painted red and makeup was applied; my hair was curled and sprayed with sugar solution. That left it stiff and heavy, so I kept my neck straight and my head still. I couldn't ruin the precisely positioned strands.

The camera stood in the middle of the room, on a wooden tripod. A small black box with a collapsible zoom made of pleated leather. Claude circled around it, moving it a few centimeters backward, forward, to one side. Searching for the right angle. I was lounging across a chair, with one arm draped over the backrest.

There were hands all over my body. Smoothing fabric, straightening necklaces, powdering my nose.

Claude barked out instructions. "Keep your head still! Twist your hand a millimeter to the right! The dress is crumpled!" When he was finally ready to take the pictures, I had to sit perfectly still until the shutters closed.

It could have ended there. With a pretty cover depicting a blonde woman in a pink dress.

But it didn't.

Once we were finished with the pictures for the magazine, Claude Levi came over to me. He asked me to pose for yet another photograph. An artistic image, he said. I kept the dress on while the makeup artists packed away their makeup, the hairdressers their brushes and bottles, the stylist and the editor the clothes and other things. The room was empty when he eventually asked me to lie down on the floor. He spread out my hair like a fan and fixed small birch leaves into it with pins. I felt proud as I lay there, proud that he had asked me. Acknowledged. He leaned over me, angled the tripod, and held the body of the camera with both hands. He told me to part my lips. I did as he said. He told me to look down the lens with desire in my eyes. I did as he said. He told me to touch the tip of my tongue to my top lip. I hesitated.

At that, he moved the camera to one side, took hold of my wrists, and held them above my head. Too firmly. His face moved closer to mine, and he kissed me. Forced his tongue between my teeth. I clenched my jaw and kicked my legs to break free. But my hair was stuck to the floor; the pins held fast. I closed my eyes, readied myself for the pain, and tore myself loose. Our heads collided, and he grabbed his forehead, swearing. I seized the opportunity, forcing my way past him and then breaking into a run. Straight through the door. Barefoot, without any of my things or even my own clothes. Wearing the dress I had been photographed in. He shouted *"Putain!"* after me, and the word echoed between the buildings. Whore!

I ran and I ran. Straight through the industrial area, in among the buildings. I cut myself on shards of glass, on stones. The soles of my feet were bleeding, but I didn't stop. The adrenaline made me keep going until I knew I was safe.

But I was completely lost. I sat down on a stone wall. The pink dress was drenched in sweat, and the fabric felt cold against my skin. As well-dressed Parisians passed by, I hid my bloody feet by pressing them against the wall. No one stopped. No one asked whether I needed help.

Day turned into evening, and I stayed where I was.

Evening turned into night, and I stayed where I was.

The torn soles of my feet had stopped bleeding when I eventually, very slowly, limped into a courtyard and stole a bicycle. An unlocked, rusty men's bike. I hadn't cycled since my childhood in Stockholm, and even then I hadn't done it especially often — only when the postman finished his round and let us children have a go on his. I wobbled down street after street. Saw the red sun rise and people wake. Caught the scent of bread ovens and wood stoves being lit. Tasted the salt of my own snot and tears. The streets felt more and more familiar, and I eventually saw Nora leap up from a bench by the rue d'Auteuil metro station and come running toward me. She cried out when she saw me. I was shaking from exhaustion.

We sat down on the sidewalk, close together as always. She pulled a cigarette from her pocket and listened patiently as I told her, between deep puffs, what had happened.

"We're not working with Claude anymore. I promise," she said, leaning her head against mine.

"We're not working with him anymore." I sniffed.

"It doesn't matter if it is *Vogue*."

"No, it doesn't matter if it is *Vogue*."

But it did matter. It wasn't the last time Nora worked for Claude. And it wasn't my last time either. That was just what life was like as a live mannequin. We didn't question it. A good job was a kind of affirmation, and saying no wasn't an option. But I made sure I was never left alone with him again.

The Red Address Book
N. NILSSON, GÖSTA

I was bedridden for weeks, with thick bandages around my feet. The room filled with the rank stench of pus and sickness. Monsieur Ponsard was furious because he had no replacement for me at the department store. He came to see me every day and muttered to himself when he noticed I wasn't making progress. I never dared tell him what had happened. That kind of thing just wasn't done back then.

One day, I received a letter from Gösta. It contained just one line, written in sprawling uppercase letters in the middle of the page.

I'M COMING SOON!

Soon, when was soon? The thought of possibly seeing him filled me with expectation, and I hoped I would finally get to walk with him through the city I had come to call my home. To see his Paris, to show him mine. I waited for him every day, but he never came. Nor did I receive any further letters providing an explanation or an arrival date.

Before long, my feet had healed and I could walk again. But Gösta remained silent. Every day when I came home, I would eagerly ask the matron whether there had been any visitors, any phone calls or letters. But the answer was always no. I can still remember the sarcastic, lopsided smile she gave me every time she stated the bad news. Her complete lack of compassion was infuriating.

Nora and I detested the matron as much as she detested us. When I think back, I can't even remember her name. I wonder whether I ever knew. To us, she was just *gouvernante*. Or, when she couldn't hear us, *vinaigre*.

Months passed before Gösta's next letter arrived.

Dear Doris,

These are difficult times in Stockholm. Perhaps the same is true of my beloved Paris? Unemployment is high, and people are saving their money rather than buying art. The payment for three canvases I sold has failed to materialize. I lack even the money to buy milk. I have no choice but to swap my paintings for food. As a result, a ticket to Paris is currently an unachievable dream. My dearest little Doris, once again I will not be able to come to you. I shall remain here. At Bastugatan 25. I wonder whether I will ever be able to leave this address. I continue to dream of the day I shall see you again.

Live! Astonish the world. I am proud of you.

Your friend,

Gösta

I'm sitting with that letter in my hand now; it is still in my possession. Please, Jenny, don't throw away my letters. If you don't want the tin box, bury it with me.

My longing for Gösta grew stronger and stronger. I could still see his face when I closed my eyes, could hear his voice. The one that had talked to me while I cleaned Madame's apartment at night. The one that asked so many questions, that took an interest in my mind.

That remarkable man, with the strange paintings and the boyfriends he tried to hide from the world, became a fantasy figure. A link to my old life. A feeling that there was, despite everything, someone who cared about me.

But his letters became more infrequent. And I wrote to him less and less. Nora and I had left behind those lonely nose-in-a-book nights, swapping them for luxurious parties at lavish addresses. With rich young men who would do anything to have us.

The Red Address Book
P. PESTOVA, ELEONORA

Every day, we witnessed the transformation as our faces were made up and our hair was curled. As the beautiful dresses were draped over our bodies. The makeup back then was completely different from today's. Thick layers were painted and powdered onto our skin; our eyes were lined with heavy black strokes. The shape of our faces changed as natural fine lines and angles were smoothed over. Our eyes became big and glittering.

Beauty is the most manipulative force of all, and we quickly learned to exploit it. With our makeup on, and stunning dresses, we stood up straight and enjoyed the power. A beautiful person is listened to, admired. This became all too clear to me later in life, when my skin suddenly lost its elasticity and my hair started to turn white. When people stopped looking at me as I walked through a room. That day will arrive. For everyone.

But in Paris, it was my appearance that carried me through life. And as we mannequins got older, as we worked at better jobs that paid more, our self-confidence grew. We were independent women; we could support ourselves and even afford a little luxury. The matron had long since disappeared. We liked to leave the apartment in the evening, making our way out into the Paris night, where the intellectuals and the wealthy entertained themselves to the tones of jazz. We entertained ourselves too.

We were welcome everywhere, but it wasn't the parties themselves that tempted Nora; she was far more interested in the champagne. We were never alone, never without a glass of bubbly in hand. We arrived together, but usually parted soon after. Nora would linger by the bar while I danced. She preferred intellectual conversations with men who offered her drinks. She was well read, could talk about art and books, about politics. If the men stopped ordering her drinks, she would stop talking. Then she would track me down, discreetly pull at the fabric of my dress, and we would leave with our heads held high, before the bartender had time to realize that no one was planning to pay.

We were women by this time and could take care of ourselves. Should have been able to take care of ourselves. The neighbors would flash us disdainful looks when we came home late at night, sometimes in the company of an admirer or two. We were young and we were free, but we were looking for real men. That was what you did back then. Someone who was kind, handsome, and rich, as Nora used to say. Who could take us away from the heavily made-up superficiality that surrounded us. Who could give us security. And we found plenty of candidates. Men came to see us in our apartment with hat in hand, with roses held behind their back. Asked us out for coffee in one of Paris's many cafés. Some even dropped to one knee and proposed. But we always said no. There was always something that didn't seem right. It might be the way they spoke, their clothes, their smile, or their scent. Nora was looking for perfection rather than love. She was firm on that point. She didn't want to return to the poverty she had grown up with in Czechoslovakia. I realized, however, that there had been a childhood sweetheart. I saw the sorrow in her eyes as she placed a newly arrived letter on the stack of unopened envelopes at the back of her wardrobe. As it turned out, reason would prove defenseless against love, even for her.

Nora always asked someone else to answer the door whenever the bell rang, so that, if it was for her, she could decide from a distance whether she wanted to see whoever was standing there. If someone was looking for her and she didn't show up, we were meant to say she was away. One evening, I was the one to answer the door. The man standing in front of me had kind nut-brown eyes, a short black beard, and a loose-fitting suit. He took off his cap and ran his fingers through his rough crewcut, nodded faintly. He looked like a farmer who had accidentally wandered into the city. In one hand, he was holding a white peony. He said her name. I shook my head.

"I'm afraid she isn't home."

But the man didn't reply. His eyes were fixed somewhere behind me. I turned around. There was Eleonora. It was as if the energy between them formed a physical bridge. They started to speak in a language I couldn't understand. Eventually, she threw herself into his arms, crying.

The very next day, they were gone.

The Red Address Book
P. ~~PESTOVA, ELEONORA~~ DEAD

Life was empty without Nora. I had no one to laugh with, no one to drag me out into the Paris night. Books became my company once again, though now I could afford to buy my own. I took them to the park on my days off and read them in the sun. I read modern authors: Gertrude Stein, Ernest Hemingway, Ezra Pound, and F. Scott Fitzgerald. They kept me far removed from the glamorous life Nora and I had shared. I was happier among the trees and birds; things felt calmer there. Sometimes I would bring a small bag of bread crumbs and scatter them on the bench where I was sitting. Small birds would come and keep me company then. Some so tame that they ate straight from my palm.

Nora had left a forwarding address when she disappeared. To begin with, I wrote her long letters; I missed her. I never got a reply. I fantasized about what she was doing, what her days were like now, about the man with the nut-brown eyes and their life together. I wondered whether her love for him was strong enough to compensate for losing a life of money, luxury, and admirers.

One night, there was a knock at the door. When I opened it, I barely recognized her. Nora's face was tan and her hair was lank. Seeing my alarm, she just shook her head and pushed past me. Answering the question I still hadn't asked, she whispered:

"I don't want to talk about it."

I hugged her. There was so much I wanted to know. Nora's swollen cheeks overshadowed her pretty features. Her heavy shawl couldn't hide her belly. I felt it bulge against my own.

"You're having a baby!" I took a step back and placed both hands on her stomach.

She shuddered and pushed them away. Shook her head and pulled her shawl tighter.

"I have to start working again; we need money. The harvest failed this year, and I used the last of our money for the train ticket."

"But you can't work looking like this. Monsieur Ponsard will be angry when he sees you," I said, astonished.

"Please don't tell him," she whispered quietly.

"I won't have to, my love. It's so obvious; there's no hiding it now."

"I should never have gone home with him!" She started to cry.

"Do you love him?"

She paused, then nodded.

"I'll help you, I promise. You can stay here a few days, then I'll make sure you get home," I said. "Go back to him."

"Life is so much harder there," she sobbed.

"You can always come back here once you've had the baby. All this will still be here! And you'll still have your beauty, you'll be able to work again."

"I have to be able to work again," she whispered.

That night, she fell asleep in my bed. We slept close together, and I could make out the faint scent of alcohol on her breath. Quietly, I crawled out of bed and shamelessly rifled through her handbag. I found a hip flask at the bottom, unscrewed the lid, and sniffed. Nora had swapped champagne for cheap spirits. She had continued to drink, even when the partying stopped.

She avoided meeting Monsieur Ponsard. We spent our last time together conversing intimately and taking long walks through Paris. One week later, she went back. I stroked her rounded belly before I waved her off at the platform. Strong, beautiful Nora — in only a few short months, a shadow of her former self. Just before the train departed, she leaned out the window and pressed into my hand a small golden angel made of porcelain. She didn't say anything, just held up her hand in a slow wave. I ran alongside the train, but it picked up speed and I dropped back. I shouted, asked her to write to me and tell me all about the baby. She heard, and every now and then a letter would appear in my letterbox. She told me about the baby girl, Marguerite, and about the hard work on the farm, how she longed for Paris and the life she had left behind. But as the years passed, the letters became more and more infrequent, and eventually I received one from a different sender. It contained a short message in misspelled French: *Eleonora et maintnant mort.* Eleonora is recent dead.

I never did get an explanation. Maybe the alcohol killed her. Or having a second child. Maybe she just couldn't cope any longer.

But ever since the day she left, I have thought of her whenever I see an angel. All angels remind me of the small golden one that she pressed into my hand.

When I heard the news, I opened my address book, slowly crossed out her name, and wrote the word *DEAD* in golden ink. Golden like the sun.

The Red Address Book
S. SMITH, ALLAN

Do you remember the man in my locket, Jenny? The one you found in a drawer last time you came to visit?

He turned up in the park one day. I was sitting on a bench beneath a linden tree. The bright sunlight found its way between the leaves and branches, spreading light across the white pages of my book. Suddenly, a shadow fell over me, and when I looked up, I found myself staring straight into a pair of eyes. They glittered, as though the man was laughing. Even now, I can remember exactly what he was wearing: white shirt, crumpled; red lamb's-wool sweater; beige trousers. No suit, no stiff collar, no belt with a golden buckle. No outward signs of wealth. But he had silky smooth skin, and his serious mouth was so beautifully shaped, I immediately wanted to lean forward and kiss him. It was a strange feeling. He glanced at the empty space next to me as if asking a question; I nodded and he sat down. I struggled to keep reading, but all I could focus on was the energy pulsing between us. And his scent — he smelled so delightful. It found its way into my soul.

"I had been planning to go for a stroll." He raised both feet in the air and showed me his worn canvas shoes, as if to explain. I smiled into my book. We listened to the rustling of the treetops in the breeze, to the birds twittering to one another. He glanced over at me; I could feel his gaze.

"The lady wouldn't by any chance want to join me for a while, would she?"

After just a moment's hesitation, I said yes, and that afternoon we walked until the sun disappeared behind the trees. The world came to a standstill; everything else lost importance. It was just he and I, and that much was clear from the moment we took our first steps, side by side. He kissed me farewell by my door. Held my head between his palms and came so close that it almost felt like we had merged. His lips were soft, warm. He breathed in wonderfully, a deep breath, with his nose against my cheek. Held me tight. For a long time. Whispered into my ear: "Meet me tomorrow, same time, same place." Then he quickly backed away, looked me up and down, blew me a kiss, and vanished into the warm night.

His name was Allan Smith and he was American, but he had close relatives in Paris and was there to visit them. He was full of enthusiasm and grand plans, studying to become an architect and dreaming of changing the world, of redrawing the silhouette of the city.

"Paris is turning into one big museum. We need to inject some modernity, something scaled back and functional."

I listened admiringly, found myself drawn into a world I had never even been aware of. He spoke about buildings, about exciting new materials and how they could be put to use, but also about the way we humans lived, and how we might live in the future. A world in which both men and women worked, where the household could be managed without maids. He was passionate about everything he said, jumping onto benches in the park and gesturing wildly when he wanted to illustrate a particular point. I thought to myself that he must be crazy, but admired his vitality. And then he took my cheeks between his hands and pressed his soft lips to mine. He tasted of sunshine. The warmth of his lips spread to mine and then continued, through the rest of my body. He gave me such a wonderful sense of peace; I found myself breathing more calmly, and my body took on a different weight when I was with him. I wanted to stay there forever. In his arms.

Money, status, and the future couldn't mean less to me than they did right there, right then, in that French park one warm spring day, as I walked alongside the man in the tattered canvas shoes.

10

"It's awful to see you lying there like that! Are you still in pain? Should I fly over?"

"No, Jenny, what good would that do? You over here, with an old biddy. You're young, you should be out there having fun, not looking after a cripple."

She turns the computer, which the priest did actually fetch for her, and waves to the nurse, who is making the bed across the room.

"Alice, come and say hello to my Jenny."

The nurse comes over, peers curiously at the screen and Doris's only visitor.

"Skype, I see? You're certainly not afraid of technology."

"Nope, not Doris, she's always been first with the latest thing. You'd struggle to find a tougher old girl than her." Jenny laughs. "But you're looking after her, aren't you? Will her leg be OK?"

"Of course we are, we're giving her the best care possible, but I can't say how she's doing. Would you like to talk to Doris's doctor? If so, I can book you in for a call."

"Sure. If that's OK with you, Doris?"

"Yes, you've never believed what I tell you anyway. But if he says that I'm going to die soon, you'll have to tell him I already know."

"Stop talking like that! You're not going to die. We've already decided that."

"You've always been naive, Jenny dear. But you can see what I look like, can't you? Death waiting in every little wrinkle, clinging to my body. It'll break me down soon enough. That's just how it is. And you know what? It'll actually be very nice."

Jenny and the nurse glance at each other; one raises an eyebrow and the other puffs out her cheeks as though she is slowly sighing. The nurse does, at least, have somewhere to go; she straightens Doris's pillow and disappears through the doorway.

"You have to stop talking about death now, Doris. It's too sad, I don't want to hear about it." Suddenly, Jenny switches to English. "Jack! Come here, say hi to Auntie, she's badly hurt and in the hospital."

The lanky teenager shuffles over to the computer. He waves and smiles. His quick smile reveals a flash of silver braces before he comes to his senses and closes his mouth.

"Look," he tells her in Swedish, before switching back to English, "check this out." He turns the computer to face the floor in the hallway. Then he steps onto his skateboard, with his feet wide apart. He pulls back one foot, kicks up the board, spins it beneath him, and lands. Doris applauds and cries bravo.

"No skateboarding in the house, I've told you!" Jenny hisses. She turns back to Doris.

"He's totally obsessed with that thing. What is it with him? A piece of wood on wheels takes up his entire day. If it's not wheels that need tightening or changing, it's tricks that need practicing. You should see his knees, the scars he'll have to live with for the rest of his life."

"Leave him be, Jenny. Can't you just buy him kneepads?"

"Kneepads? On a teenager? No, I tried, but he refuses. And I can hardly staple them to his skin. Protection isn't cool, you see." She rolls her eyes and sighs.

"He's young, let him be young. A few scars aren't going to kill him. Better to have them on the surface than on the inside, on his soul. He seems happy, anyway."

"Yeah, he's always been happy. I've been lucky, I guess. They're good kids."

"You have wonderful children. I wish I could fly over and give the whole gang a hug. It's great to be able to see you like this. It always used to be so difficult to stay in touch. Have I ever told you how young I was when I last saw my mother?"

"Yeah, you have. I know it must have been hard. But at least you made it back to Sweden in the end, like you always wanted."

"Yes, I came back. Sometimes I wonder whether it wouldn't have been better if I had stayed with you, with you and your mother."

"No, uff, don't say that. Don't start regretting things now; you've got enough to think about as it is. If you feel like being nostalgic, think about all the good things instead." Jenny smiles. "Do you want to come over here? Should I find you a nursing home here in San Francisco?"

"You really are the sweetest. I'm so glad I have you, Jenny. But no, thank you, I'll stay here like I planned. I don't have the energy for anything else . . . And speaking of energy, I need to get some rest now. Sending you hugs, my love. Tell Willie I said hello, and speak again soon?"

"Hugs to you, Dossi! Yeah, same time in a week? You'll just be out of the operation then . . ."

"Yes," Doris sighs, "I will be."

"Don't worry about it, it'll be just fine. You'll be back on your feet in no time, you'll see." Jenny nods, her eyes widening, encouraging.

"Same time next week," Doris mumbles, blowing the usual kisses. She hurries to disconnect Jenny and her enthusiasm, but the silence falls over her like a heavy, damp blanket. She stares at the dark screen. Doesn't have the energy to move her hands and get some writing done, as she had planned. Her breathing is strained, and there is an acrid taste of bile in her mouth. The pain medication they've put her on has upset her stomach, which is bloated and aching. She pushes the still-warm computer onto her belly, closes her eyes, and allows the heat to work its magic.

A nurse comes into the room. She places the computer on the lower shelf of the bedside table. Then she pulls the blanket over Doris's sleeping body and turns out the light.

The Red Address Book
S. SMITH, ALLAN

It was like carbon dioxide in my veins. I could barely sleep that night, and the next day, at work, I was in a cloud. When I finally finished, I ran from the warehouse, threw myself down the stairs three at a time. By the time I got to the park, he was already waiting for me on the bench. Sketchbook in hand. He was busy drawing with his pencil. A woman, with long hair flowing down over her shoulders. She looked just like me. He turned the pad away when he saw me watching. Smiled bashfully.

"I was just trying to capture your beauty," he mumbled.

He flicked through his pad with me by his side, showing me other pictures, most of them buildings and gardens. He was good at drawing, captured details and angles with sweeping lines. On one page, he had sketched a magnolia, its thick branches overloaded with elegant, delicate flowers.

"What's your favorite flower?" he asked as he absent-mindedly continued to draw.

I thought about his question, remembered the flowers back home in Sweden, the ones I missed so much. Eventually I said, "Roses," and told him about the white ones that had grown outside my father's workshop. I spoke about how much I missed him, about his death and how it happened. Allan wrapped his arms around me and pulled me close, so that my head was resting on his chest. Slowly stroked my hair. There, in that moment, I no longer felt alone.

Darkness fell over the park and the bench where we were still sitting. I remember a sweet scent of jasmine in the air, the birds falling silent and the streetlights coming on, casting their dim glow onto the gravel path.

"Can you feel it?" he suddenly asked, unbuttoning the top two buttons on his shirt. "Can you feel the warmth?"

I nodded, and he took my hand in his, pressing it against his forehead. The droplets of sweat were glistening on his hairline; he was damp.

"Your hand is so cool, my love." He took it between his and kissed it. "How can you be so cool when the heat is so oppressive?"

His face lit up. The way it always did when he had an idea. As though he was amused by his own imagination. He pulled me up from the bench, spun around with me pulled tight to him.

"Come on, I want to show you a secret place," he whispered, with his cheek against mine.

We wandered through the night, slowly, as though we had all the time in the world. It was so easy to talk to Allan. I could share my thoughts with him. Tell him about my longing. My sorrow. He listened. He understood.

Eventually, we caught sight of the grand Pont Viaduc d'Auteuil. The two-level bridge that allowed the railway to cross the wide river. He took me down several flights of stairs, toward the beach where the riverboats rested for the night.

I hesitated, stopped halfway down. "Where are you taking me, what is this secret place?" Allan ran back up to fetch me. Eagerly.

"Come on, you're not a Parisian until you've taken a dip in the Seine."

I stared at him. A dip? How could he suggest something like that?

"Are you crazy? I'm not going to get undressed in front of you. You can't think I will?"

I pulled away from him, but his hand clung to mine; he was so irresistible. It wasn't long before I was in his arms again.

"I'll close my eyes," he whispered. "I won't look, I promise."

We clambered over the boats. Three were moored in a row. The farthest had a ladder at the stern. Allan took off his shirt and trousers and cut through the surface of the water in a perfect dive. Silence descended over me, and the ripples on the surface of the black water became still. I shouted his name. Suddenly, he reappeared by the boat. He hauled himself up to the edge and hung there from his arms. Water was running from his dark hair. His white teeth, visible thanks to his wide smile, glittered in the night.

"I stayed away so the lady could jump in unobserved. Come on, hurry," he laughed, disappearing again.

I knew how to swim; I had learned in Stockholm. But it was so dark, I can remember that I hesitated, that my heart was racing with fear. Eventually, I kicked off my shoes and allowed my dress to drop to the boat. I was wearing a corset; they were common at the time. Made from thick silk, skin-colored, with rigid cups. I kept it on. When I moved my foot toward the surface of the water, Allan grabbed hold of it. I shouted loudly and fell into his arms with a splash. His laughter echoed beneath the arches of the bridge.

The Red Address Book
S. SMITH, ALLAN

Allan made me laugh. He turned my entire worldview upside-down, though I still used to think he was a little crazy. It's only now, with hindsight, that I realize his opinions were based on genuine knowledge of people and the direction in which the world was heading. When I look at today's young families, I see the people he talked about so long ago.

"Your home is your own little world," he used to say. "Your own dominion. That's why a home should be adapted to the way you live your life. A kitchen should be adapted to the type of food that's cooked in it, to the people who actually live in the house. Who knows, in the future, maybe our houses won't even have kitchens. Why should we have them when restaurants cook better food than we ever could?"

It amused me greatly to hear him talk about homes without kitchens just as the first refrigerators and other large appliances became available. While everyone else strove to fill their kitchens with as many modern conveniences as possible.

"Maybe in the future, our kitchens will look like they do in restaurants." I laughed. "Maybe it'll be the norm to have your own chef and a waitress or two?"

He always ignored the sharp hint of sarcasm in my comments, and remained serious.

"I mean that everything is changeable. Old buildings are torn down, replaced by new ones. Decoration is replaced by functionality. As a result, rooms will take on new meaning."

I shook my head, unsure whether he was joking or serious. I loved his ability to use his imagination, to create abstract images as surreal as some of the art being produced in Paris at the time. To

Allan, architecture was the basis of all human relations, and consequently also the solution to all of life's mysteries. He lived for materials, angles, façades, walls, and nooks and crannies. Whenever we went for a walk, he might suddenly stop and stare at a building until I threw something, a scarf or a glove, at him. Then he would pick me up in an embrace. And spin me round, like I was a child. I loved that he laid claim to me as if I was a possession, loved it that he took the liberty of kissing me in the middle of Paris's crowded streets.

Sometimes he would sit and wait outside the studio where I was working. When I came out at the end of the day, fully made up, he would proudly wrap an arm around me and escort me to a restaurant somewhere. It's strange. Allan and I had so much to say to each other; there were never any awkward silences. We strolled through Paris, oblivious to the bustling life surrounding us, engrossed in each other.

He didn't have much money of his own. He also had absolutely no idea how to behave in fine company. He couldn't even get into the more upmarket places because the only real set of clothes he had was far too big for him and rather old-fashioned. He looked like a teenager wearing his father's suit. In fact, if he hadn't radiated such charm when we first met on the park bench, I probably wouldn't have even talked to him. The memory of that meeting has always made me try to avoid judging people by their clothes.

Sometimes you don't need to have the same interests or the same style, Jenny. Making each other laugh is enough.

The Red Address Book
S. SMITH, ALLAN

I continued to work hard. Smiled with blood-red lips, posed as I was told to, appealed to Paris's society ladies, cocked my head for the photographer's square box. But my mind was full of love and longing. I thought about Allan constantly when we were apart. When I sat next to him on the bench in the park, he would sketch lines in his pad, lines that became buildings. There was an entire city in that little sketchbook of his, and we often used to fantasize about which of the houses we would live in.

Every so often, I had to leave Paris for work. Both he and I hated that. On one occasion, he came to pick me up from my place in a borrowed car — I can remember the model even today, a black Citroën Traction Avant. He said he would drive me all the way to the castle in Provence where I would be modeling dresses and jewelry. He was an inexperienced driver; it might even have been his first time driving. The journey was a bumpy one, and at first he kept stalling the engine. I almost laughed myself silly.

"We'll never make it if you keep bouncing around like this!"

"My darling, I would drive you to the moon and back on a bicycle if I had to. Of course we'll make it. Hold on now, I'm accelerating!"

And with that, he pressed the pedal to the floor, and we sailed forward in a cloud of black fumes. When we eventually turned onto the road leading to the castle, several hours late, I was both dusty and sweaty. We were still in the car, kissing, when Monsieur Ponsard suddenly tore open the door. He stared at Allan. The fact that I was kissing a man I wasn't married to was scandalous, and he let Allan know. He had to run off, down the gravel road, to avoid being punched. Despite the gravity of the situation, I could hardly stop laughing. In the distance, Allan turned and blew me a kiss.

Once the viewing was over, I sneaked out and found Allan asleep in the grass on the castle grounds. I dragged him to the car and we escaped before Monsieur Ponsard had time to realize it. That night, we slept beneath the stars in the warm air, curled up tight. We counted the shooting stars and imagined each of them representing a child we would one day have.

"Look, a boy." Allan said, pointing to the first one.

"And a girl," I said excitedly when the next one appeared.

"Another boy." Allan laughed.

As the seventh star fell, he kissed me and said that was enough babies. I gently stroked his neck, buried my fingers in his hair, breathed in the scent of him, and allowed it to become a part of me.

The Red Address Book
S. SMITH, ALLAN

We had known each other for just over four months when he suddenly and unexpectedly disappeared. Just like that, he was gone. There was no more knocking at my door. No one waiting for me with kisses and smiles after work. I didn't know where he lived, I didn't know his relatives, I didn't know who to get in touch with to find out what had happened. I had noticed that he seemed anxious the last time we met, that he wasn't his usual happy and exuberant self, and he was dressed more soberly. I had assumed it was for my sake that he had bought a jacket and some glossy leather shoes. But maybe there was another reason? My worry and despair grew with every day that passed.

I went back to the bench in the park, the one where he used to sit while he sketched his buildings. Other than a one-legged pigeon hopping back and forth in the hope of finding a crumb or two, it was empty. I kept going back, sitting there for hours every day, but he never returned. As I waited, I could almost feel his presence; it felt like he was right there beside me.

The days passed. I walked our usual route, alone, hoping he would turn up. He started to seem more and more like a distant dream. I cursed myself for having been so naive, self-absorbed, infatuated. For asking too few questions, for not demanding to know more about him.

Where had he gone? Why had he abandoned me? We were supposed to be together forever.

The Red Address Book
A. ALM, AGNES

After Allan's sudden disappearance, I was lost. Dark, swollen bags formed beneath my eyes, and my skin turned dull and pasty after so many sleepless nights and salty tears. I couldn't eat, and I became weak and thin. Every minute, conscious and unconscious, was taken up by thoughts of him.

Separation is the worst thing on earth, Jenny. Even now, I hate saying goodbye. Being separated from a person you hold dear always feels like a wound to the soul.

It pains me to admit it, but the memory of most people tends to fade after a while. Not to the extent that they disappear or no longer mean anything. But that initial, panic-stricken sense of loss at their absence becomes dulled and is eventually replaced by something slightly more neutral. Something you can, somehow, live with. In certain cases, you no longer even want to rekindle an old friendship, and any remaining link is tinged with obligation more than enthusiasm. Such friends become people to keep in touch with — letters to be written, letters to be read and pondered for a moment — before you fold up the memory, shove it back into the envelope, and mostly forget it.

After a few years in Paris, even the memory of my own mother had faded. My recollection that she had once dissociated herself from me, throwing me out into an adult world I knew nothing about while she let my sister stay . . . that took over. To me, she became someone who had chosen between her children. I thought about her from time to time, I did. But the longing I felt for her gradually vanished.

Allan didn't fade, not even slightly. He was almost always in my thoughts. The pain lessened slightly, but not the love. It was overwhelming.

At first I went through life one day at a time, one hour at a time. I searched for faults in myself, reasons why he had abandoned me. Eventually, I put more energy into plucking my eyebrows and sucking in my stomach than I did to thinking about the future. Seven years had passed since I left Sweden. I had money and I was independent; few women at the time were so lucky. My life became the clothes and the makeup that transformed me into someone else, someone to admire. Someone who was good enough. I filled my days with the pursuit of perfection.

The truth is, on the day that an ill-fated telegram arrived at my apartment, I had devoted hours to buying a pair of leather pumps in the exact same shade of red as my new dress. I went from shop to shop, comparing them with the fabric, asking the shopkeepers to polish the leather until it shone, only to reject the shoe a second later because the buckle was ugly. It was a carefree life I was living and, looking back now, I do feel ashamed. Transforming young women into egocentric, self-obsessed witches is easy. Then and now. Many are tempted by the glitter of gold, but few actually stop to think. Many of the live mannequins of the time came from rich aristocratic families. It was thanks to them that mannequins gained status, that we became something to look up to, did you know that?

In any case, back to the telegram. It was from my mother's neighbor, and it effectively ended my destructive life.

Dear Doris,

It is with great sadness that I must inform you of your mother's passing after a long illness. Together with her friends and workmates, I have scraped together enough for a ticket for young Agnes. She will arrive in Paris by train at 13.00 on 23rd April. I pass her into your care. Your mother's belongings are being stored in one of the attics.

Hoping that luck will shine on you both.

With affection,

Anna Christina

A dead mother I no longer knew. A little sister, crashing into my world like a parcel sent to the wrong address. When I last saw her, she had been a small child. Now she was a lanky fourteen-year-old wandering along the platform, looking lost. She was carrying a battered suitcase in one hand, strapped shut with a thick leather belt. It looked like Pappa's old belt, flecked with white paint. Her eyes scanned the crowd, searching for me, her sister.

When she spotted me, she stopped dead and stared as people continued to surge past her. They pushed and shoved her, and her body swayed back and forth, but her eyes were fixed on mine.

"Agnes?" The question was unnecessary because she was the spitting image of me at that age. Just a little heavier, with slightly darker hair. She met my gaze, her mouth half-open and her eyes wide. As though I was a ghost.

"It's me, your sister. Don't you recognize me?"

I held out my hand and she took it. Right then, her body started to shake and she dropped her bag. She let go of my hand and wrapped her arms around herself. Her shoulders hunched up toward her ears.

"Come on, little one." I put an arm around her and felt the trembling spread from her small body to mine. I breathed calmly and took in the scent of her; it seemed familiar.

"Are you very scared?" I whispered. "And sad? I can understand that. It must have been hard for you when she died."

"You look like her. You look just like her," she stammered, her face against my shoulder.

"Do I? It's been so long, I can barely remember. I don't even have a picture of her. Do you?"

I slowly stroked her back, and her breathing grew calmer. She let go of me and took a few steps back. From one of her pockets, she pulled out a well-thumbed photograph and handed it to me. Mamma was sitting on a piano stool in her long blue dress. The one she always wore to parties.

"When was this taken?"

Agnes didn't reply; maybe she didn't know. Mamma's eyes looked so full of life. It was only then that it finally dawned on me that she really was gone, that I would never see her again. Anxiety washed over me. She had died believing that I didn't care about her. Now I would never get another chance.

"Maybe we'll see her in heaven." I tried to comfort Agnes, but the words just made her cry. My own tears turned inward. I felt my chest turn cold, and a shiver spread through me.

"Shh, don't cry, Agnes." I pulled her close and noticed, for the first time, just how tired she looked. Her eyelids were drooping, the skin beneath her eyes dark.

"Did you know that the best hot chocolate in the world is here, in Paris?"

Agnes dried her tears.

"And did you know that chocolate is the best cure for tears? The loveliest café happens to be right here, just around that corner," I said, pointing. "Shall we go?"

I took her hand and we walked slowly through the station. It was the same way I had walked with Madame seven years earlier. I didn't cry at all then. But my sister did now. My little sister, who, just like me, had been involuntarily thrown into the big, wide world. It was my job to take care of her. That terrified me.

Agnes turned my life upside-down. I had to act like a parent, and worry struck me immediately. She needed a good school, she needed to learn French. She would never have to clean or work as a maid. And I would never let her stand in front of the camera, flashing those fake smiles. Agnes would have everything I had always dreamed of: an education, opportunities, and, most important, a childhood lasting longer than mine had.

The very next day, I gave notice at the apartment I shared with two other mannequins. I looked through my bookings. Viewings at the department store. Photo shoots for Lanvin and Chanel. Work that at first had brought me anxiety and fear had become my everyday life.

Suitors still pursued me. I met up with them when I had time, accepted the gifts they brought, and chatted with them in a friendly enough way. But none of them could take Allan's place in my heart. None had his gaze, none looked into my soul the way he had. None made me feel so safe.

Nor could they take Agnes's place. From the day she moved in, I sold the presents these men gave me as quickly as I could and used the money to buy her schoolbooks. And I no longer spent my time trying to find shoes that exactly matched the fabric of my dress.

11

"I hope you understand?"

She turns away, stares out of the window at the clouds. The wind is playing with them, making the small white balls move at different speeds: the top layer is still, but those beneath it pass by with speed and then disappear from view.

The man sitting by her side clears his throat. A fleck of spit flies from his mouth and lands in his short beard. He says her name. She turns back and stares at him as he talks.

"You can't live alone, not while you can barely walk. How would that work? You won't even be able to get to the toilet without help, now that you've had surgery. I'm reading here that you could barely even do that before. Doris, trust me. You'll be better off in assisted living. You can even take some of your own furniture with you."

This is the third time the hospital social worker has come to see her with his form. Three times now, she has had to sit through his speech about how important it is for her to sell her apartment and put into storage any furniture and memories that won't fit into her rooms at assisted living. Three times now, she has had to fight the impulse to hit him on the head with something hard. She would never leave Bastugatan. This will be the third time he'll have to leave without her signature.

And yet he's still sitting there. His fingers are drumming the form. She turns her head, defies the pain of moving it.

"Over my dead body," she hisses. "Forget about getting me to sign, I've told you already."

He sighs deeply and whacks the form against the bedside table. Tries, anyway: one lonely piece of paper doesn't make much noise.

"But how are you going to cope on your own, Doris? Tell me that."

She fixes her eyes on him.

"I managed perfectly well before this happened. And I'll do the same after. It's just a broken hip. I'm not crippled! I'm not dead. Not yet, anyway. And when I do die, it's not going to be here or at that Bluebell place. By the way, you should be wishing me luck with my rehab rather than wasting your time and mine. Give me a few weeks and you'll see that I can walk perfectly well again. Or maybe you should try breaking your hip and having a new joint put in, and then we'll see how cocky you are in the weeks after!"

"There are worse places than Bluebell. I've had to talk the manager into taking you; they don't usually take patients in your condition. Take this opportunity, Doris. Next time you might not be so lucky; you'll end up in long-term nursing-home care."

"Threats don't work on old biddies. You of all people should know that by now, the way you've been running in and out of here. If not, then you've learned something new today. You can go and harass someone else now. I want to sleep."

"Is that how you see this?" His eyebrows are tense, his mouth a thin line. "That I'm harassing you? I actually just want to help you. You have to see that this is for your own good. That you can't live alone. You don't have anyone to help you."

When he eventually leaves the room, tears run down Doris's cheeks, sneaking between her wrinkles and finding their way into her mouth. Her heart is still pounding angrily. She raises her hand, the one bruised from the IV line, and rubs her cheek. Then she fixes her eyes on the wall. She stubbornly moves her foot, back and forth, ten times. Just like the physical therapist showed her. Next, she struggles to lift her foot a few millimeters. She stares at her thigh, visualizes her heel in the air. One short second in the air, then she lowers her foot to the pillow again. The movement took all her strength. She allows herself to rest for a moment and then moves on to the third exercise. She presses her knee into the bed so that her thigh muscles contract; then she relaxes, and repeats the sequence. Lastly, she tenses her backside so that her hips lift a few millimeters. She feels a twinge in the wound from the operation, but her hip can now manage small movements without hurting too much.

"How are you doing, Doris? How does your leg feel?" A nurse sits down on the edge of her bed and takes her hand.

"It's fine. No pain." She lies. "I want to get up and walk tomorrow, or try anyway. I should be able to manage a few short steps."

"That's the spirit," the nurse says, patting her cheek. Doris shrinks back from her touch.

"I'll write it in your chart so that the morning team knows what you want."

And with that, Doris is left alone once more. The beds across from her are empty tonight. She wonders who might be brought in tomorrow. It'll be Monday. Monday, Tuesday, Wednesday. She counts on her fingers. Just three days until she can talk to Jenny again.

The Red Address Book

A. ALM, AGNES

An apartment close to Les Halles. A room with a kitchenette. Water pump and outhouse in the yard. It wasn't the best neighborhood, but the apartment was ours and we could be ourselves. Me and Agnes. We slept together, in the same little bed. The creaking when one of us moved eventually became like a melody. I can still hear it when I close my eyes. Even the smallest movement would make the rusty springs rasp and the lopsided iron frame sway. Sometimes I actually worried that the entire thing might collapse.

Agnes was so sweet. That's the word that describes her best. Always helpful and understanding. Quiet and a little melancholy at times. She squirmed in her sleep at night, whimpered as the tears ran down her cheeks, still not waking. She would just press herself against me. If I moved away, she would follow until I was lying on only a thin strip of mattress.

One morning, as we curled up in bed with cups of tea, Agnes started to talk about her life in Stockholm. What she said helped me somewhat understand her melancholy nature. It had been awful — an experience that could have been mine. She and our mother were so poor that they didn't have enough to eat. Agnes couldn't go to school. They were thrown out of the apartment and had spent the last few months of my mother's life with Anna Christina.

"Mamma had such a terrible cough," Agnes said, her voice so faint that it barely carried. "There would be blood in her hand, dark red and thick as phlegm. We were sleeping together on the daybed in the kitchen, and I could feel her body trembling in pain with every cough."

"Were you there when she died?" I asked, and she nodded. "What did she say? Did she say anything?"

"I wish you enough sun to light up your days, enough rain that you appreciate the sun . . ." Agnes's voice trailed off. I took her hand in mine. Wound my fingers between hers.

"I tell you what we've had enough of. Enough rubbish. Don't you think?"

We could laugh about it intimately, the way sisters can, despite the fact that we didn't really know each other yet.

I'll never forget that first summer with Agnes. If you ever want to really get to know a person, Jenny, share a bed with her. There's nothing more disarming than curling up together late at night. In that moment, you're nothing but yourself, no evasion, no excuses. I thank that rusty iron bed for making us sisters once again. Sisters who shared everything.

Whenever I wasn't working, we would wander the streets of Paris, both wearing hats and gloves to protect us from the sun. We spoke French with each other. Every word she learned we found right there on the streets. *Car, bicycle, dress, hat, sidewalk, book, café.* It became a game. I would point to something and say the word in French, and she would repeat it. We searched for words everywhere. She learned quickly and was looking forward to starting school. And I got to take a few wonderful steps in childhood, something I had lost far too early.

Then the worries flared up. Rumors of a war, whispered in every café, proved true, and by September 1939 had become fact. The terrible Second World War. The heat hung heavily over Paris's streets, as did fear of what was to come. France had thus far been spared, and life in Paris went on like normal, except it seemed that someone had stolen people's smiles. *Soldier* and *rifle* were new words that Agnes and I heard on the street. Suddenly, I also found myself working less. The fashion houses were saving money, which meant financial catastrophe for us. Even the department stores stopped hiring mannequins. Agnes continued to go to school every day while I waited for the phone to start ringing again, for the familiar jobs to reappear. Eventually, I asked around about other jobs, but no one dared take anyone on. Not the butcher, not the baker, not the aristocratic families. I still had some money in savings, but the balance fell lower and lower.

We had a crackly old radio in the apartment: dark wood, yellowed fabric, and golden dials. We listened to it every evening. We couldn't help ourselves. The broadcasts reported more and more brutality, and the number of lives lost grew from the dozens to the hundreds. The war was so close, and yet it also felt so far away, so incomprehensible. Agnes used to cover her ears, but I always forced her to listen because she needed to know.

"Stop it, please stop it, Doris. It brings such horrible pictures to mind," she said. Once, she even ran straight out of the room, out of the apartment. It was when the news reporter announced that the Germans had occupied Warsaw and that the Polish resistance had been crushed.

I found her in the back yard, curled up on top of a firewood bin. Her arms were wrapped tightly around her legs, and her eyes were staring blankly. The cooing of doves sounded faintly from the rooftops. They were everywhere, and their droppings flecked the paving stones.

"They might just be numbers to you," she hissed at me, "but these are people they're talking about. People who were alive and who are now dead. Do you understand that?"

She shouted those last few words, accusingly, as though I didn't comprehend the word *dead*. I curled up beside her, right up close.

"I don't want to die," she sobbed, her head resting against my shoulder. "I don't want to die. I don't want the Germans to come here."

The Red Address Book
S. SMITH, ALLAN

One day, Agnes came home with an envelope. I'm sure it had been white at some point, but it was yellowed, dirty, and covered in postmarks, stamps, remnants of glue, and scribbled-out addresses. It contained a letter from America.

More than a year had passed since he suddenly disappeared. And now, amid the great anxiety about the war, he had finally written a letter. As though he had perceived my never-ending sorrow at having lost him. Inside the envelope was a brochure about passage to New York, plus a bundle of dollar bills. And the few lines that have etched themselves in my memory forever:

> *Darling Doris, my most beautiful rose. I was forced to leave Paris hastily and could not cope with a farewell. Forgive me. My father came to collect me, my mother needs me here. I had no choice.*
>
> *Come to me. I need you. Cross the Atlantic so that I can hold you in my arms again. I will love you forever. Come as soon as you can. Here is everything you need to travel. I shall take care of you when you arrive.*
>
> *We'll see each other again soon. I miss you so.*
> *Your Allan*

I read that letter to myself over and over again. At first, I was angry. At the fact that he had waited so long to get in touch, and that he had written so briefly when he finally did. But then joy took over. I started to live again, as the paralysis of sorrow slowly let go. He was still there, there was nothing wrong with me, he loved me.

I read the letter to Agnes.

"We're going!" she exclaimed, her eyes serious and her forehead tense. "Why stay here when all we have to look forward to is war?"

There were rumors that the Germans were taking civilians prisoner. Driving them out of their homes, seizing everything of value. We didn't know what happened to these people next, but Agnes was afraid. At school these awful stories were twisted in ways that made the situation seem even worse.

We sat in the kitchen in the evenings that followed, talking about the journey. Agnes was so certain. She wanted to leave. Couldn't handle the fear any longer. It didn't take us long to decide. We both wanted to get away. But longing, not fear, was what drove me. I sold most of my clothes, hats, and shoes, as well as our furniture and paintings. What little we had left, we packed into two suitcases, with letters, photographs, and jewelry. I emptied my bank account and gathered the large bills in an old tin chocolate box that Allan had once given to me. I kept it close, stashed away in my handbag.

Once again, my entire life had been packed up, but this time it was different. I was an adult. I felt safe and full of hope. My family was with me, and Allan and I would be reunited.

The Red Address Book
J. JENNING, ELAINE

It was a dark, rainy day in Genoa, in November 1939. I was wearing my red coat, the one made of soft cashmere. It stood out among all the other coats, which were black, gray, and brown. I had tied a gray scarf around my head, and as I walked up the gangway, I left behind Europe and my career with grace. I was still Doris, the live mannequin. The pier was full of people with and without tickets. Some of them recognized me from hand-colored images in magazines, and they whispered and pointed. Others were completely absorbed by tearful farewells to loved ones. Halfway up the gangway, I turned around and waved to the world, as though I was a film star. No one waved back. Agnes didn't turn. Paris had been nothing but a set of parentheses that briefly enclosed her life; the place would soon fade to a vague memory. But for me, Paris represented a treasured period in my life. As the ship sailed out through the entrance to the port of Genoa, one of the last permitted to leave the harbor, I watched with sadness through the window of our cabin as the coastline disappeared.

The SS *Washington* was a long, beautiful ship. We had a large cabin with a living room and a double bed. The bed didn't creak and the mattress didn't dip in the middle, which meant that Agnes and I could lie in it separately. That first night, we both lay awake.

Agnes whispered to me, "Tell me that he's handsome. And rich. Tell me everything! God, this is so romantic . . ."

I didn't know what to say. I could see Allan's face when I closed my eyes, could remember the exact scent I had breathed in so often during our embraces. But in truth, I knew almost nothing about his life now. Far too much time had passed.

"He's an architect and a visionary. He has so many strange ideas, but you'll like him because he laughs a lot."

"But is he handsome?" Agnes giggled, and I swung my pillow at her face. She never stopped asking questions. I told her everything I could remember. About how we had met, about his impulsivity, his joy, his passion. About his green eyes. His smile.

I wondered to myself why he had finally written to me. Why now and not before? Was it because rumors had finally reached him about the war coming to Paris? Though his disappearance had caused me many tears, I felt expectantly loving, now that I knew he still thought of me. My entire being was filled with longing.

Before we boarded the ship, I had posted two letters. One was a farewell to Gösta. Our correspondence had become even more sporadic, but I wanted to let him know where I was. I gave him one last intense snapshot of Paris. The second letter was to Allan. It contained the details of our arrival and a brief message, as short as the one he had sent to me. We would soon see each other again. I could just picture the scene, like something out of a spectacular film. He would be standing on the dock, waiting for us, wearing his ill-fitting suit, his shaggy hair blowing in the breeze. Me in my elegant red coat. When he caught sight of me, he would grin and wave. I would run to him, throw myself into his arms, and kiss him. My fantasy ran wild during those choppy nights. As did my nerves.

Our days at sea were full of activity, planned down to the very last detail by an enthusiastic crew: clay pigeon shooting, bowling, dancing, quizzes. We got to know many new friends. Before we left Paris, I hadn't given a single thought to the English language; my impulsive decision had been made on the basis of love, not language. I knew only a few words of English, and Agnes none at all. But, as luck would have it, we met Elaine Jenning, an elderly American lady who spoke French, and she became our guardian angel. She gave us language lessons in the dining room every day. With Elaine,

Agnes and I played the same game that we had played on the streets of Paris. We pointed, she said the word in English, and we repeated it. Soon enough, we knew the English words for all kinds of items on board the ship. Elaine enjoyed teaching us her mother tongue, giving each word its own weight and articulating it carefully so that we could follow her meaning.

Elaine was recently widowed. Her husband had been a salesman, and they had lived all over the world, spending the past ten years in France. Like me, she had experienced the good life in Paris. Her dresses were all tailor-made, and she wore several strings of pearls around her neck. Sometimes I imagined that I had seen her in the department store, that she was among the ladies who had pulled at my clothes in search of something that would make them look equally elegant. The white powder on Elaine's face clumped in her wrinkles when she perspired, and she used an embroidered handkerchief to wipe it away, leaving streaks on her skin. Her hair was carefully arranged in a smooth silver-gray bun at the nape of her neck. Every now and then, she would reach up to steady a hairpin that was about to succumb to the weight of her hair. We enjoyed spending time with her. She was our great comfort out there at sea, on our way toward the unknown.

Most people onboard that ship were traveling to leave something behind, but Elaine was heading home. To a life she had been absent from for over thirty years.

The Red Address Book
S. SMITH, ALLAN

Agnes and I stood on the deck, sharing a black umbrella, amazed by the skyscrapers towering up against the overcast sky. It was misty; dense droplets found their way beneath the umbrella, with the help of the wind. I pulled my red coat tight at the throat, buried my chin in my shawl. Angled the umbrella slightly to shield us better, but Agnes firmly straightened it again, so that we wouldn't miss a single detail on our way to the docks. She squealed when she saw the Statue of Liberty, that powerful gift from France. The statue looked out to us with torch raised high, and right there and then I felt fairly certain that we would have a good life in America. Despite that, I still had to visit the bathroom several times. Agnes laughed when I returned from my fourth trip.

"You're nervous, aren't you?" She smiled, her eyes still fixed on land.

Her words hardly made things easier, and I snorted. "Of course I'm nervous, I haven't seen him in so long. What if I don't recognize him?"

"Just go slowly. And smile. Look like you know where you're going. Everything will work out."

"What do you mean, go slowly and smile? That sounds like something Mamma would say. She was full of strange ideas."

Agnes laughed. "Yeah, she was. Did she say 'Be strong' to you? That was her favorite."

I nodded and laughed, those words were so familiar. And when it was finally time to leave the ship, I did exactly as she said. We said goodbye to Elaine, giving her a big hug. She pressed a slip of paper into my hand. On it was an address, written in ornate script.

"If you ever need help, you know where I am," she whispered.

• • •

After giving a kiss on the cheek to passengers we had come to know, I slowly made my way down the narrow gangway. Because of my red coat he would be able to see me immediately. I smiled, certain that I was being watched.

We paused after passing through immigration. The room was full of people waiting for someone. The minutes that followed felt more like hours. Words and phrases in languages we barely under-stood swirled around us. We sat on our suitcases, which a porter had carried down from the ship. The icy wind crept up my stocking-clad legs and beneath my skirt. I shivered. Agnes stared at everyone who passed. There was hope in those blue eyes of hers. There were tears in mine. None of the people we saw were Allan.

Almost an hour had passed when a man in a dark suit came for-ward. He was wearing a peaked cap, which he took off when he spoke to us.

"Miss Alm? Miss Doris Alm?" he asked. I leapt up from my suit-case.

"Yes, yes," I replied eagerly in English. I held out the only picture of Allan that I had, the one I had pushed into an antique locket. I often wore it around my neck, but I had never opened it to show anyone before. Agnes leaned forward with curiosity.

"Why didn't you tell me you had a picture?" Then she pointed to the man. "But that's not Allan. Who is he?"

He mumbled something in English. From the inner pocket of his jacket, he pulled out an envelope, which he thrust toward me. My eyes scanned the few lines of French.

Dear Doris,

It was with dismay that I received your letter. I don't know what has brought you here, over a year has passed. Doris, my love, why have you come now? I waited months for you. In vain. I had to stay here; my mother was terribly ill and I could not abandon her.

*Eventually, I couldn't wait and hope any longer. I thought
you had forgotten me. I moved on. I am now married, and un-
fortunately cannot see you. The driver will take you to a hotel
where you will find a room booked in your name. You can stay
there for two weeks at my expense. We cannot meet. I'm so terribly sorry. A.*

I fainted.

Agnes slapped my cheeks.

"Doris, you have to pull yourself together! We don't need him.
We managed before, and you've managed all these years. That dream
isn't coming true. Get up."

I couldn't breathe, felt a heavy weight on my chest. Was that all
he was to me now? A dream? Agnes helped me to my feet. She had
to lead me to the man's car. I don't remember anything from the journey. None of the streets, none of the people, no scents, no words. An
entire year had passed since he sent his letter. I should have realized,
given how unreliable the mail service had become. Imagine — if it
had arrived in time, I would have been the one to marry him. Now
there was another woman at his side. I felt my stomach contract at
the thought. I wanted to throw up.

Agnes and I curled up in the big, soft hotel bed, hiding from the
frightening world. For the second time for each of us, we found ourselves in a foreign country whose language we barely spoke. We had
no plans and far too little money. But we couldn't return. We had
left behind a Europe at war.

Outside our window, just thirty centimeters away, was the brick
wall of the neighboring building. I stared at it until the rows of
bricks started to sway. On the fourth day, I got up. I washed and
powdered my face, applied some red lipstick, and put on my pret-

tiest dress. Then I stepped out onto the city streets, which bustled with life and voices. In broken English, I managed to find out where the department stores were in the closest neighborhoods. I visited them one by one, but it turned out that live mannequins were different in America. They behaved more like hostesses, talking to the customers, showing them around. Back in Paris, we hadn't needed to say a thing. In fact, we hadn't been allowed to talk. But here, they were expected to sell while they showed off the clothes.

After wandering street after street, I eventually managed to get myself a test position, for at least one day, at Bloomingdale's. I would be in the warehouse. This celebrated Paris mannequin would use her delicate fingers and red polished nails to unpack goods and iron dresses. But I was determined to manage the work and keep the job. Then all we would need was a place to live.

12

The man is at her side again, and her head is turned obstinately to the wall, as before.

"You can't stay here. And you can't go home. That's why we need to move you to assisted living. Call it temporary if you like, but as things stand, you can't manage on your own. The nurse told me you couldn't walk when you tried today. How would you be able to live in your apartment, if that's the case? And alone?"

She continues to stare at the wall in silence. The only sounds come from the faint beeping of an alarm out in the corridor and the soft tread of the nurses' shoes.

"It would feel much better if we could talk about this, Doris. If you could try to understand. I know you're used to coping on your own, but your body has given up. It's difficult, I do understand."

She slowly turns her head and glares at him.

"You understand? What exactly is it you understand? How miserable it is to lie here in this bed? How it feels to desperately want to go home? How much my hip hurts? Or maybe you understand what I want and don't want? I think it would feel much better if you went away. Just go." She snorts. She purses her lips and feels the skin on her chin straining. The hospital blanket is half-covering her, and she makes an attempt to pull it over her legs, but the pain prevents her.

The man gets up and stands for a moment, watching her in silence. She can feel his eyes on her and she knows what he's thinking. That she's a stubborn old woman who'll never be able to cope on her own again. Well, he's free to think that. But he can't force her to do anything, and both of them know that. She wishes he would just go away, and as though he has read her thoughts, he takes two steps back and then turns to leave without saying another word. She hears the sound of paper being torn in two. Once again, his form ends up in the wastebasket. She smiles. A fourth minor victory.

The Red Address Book
S. SMITH, ALLAN

It was our fifth day in New York. We needed to start thinking about the future, but we had few ideas about how to survive in our new country. Terrible homesickness struck both of us. Me for the familiar streets of Paris, Agnes for Stockholm. We longed for everything we had left behind. I wrote to Gösta. Complained in a way I couldn't with anyone else. Asked him for help, though I knew he would not be able to give it.

I set off for Bloomingdale's and my first day in the warehouse. I was prepared for a stark contrast to my working life in Paris, knew that this wouldn't be something I could smile my way through. I left Agnes in our little room with nothing but a handful of orders to keep her company: *Don't leave the room, don't open the door, don't talk to anyone.*

There was noise everywhere. And unfamiliar words. People shouted, cars sounded their horns. Many more cars than in Paris. As I walked the few blocks to the warehouse, steam rose from the grates on the streets. I skirted them, not daring to walk over.

The manager who welcomed me spoke quickly. He pointed, gestured, nodded, smiled, talked again. And frowned when he eventually realized that I hadn't understood. His pronunciation was a long way from Elaine's clear articulation. Lacking the ability to speak lands you at the very bottom of the hierarchy, and that was where I found myself that day. I apologized for my ignorance by lowering my head.

I had been strong and hopeful before my first shift, but as the days passed, my feet grew heavier and the ache in my shoulders from all the lifting became worse. I was allowed to continue for a few more days, but then the manager shook his head and handed me my wages in cash. There had been too many issues with language; I didn't carry out my tasks properly. I argued, but he just shook his head and pointed to the door.

What were we going to do now? We had only two nights left at the hotel. During my walk back, I became increasingly confused, increasingly full of worry. Where would we live, how would we manage to make a life for ourselves in this new country?

I recognized the messy brown hair from a distance. I stopped and stared, letting people pass. Although he had seen me, he too remained completely still. The bond between us was like a magnet pulling me toward him. When he got up from the steps outside the hotel, I started to run. I threw myself into his arms and cried like an abandoned child. He reciprocated my embrace and kissed away my tears. But that intense feeling of joy quickly turned to anger, and I started to beat his chest with my fists.

"Where have you been? Why did you leave me? Why did you leave?"

He stopped me by taking a firm grip of my wrists.

"Calm down" — his French was like music to my ears — "calm down, *ma chérie*. My mother was ill, as I wrote." He whispered into my hair. "I had to be by her side. I wrote that letter to you the minute I got back. Why did you take so long?"

His arms were tight around me.

"I'm sorry. Oh, I'm so sorry, Allan ... darling ... I only recently received your letter. I came straightaway."

He stroked my head. I buried my face in his jacket, breathed in the scent of him. It was just like I remembered. So many memories. So much comfort.

He wasn't dressed the way I was used to seeing him dress. His pinstriped suit was double-breasted, and it fit him properly. Not at all like it was in Paris. I ran my hand over his jacket.

"Take me up to your room," he whispered.

"I can't, my sister is with me. She came to live with me in Paris after you left, and she's up there now."

"We'll get another room. Come on!"

He took my hand and pulled me inside. The receptionist recognized me and nodded, listened attentively as Allan spoke. He was handed a key and we tumbled into the elevator. As the doors closed, he took my head in his warm hands and our lips met. It was one of those kisses that make time come to a standstill. I haven't experienced many of them in my life. When we reached the room, he carried me to the bed, slowly lowered himself on top of me, and pressed his body against mine. Unbuttoned my blouse and gently caressed my bare skin, kissed me. We made love, and it felt like we had become one.

Afterward, we lay quietly, breathing in sync. We were so close. Even now, my heart beats more quickly when I think about that moment, how it felt. How happy I was when I fell asleep in his arms.

When I woke, it was night. He was awake beside me, his hands behind his head. I shuffled closer and lay my head on his chest.

"I'm leaving for Europe tomorrow morning," he whispered, slowly stroking my back, tenderly kissing my forehead.

I turned on the bedside lamp and met his gaze.

"Sorry, what did you say? Europe? But you can't, the continent is at war. Didn't you know?"

"It's because of the war that I'm going back. I'm a French citizen; it's my duty to be there. My mother was French, and I was born in France; it's where my roots are. I can't betray my family, my blood. They're counting on me."

He stared gloomily at the wall. The intense gaze I was used to had dimmed, and now all I could see was sorrow. I whispered the words.

"But I love you."

He sighed deeply and sat up on the edge of the bed with his head in his hands. I crept up behind him and kissed his neck. Wrapped my legs around his hips.

"You're going to have to cope without me, Doris. When I come back, I'll still be married."

I leaned my face against his back. Kissed his warm skin. "But I love you, don't you hear me? I came over here for you. I would have come sooner, but your letter arrived too late. I thought it was the war that made you write. Agnes and I came as soon as we could."

He pulled himself free from my embrace, got up, and started to button his shirt. I reached for him and asked him to come back. He bent down and kissed me, and I saw his eyes brim. Then he let go and pulled on the rest of his clothes.

"You'll always be in my heart, my darling Doris. I wish I had written again when I didn't hear from you, but I thought you didn't want me."

I got up from the bed, tried to hold him there. I was completely naked, and I remember that he first kissed one of my breasts, then the other, before abruptly turning away. From his wallet, he pulled out a wad of bills. I shook my head at him, appalled.

"Are you crazy? I don't want your money. I want you!"

"Take the money, you're going to need it. Besides, I have it to give — I know I looked like a bum in France, but my family, well, my family has money to spare." His voice sounded firm, but I could hear him fighting back the tears.

Now I understood the fancy suit, the ability to pay for the room. "When do you have to go?"

"Now. I have to leave. Take care, my darling. My most beautiful rose. Never let life or circumstances get you down. You're strong. Stand tall, be proud."

"We'll see each other again, won't we? Please, tell me I'll see you soon."

He didn't answer my question, and I have always, over all the years that have passed, wondered what he was thinking. How he could manage to be so cold. How he could leave. How his hand managed to close the door.

I was left behind. Sitting on an unmade bed that smelled of sweat and love.

The Red Address Book
J. JENNING, ELAINE

Everyone experiences setbacks in life. They change us. Sometimes we notice; other times they happen without our knowledge. But the pain, that's there the whole time, piled high in our hearts, like clenched fists ready to break free. In our tears and anger. Or, in the worst cases, in our coldness and introversion.

Even now, every time I see a TV program or hear someone talk about the Second World War, I imagine how he died. I have seen him riddled by bullets, seen his blood spray in every direction and his voice cry out in despair and terror. I have seen him running over fields, fleeing a tank that will eventually mow him down and leave him mutilated, his face pressed into the mud. I have seen him pushed overboard and drowned. Seen him freezing to death, lonely and afraid, at the bottom of a trench. Seen him stabbed in a dark alleyway, discovered by SS soldiers. I know it's unusual, but the images continue to come to me. I can't help it. His shadow has followed me through life.

That night is forever etched in my memory.

My love . . . we were meant for each other, and yet we weren't. That thought still confuses me.

After Allan left, I spent a long time sitting on the floor, my back against the edge of the bed and his dog-eared dollar bills spread out around me. I couldn't get up. I couldn't cry. And I couldn't bring myself to believe that this had been the last time he would ever hold me in his arms. Eventually, sunlight found its way between the curtains and woke me from my thoughts. I left the scent of Allan, of us, behind a door bearing the number 225 in gold. While he was getting on a boat to Europe, heading toward war, I desperately tried to bury the memory of him in that hotel room.

Agnes shouted at me when I appeared. She was ashen-faced, exhausted from an anxious, sleepless night in a foreign land.

"Where have you been? Answer me! What happened?"

I couldn't find the words to reply, and she continued to shout. I couldn't explain what even I found difficult to understand. Instead, I frantically searched our luggage to find the tiny scrap of paper on which Elaine, our friend from the boat, had written her contact details. I threw things everywhere, onto the bed and onto the floor, but though I turned every pocket inside-out and shook everything I owned, I couldn't locate it.

"What are you looking for? Answer me!" Agnes's voice was louder now, as though my sense of panic had spread to her. Eventually, she grabbed my arm and forced me to sit on the bed.

"What happened? Where have you been?" she asked gently.

I shook my head, the tears welled up. She sat down and wrapped an arm around me.

"Tell me now, please tell me what happened. You're making me so worried."

I turned to look at her, but all I could manage was a single word. His name.

"A . . . Allan . . . Allan."

"Doris, let him go . . ."

"I was with him. All night, here at the hotel. Forgive me, I didn't think . . . I forgot . . . but he came to me."

Agnes's grip on my arm tightened. My head slumped against her shoulder.

"Where is he now?"

Her sweater against my cheek, wet from my tears.

"He's gone . . . left me again. He's going to Europe. To war."

I sobbed uncontrollably. Agnes held me tight, and neither of us spoke for quite some time. At last I raised my head and met her eye. It calmed me, and I managed to find my voice again.

"This is our last night at the hotel," I said weakly. "Though we have enough money for a few more nights, we need to find somewhere to live. I had a piece of paper with Elaine's surname and address, but I can't find it."

"I remember it. Her name is Jenning."

I sat in silence for a moment, trying to bring order to my swirling thoughts.

"Did she say where she lived?"

"No. But her son was a fisherman and lived somewhere on the coast. On a peninsula, I think. She said he lived right at the tip, looking out to sea."

"My God, that could be anywhere. America is a big country; there must be hundreds of peninsulas! Where is that piece of paper!"

Agnes stared back at me. Neither of us spoke. We rummaged through bags and pockets. Suddenly, my sister exclaimed: "Hold on! When we were saying goodbye to her, she said she was looking forward to being home, that she only had a few hours to go . . . That must mean she lives somewhere close to New York?"

I held my tongue, my head full of worry.

But Agnes didn't give up. She asked me what the English word for fish was.

I thought back to Elaine pointing to the types of food on the boat.

"Fish."

Agnes rushed out of the room. A few minutes later, she returned with a map. She eagerly held it out to me. Three locations by the sea were circled.

"Look, it could be here! The receptionist circled a few places, but this is the only one on a peninsula. Which means it's here, Montauk."

In that moment, I didn't have much choice but to listen to my little sister and allow her enthusiasm to drown out my worry. We packed our things, placed our bags by the door, and spent one last night at the hotel. I can still remember the cracks in the ceiling, how my eyes traced their lines as if searching out new routes across a brownish-gray sky. Agnes later told me that she too had not slept. We laughed at the fact that we hadn't spoken, that we had both tried to lie as still as possible so as not to wake the other. Talking might have made our concerns and loneliness easier to bear.

The skirt I put on the next morning was loose around my waist. I rolled up the bottom of my blouse twice beneath it to try to fill it out, but it didn't help. It slipped down to my hips all the same. Life in America was taking its toll on me.

We carried the bags together, each gripping one handle on the heavier suitcase. We took turns carrying the other one for short distances. Our hands, arms, and shoulders ached, but what choice did we have? Somehow we made it to the right station. Using the map and Agnes's sign language, we managed to buy bus tickets to Montauk. We had no idea what we would do if Elaine didn't live there — we didn't even dare consider the possibility. As the bus pulled out of the station, we sat in separate seats, up against a window, staring out. Fascinated by the tall buildings we could barely see the tops of, by the streetlights and power lines strung across the roads, by the bustle of the people and cars.

13

The laptop is on her stomach, and it moves with every breath she takes. It has been balanced there all morning. The painkillers are making her sleepy, but she fights to keep her eyes open. If she nods off now, the night will be an anxious one. A Word document takes up most of the screen, though she has left a little space for the Skype window in the top right corner. She is waiting for Jenny, counting down the endless hours that remain of the San Francisco night.

She writes a few words, sorts some memories, wonders whether she has managed to get things in the right order, whether she is repeating something already mentioned in an earlier section. There are so many events to keep track of, so many people, now dead, who meant so much to her. The names in her address book — people who, passing through, made an impression on her — she gives them life again. So few of them lived for as long as she has. A shudder passes through her, and the loneliness of the cold room feels more tangible than ever.

Her breakfast is still on the tray table next to the bed, and she reaches for the half-full glass of the hospital's brown apple juice. She has taken only a single bite of the cheese sandwich on the plate next to it. The bread tasted of rubber. She still hasn't gotten used to Swedish bread: it doesn't crumble, doesn't crunch, doesn't taste like bread should. Her tongue feels rough and dry, and she smacks it against the roof of her mouth several times before raising the glass to her lips and letting drops of juice run down her throat. She feels the wave of liquid spreading, quenching her thirst. She greedily takes another sip, then another. She glances at the time. It's finally almost morning in California, and Jenny and the kids will soon be waking up. They will crowd into the light-green kitchen, wolf down their breakfast, and then rush out to whatever adventures the day has in store. Doris knows that Jenny always connects to Skype when only she and the little one are left at home. Just a few more minutes now.

"Time to get some rest, Doris. You can put the computer down for a while." The nurse gives her a stern look and closes the lid of the laptop. Doris protests and reopens it.

"No, I can't. Leave it alone, I'm waiting for someone." Her fingers brush the Wi-Fi dongle sticking out of a USB port. "It's important."

"No, you need to rest. You aren't getting sleep if you're always on the computer. And you really do look tired. Your body needs as much rest as possible if you want to get back on your feet. So that you have the energy to start walking again."

It's difficult being old and unwell, unable to decide for yourself when you're rested, tired, or somewhere in between, and what you should or shouldn't do about it. Doris gives in and lets go of the computer, and the nurse places it on the bedside table. But she says, "Leave it on, with the lid open. So I can see if anyone tries to contact me."

"Let's do that." The nurse angles the screen toward Doris and then holds out a cup of pills. "Here, you need to take your medicine before you doze off."

Doris obediently washes them down with the last of her apple juice. "There, happy now?"

"Are you in a lot of pain?" the nurse asks gently.

"It's fine," Doris replies, waving her hand in the air. She squints, fights the sedative effect of the medicine.

"Get some sleep now. You need it."

She nods and lets her head slump to one side, her chin grazing her bony shoulder. Her eyes are fixed on the computer screen, but everything is becoming blurred. She breathes in her own scent. She smells like a hospital. Not like her own washing powder, not like her perfume. Just a faint scent of cheap detergent and sweat. She closes her eyes. The last thing she sees is an orange curtain fluttering.

The Red Address Book
J. JENNING, ELAINE

The rounded window at the back of the bus was almost completely covered by a short curtain made of thick orange fabric. It fluttered back and forth as the bus bounced along the uneven road. I gazed out the window, unable to stop looking at what we were leaving behind. The tall buildings of the Manhattan skyline. The cars. The suburbs and their beautiful houses. The choppy waves. I dozed for a while.

We got off the bus a few hours later, at a stop that was nothing more than a simple sign on the side of a country road and a weather-beaten bench. The air smelled strongly of salt and seaweed, and the wind carried small grains of sand, which stung our cheeks like small, sharp pins. We hunched our shoulders and walked slowly along the deserted road, accompanied by waves crashing on the beach. The wind was so fierce that we had to lean sharply to the right to keep our balance.

"Is this really the right place?" Agnes whispered the words, as though she didn't dare say them aloud. I shook my head and shrugged, and though I wanted to reproach her, I didn't. Our situation hadn't really changed, I tried to tell myself; it was neither better nor worse — we were still lost in a strange country, and in desperate need of help. We needed a roof over our heads and an income of some kind. The tin box in my suitcase was empty, and what little money we did have was rolled up in my bra. It was safer that way. Our last few dollar bills had been joined by the money from Allan's wallet. That gave us a good wad of cash, and its weight was a constant presence against my breast. If we didn't find Elaine, we would just have to do something else. We could manage a few more nights yet.

That said, as we began to pass boarded-up windows, we realized that we were more lost than ever. The wooden houses towered up like empty shadows, devoid of beachgoers, laughter, and life.

"There's no one here. It's a ghost town," Agnes muttered, coming to a halt. I paused too, and we sat down on the larger suitcase, squashed up together. I picked up some gravel from the ground, sieving it between my fingers. From a blossoming career as a model in Paris, with high heels and dresses lined up in my wardrobe, to blisters and a sweaty blouse on a deserted road somewhere in rural America. In just a few short weeks. There was no holding back the tears that those thoughts brought up. They flowed freely, like a flood delta, down my powdered cheeks.

"Let's go back to Manhattan. You can keep looking for a job. I can work too." Agnes leaned her face against my shoulder and sighed deeply.

"No, let's go a little farther." I could feel my strength returning, and I wiped away my tears with the arm of my coat. "There are buses coming out here, so someone must live here. If Elaine's here, we'll find her."

The suitcase we were carrying between us swung as we continued our walk. The bottom corner struck painfully against my shin whenever we lost our balance, but we continued to walk down the road. I could feel the gravel through the soles of my shoes, and somehow it seemed as painful as walking barefoot. But eventually, thank God, the number of houses increased and the gravel was replaced by asphalt. We spotted a few people wandering along the sidewalks, dressed in thick wool coats and knitted hats, their heads bowed.

"Stay here and watch the bags," I said to Agnes when we reached what seemed to be the center of a town. There were a couple of men sitting on a bench. As I approached them with a smile, I was met by a long tirade of words I didn't understand. The man saying them had a thick white beard and kind, wrinkled eyes. I replied in Swedish, but he shook his head. I came to my senses and switched into broken English.

"Know Elaine Jenning?"

He stared at me.

"Look Elaine Jenning," I continued.

"Aha, you're looking for Elaine Jenning?" he said, followed by more words I didn't understand. I stared at him helplessly. He paused, took my hand, and pointed.

"There. Elaine Jenning lives there," he said slowly and clearly, pointing to one of the houses farther down the street. A white wooden building with a cornflower-blue door. The building was narrow, with a round tower at one end, reminding me more of a boat than a house. The paintwork had peeled on the front, making the façade patchy. White shutters protected the windows from the strong wind. I nodded and curtsied in thanks, then took a few steps back and ran to Agnes.

"There!" I exclaimed, pointing. "She lives over there! Elaine lives there!"

The French words that came streaming out of Elaine's mouth as she opened the door and saw us standing there felt like a big, warm, welcoming embrace. She herded us inside, gave us blankets and tea, and allowed us to calmly tell her everything that had happened since we parted ways on the dock. About Allan. About the letter that had arrived too late. About our days at the hotel in Manhattan. She sighed and hummed, but said nothing.

"Could we stay here a few weeks? To learn more English?"

Elaine got to her feet and started to clear away the teacups. I waited for her reply.

"We need to make some kind of life for ourselves in America, and I don't know how," I continued after a moment.

She nodded and folded up the lace tablecloth.

"I'll try to help you. Language first, then a job, then somewhere to live. You can stay here, but you'll have to be careful. My son can be a little particular."

"We don't want to cause you any trouble."

"He doesn't like strangers. You'll have to keep hidden if you're going to stay here. Otherwise it won't work."

Silence descended over the room. We had found help, but perhaps not in the way we'd been expecting it.

Suddenly, Elaine got to her feet and fetched a rectangular box, which she placed on the table.

"Let's leave all that seriousness behind for now. Shall we play Monopoly?" she exclaimed. "Have you ever played? There's nothing better for sorrow and grief than a good game of Monopoly. One of my neighbors gave it to me as a welcome present when I arrived here."

Her hands shook as she unfolded the board, set out the pieces, and grabbed a small crystal bottle filled with dark-red liquid. She held out what looked like a small dog to Agnes.

"This one could suit you, Agnes? We call it *dog* in English."

Agnes repeated the word and took the piece in her hand, studying the little pewter figurine. Elaine gave her an approving nod.

After a moment's hesitation, I picked up a piece of my own.

"*Boot*," said Elaine, but I was lost in thought.

"Say it after me, *boot*."

I jumped. "I don't want to play games, Elaine!" I dropped my "boot," and it clattered onto the game board, then fell to the floor. "I want to make sure we can stay. What do you mean, hidden? Where are we meant to hide? Why?"

"Phew, we're probably going to need a drop of this sherry if we're going to do this." She flashed us a strained smile and got to her feet to fetch some glasses. We sat in silence, watching her movements in the little kitchen.

"There's a room in the attic; you can stay there. You can't come down when my son is home, only during the day. He's just a little shy, that's all."

She took us up to the attic room. There was a narrow mattress propped against one wall, and she pushed it over. We stood, watching the dust swirl as she got blankets and pillows. We helped one another carry up the suitcases. Once everything was ready, she gave us a bedpan and then locked the door.

"See you in the morning. Try to keep quiet," she said before she pulled the door shut.

That night, we slept topped and tailed beneath the thick wool blankets. The wind wailed outside the window. Through its cracks, faint gusts of icy air entered, and we pulled the blankets tighter around our bodies, up to our ears, above our chins, and eventually over our heads.

The Red Address Book
N. NILSSON, GÖSTA

We quickly established a routine in that little white house by the sea. Every day followed the exact same pattern. When Elaine's son closed the front door behind him in the morning, she would immediately come up to the attic and unlock our door. We emptied the bedpan in the outhouse in the yard and then sat down at the kitchen table, where we would be handed a cup of hot tea and a slice of plain bread. After that, the day's English lesson would begin. Elaine would point and talk as we helped her with chores around the house. We cleaned, baked, sewed, darned socks, and aired rugs, always with Elaine chatting away and our own voices repeating everything. By the end of the second week, she had stopped speaking any French at all. We carefully followed the nuances of her language and the pronunciation of individual words, which we shaped into simple sentences. She asked us to fetch things or do certain chores. Sometimes we didn't understand what she meant, but she never gave up. Occasionally she simplified a lesson by using fewer words or by gesturing and acting out a meaning until we laughed. Only then, with a wink, would she explain herself. Our lessons with Elaine were a welcome break from reality.

As dusk approached, she would shoo us back up to the attic. We heard the rattle of the key as she locked us in, followed by her footsteps down the stairs. She always went out to the porch to wait for her son, Robert, regardless of the weather. From the window in the attic, through a gap in the thin lace curtain, we could see her. She always got up and smiled warmly when Robert arrived, but he never said a word to her, just walked moodily past, his eyes focused on the ground. Day in and day out, we saw him punish her with silence; night after night, we saw her ignored.

Eventually, Agnes couldn't help herself. "Do the two of you never talk?"

Elaine shook her head unhappily.

"I left him behind. My new husband got a job in Europe, and I couldn't do anything but follow him there. Robert has never forgiven me for that. I came back when I got the chance, but too many years had passed. Now it's too late. He hates me."

He took out his anger on her. We heard him shouting whenever something went wrong. We heard her put up with it all, apologies for one thing after another. Swear her love and beg for forgiveness from the son she had lost forever. Her situation was much like ours — she was alone, a new arrival. Living in a country she no longer knew, confronting someone who no longer wanted anything to do with her.

The hours we spent in the attic passed more slowly than our time in Elaine's company. I can still remember being trapped up there in the stale air. My sorrow and longing for Allan. He was constantly in my thoughts. I couldn't understand how he could abandon me again. How could he move on to another woman so quickly, how could he be married? I wondered who she was, and whether time also came to a standstill when they were together.

Worries became overwhelming in that cramped space, and I tried to take my mind off them by getting in touch with Gösta. Every night, by the glow of a small oil lamp, I wrote long letters telling him all about our new home. About the sea and the sand we could see from the house, about the wind that whipped my face whenever I went out to the garden to get some air. About the English language and how it sounded to my ears, how the words mixed together to become noise when people spoke quickly, as Americans always seemed to do. I had experienced the same thing with French when I first arrived in Paris. I told him about Elaine and her strange son. She mailed the letters for me every day, and I waited patiently for a reply. But Gösta remained silent, and I became afraid that something had happened to him. I knew that the war was still raging in Europe, but it was hard to find out more than that. In America, everyday life continued as though nothing had happened, as though Europe wasn't burning.

Then, one day, it arrived. The envelope contained a handwritten note with a few lines of text and a page torn from a newspaper. It was a review of Gösta's paintings. The tone was critical, and the text finished by stating that the current exhibition would likely be Gösta's last. Now I can't claim that I ever truly understood his paintings, even if I did like the colors, so I wasn't all that surprised by the negative review. That kind of modern art — abstract explosions of twisting color, surreal geometric perfection — certainly wasn't for everyone. But the article helped me understand his silence, and the few short lines from Gösta himself revealed his frame of mind. I understood why he had written just one polite phrase about how we were doing, why he only briefly added that he was happy we were alive.

I remember feeling so sorry for him then. He was determined to cling to something he clearly lacked the talent for, which only made him unhappy. I missed him more then than I ever had before. Missed our conversations. Nine years had passed since I'd last seen him. There was a picture of him in the article, and I tore it out and pinned it up next to the bed. He stared down at me with a serious face and sad eyes. Every night, as I blew out the oil lamp, I wondered whether I would ever see him, or Sweden, again.

The Red Address Book
J. ~~JENNING, ELAINE~~ *DEAD*

Our secret existence in the attic had to come to an end; we had probably known that all along. And sure enough, early one morning, we were discovered. Agnes had left her cardigan on a chair in the living room, and we heard Robert shout:

"Whose cardigan is this? Who's been here?"

"A friend, she stopped by for tea yesterday afternoon," Elaine said quietly.

"I've told you that you aren't to let anyone into this house! Not a single soul should cross my threshold! Do you understand?"

Agnes crept closer to me, and her movement caused the floorboards to creak. The voices downstairs immediately fell silent. We heard loud footsteps on the stairs, and the door was kicked open with a single blow. When Robert saw us there on the mattress, his eyes were full of rage. We quickly jumped up and fumbled for our clothes in the semidarkness. Half-dressed, we ran past him, out onto the street. He came after us, throwing out our bags. The hinge on the bigger suitcase broke, and the lid skidded across the road. Next came the clothes. Beautiful dresses from Paris landed in a heap in the mud. We grabbed them and shoved them into the bags. But what I remember most distinctly from that moment is how fast my heart was beating. From behind the new lace curtain that Agnes had sewn during our quiet hours in the attic, I saw Elaine peering out. She held up a hand, but didn't wave. She had given us so much. Not least of all, her language. That was the greatest of gifts. Those terrified eyes behind the lace curtain were the last I ever saw of her. Robert stood on the steps, hands on his hips, as we picked up our bags and left. Only when the bus pulled up, at the stop farther down the street, did he turn and head back into the house.

The steel-gray flank of the bus reflected the day's first sunlight, blinding us as we climbed on board. The red-and-white vinyl seats were already warm from its rays. We sat at the very back, peering through the window as the bus slowly trundled on. Sitting there, we had no idea what was going on back in the little white house. Despite everything, we actually felt a certain sense of relief. The language the other passengers were speaking was no longer entirely foreign to us; we could talk to the driver, tell him where we were going. Back to Manhattan. Our months in the house in Montauk had hardened us and prepared us for a life of freedom. Completely without warning, Agnes even started to laugh. Hilarity washed over her, and it drew me in.

"What are we even laughing at?" I said when I eventually managed to stop.

Agnes grew serious again. "It feels like we just escaped from prison."

"Yes, that attic had started to feel a bit shut in. Maybe it's for the best, who knows?"

Morning was passing. By the time we reached Manhattan, it would almost be evening, and we had nowhere to go. When the bus finally pulled up to the station, Agnes was sleeping deeply against my shoulder. We gathered up our things, left the bus, and started making our way toward the bright arrivals hall. We put down our bags in one corner.

"Where are we going to go now? Where will we sleep?" Agnes sounded dejected.

"We'll have to stay awake tonight if we can't find anywhere to stay. You watch the bags, and I'll go and look for an inexpensive hotel."

Agnes sat down, leaned against the wall.

A man with ash-blond hair suddenly appeared before us. "Excuse me, but you wouldn't happen to be Swedish, would you?"

I recognized him from the bus. He was wearing a simple black suit and a white shirt. Agnes replied in Swedish, but he shook his head and said, "No, no." He wasn't from Sweden, but his mother was. We spoke for a while, and he offered to help us, to give us a place to stay until we found someplace of our own.

"I'm sure my mother would be happy to speak a bit of Swedish," he said.

Agnes and I glanced at each other, hesitating. Following this strange man home wasn't the obvious best choice. But he looked kind, and he seemed honest. Eventually, Agnes nodded and I thanked him for the offer. He picked up the heavier suitcase and we followed him out of the station.

We didn't find out more about Elaine until much later, when we returned to visit her. The house was boarded up, and we had to ask a neighbor what had happened. Shortly after we left the house that day, the neighbor told us, Elaine's heart had suddenly given out during an argument with Robert. He had been crushed. For the first time, he was able to express his sorrow at having lost his mother all those years ago. The neighbor said he had left the house and gone to sea that same week. No one had seen him since.

14

On the other side of the curtain, the woman who was admitted last night coughs. The sound echoes off the walls. She has pneumonia and shouldn't really be in this room, but they couldn't put her in the infection ward because of a bedsore. When she coughs, it sounds as though the contents of her stomach are about to reappear. Doris shudders in disgust and covers her ears with her hands.

"Can I have my computer?"

Doris shouts out into the empty room, then repeats the question in a voice that barely carries. Because of her dry throat, the sound creaks and cracks against the roof of her mouth. The cool hospital room remains quiet — no footsteps of nurses coming to help.

"Press the alarm button," pants the woman with the cough, when Doris shouts for help a third time.

"Thanks, but it's not that important."

"It's clearly important enough for you to lie there shouting. Press the button," the woman snaps irritably.

Doris doesn't reply. When she doesn't want help, the nurses are always there to nag her, but now that she really needs them, they're nowhere to be seen. What if she tried to get the computer herself?

She can see it, its lid now closed, on the table where the nurse placed it earlier. She had told the nurse to leave it open; why couldn't they just do as she asked? Surely she can manage to get over there and fetch it herself? It's not far at all. If she ever wants to go home, she will need to practice getting up. She picks up the remote control for her bed and tries pressing one of the buttons. The bed jolts and the foot end starts to rise. She tries to stop the movement by pressing one button after another. Now the head end starts moving, and the lower half starts rising beneath her knees. In panic, she presses the red alarm button as she shakes the remote control and continues to press every button she can. Eventually the bed stops.

"Goodness, what's going on here?" laughs the nurse who comes running. Doris is sitting upright, with her legs raised high, posed like a half-open pocketknife. But she doesn't laugh; she's blinking away tears of pain.

"The computer over there, I need it." She points as her legs are slowly lowered and the pain in her back gradually decreases.

"Why didn't you press the alarm? We come running if you do that. You know that, Doris."

"I wanted to practice walking. I want to get out of here. Just doing physical therapy isn't enough, it's too slow."

"Patience, Doris. You need to accept your limits. You're ninety-six, you're not a spring chicken anymore." The nurse is talking slowly and a touch too loudly.

"Patience and stubbornness," she mutters. "If you knew how stubborn I am."

"So I've heard. Should we try it, then?" Doris nods and the nurse slowly swings Doris's legs over the edge of the bed and lifts her upper body into a sitting position. Doris screws her eyes tight.

"Was that too fast? Do you feel dizzy?" The nurse gives her a sympathetic look and gently strokes her hair. Doris shakes her head.

"Patience and stubbornness," she says, pressing her hands against the soft mattress.

"One, two, three, and up," the nurse says, pulling Doris into a standing position, with her hands firmly beneath Doris's armpits. Doris feels a jolt of pain in her hip, which then shoots down one leg. "One step at a time, OK?" Doris doesn't say anything, just moves the foot of her bad leg forward a few millimeters. Then the other, a few millimeters. The computer is just over there, almost within reach. Her eyes are fixed on it. It's only two meters away, but at that very moment, it might as well be on the opposite side of an abyss.

"Do you need to rest? Sit down a minute?" The nurse hooks her foot around a stool and drags it toward them, but Doris shakes her head and laboriously inches toward the table. When she finally makes it, she rests both hands on the computer and breathes out, her head hanging over her chest.

"My word, you really are stubborn." The nurse is smiling as she places an arm around Doris's shoulders. Doris is breathing heavily. She can no longer feel her legs, and she wriggles her toes to wake them up. She looks up and meets the nurse's eye. Then she collapses.

The Red Address Book
A. ANDERSSON, CARL

Carl led us through the station and out onto the street, chatting nonstop. He said that he had heard us talking on the bus, that he understood a few words of Swedish. There was a line of yellow Checker taxis outside the station, but he walked straight past them, ignoring the drivers who called to us as we passed. He walked quickly, with long strides, and was always a few steps ahead of us.

"What if he's conning us? What if he's dangerous?" Agnes whispered, tugging at the suitcase we were carrying between us to make me stop. I pulled back, fixed my eyes on her, and nodded for her to keep going. She grunted before she reluctantly started moving again. We continued, following the blond head, which was at least ten centimeters higher than any other on the street. He did look Swedish, and maybe that was what made me decide to trust him.

We walked and walked. Every now and then, Carl would turn around to check that we were still there. I had blisters on my hand by the time he came to a halt outside a narrow brick building. There were two iron pots of daffodils outside the red front door. He smiled at us.

"Here we are. She isn't too well," he explained before he opened the door.

The house had three stories, with just one room on each floor. We walked straight into the kitchen. Inside, an old woman was sitting in a rocking chair. Her hands lay in her lap and she was staring straight ahead.

"Mom, look who I have with me. Two girls from Sweden." He nodded toward us. She didn't look up, didn't seem to notice that anyone had come in.

"Mom, they can speak Swedish with you." He stroked her cheek. Her blue eyes seemed glassy, her pupils small. Her hair hung limp over her shoulders, and a few strands had come loose, covering one of her eyes. A thick knitted shawl was draped over her shoulders. It didn't look clean.

"Her name is Kristina. She hasn't really spoken since my father disappeared. Sometimes she says a few words in Swedish, and I just thought that . . ." He turned his back to hide his sorrow, cleared his throat, and continued.

"I just thought you might be able to get her to talk. Maybe you could help out with the housework too."

"Let me try." Agnes cautiously approached the rocking chair. She sat down on the floor, with her back turned to the woman.

"I'm just going to sit here a while," she said in Swedish. "I can sit here all night if I have to. If you want to say anything, I'm listening."

The woman didn't reply. But after a while, her chair began to rock gently. I sat down too. The house was silent except for the gentle creaking of the rocking chair and the distant street noise. We agreed that we would stay a few days, and Carl made up a bed for us in the living room, on the second floor. He even pulled out a mattress for Kristina and gently lowered her onto it. She was too heavy to carry up the two flights of stairs to the bedroom.

Carl often came up to the living room to talk to us. Never about Kristina. He told us stories about what he had done that day, about the bank where he worked. And about Europe and the war. The situation had worsened during the months we had spent with Elaine, and Carl kept us up-to-date, but he didn't know whether Sweden was involved. In America, people talked about Europe as if it was one big country.

At first we didn't want to ask Carl where his father had gone, but the more we got to know him, the more personal our conversations became. After a few weeks, we finally worked up the courage. The reply wasn't surprising.

It had all been very sudden. One day, when he and his mother got home, his father was waiting, with his bag packed. He said a few words and then just left Carl and Kristina without any money, but in a house they could keep.

"He left my mom for someone else. Something inside her died when he disappeared. She had always felt so lost in New York, and he was her refuge. He looked after everything; he even spoke for her."

We listened in silence.

"It's been three years since he left. I don't miss him. I don't miss his moods or his overbearing nature. We're actually much better off without him. I just wish Mom could see that too. But she gradually got more and more depressed. She stopped seeing anyone, stopped caring about our home and her appearance. Eventually, she sat down in the rocking chair and she hasn't gotten up since. She's barely uttered a word."

We took turns sitting next to Kristina, talking to her. She didn't like to move from her chair, and I sometimes worried that she would turn to stone, sitting there. How long could a person remain still like that, saying nothing? As more weeks passed, Carl insisted that we stay; he said we were good for Kristina. And he was right. Eventually, early one morning, as we were heating water for tea, it finally happened.

"Tell me about Sweden," she said faintly. It was wonderful to hear those Swedish words.

Agnes and I hurried over, sat on either side of her, and started to talk. About the snowdrifts we used to play in. About the potatoes and the herring. About the smell of the soft spring rain. About the first coltsfoot. About the lambs skipping about on the lush green island of Djurgården in central Stockholm. About the bicycles swaying along Strandvägen on a bright summer's night. With every image we described, a glimmer came to her eyes. She didn't say anything else, but she started to look at us more and more often. If we fell silent, she would raise an eyebrow and nod for us to continue.

The days passed, and we continued our struggle to make Kristina happy. One day, when Carl came home, he found the rocking chair empty.

"It's empty." He stared at us. "It's empty! Where is she? Where's my mother?"

We laughed and pointed to the sink. There she stood, washing the plates from lunch. She was pale and thin, but she was standing on her own two feet, and her hands still worked. When Carl walked over to her, she smiled gently. He hugged her tight and glanced at us over her shoulder, his eyes full of tears.

We tried to find information about what was happening in Sweden, but no one could give us answers. The news reports discussed Hitler and how his armies were advancing, how the French men and women cried as German soldiers marched into Paris and occupied the city. We stared at the black-and-white newspaper images; it was hard to make sense of events in the city I loved and missed. It was nothing like when we left it; everything had changed. I wrote a few lines to Gösta but, as so often before, heard nothing in reply.

We were still living with Carl and Kristina. We didn't have to pay rent; it was Carl's way of thanking us. But we helped with the cooking and cleaning. We would talk to Kristina while Carl was at the office. She couldn't explain why she had been silent for so long; she said it felt like she had been sleeping for months. But as the days passed and she got better and better, I started to think about the future once again. Agnes and I needed to find work and a home of our own. We needed to venture out into the world, after almost a year in exile.

Agnes wasn't interested in my plans, and I often felt frustrated with her. She stopped telling me things, and whenever I brought up the future, she seemed absent-minded, wistful. She started replying in English, even when I spoke to her in Swedish. Over time, I noticed that she would seek out Carl rather than me. They would linger on the sofa in the kitchen in the evenings, whispering together at night. Just like Allan and I once had.

It was late one evening. Kristina was in her rocking chair, hand-stitching a tablecloth. I was reading the daily paper, searching, as always, for the latest news about the war. I imagined that every dead soldier listed was Allan. I was so absorbed that I didn't even notice the two of them standing in front of me, hand in hand. Agnes had to repeat what she had just said.

"Carl and I. We're getting married."

I stared at her. Stared at him. Didn't understand. She was so young, far too young to be getting married.

"Aren't you happy?" Agnes exclaimed, holding out her hand to show me her smooth gold ring. "You're happy for us, aren't you? It's so romantic! We want to have a spring wedding at the Swedish church. And you're going to be my bridesmaid."

So it was. The cherry blossoms had just bloomed, and Agnes's bouquet was the same color: a playful, straggling bunch of pink roses, ivy, and white mimosa. I took it from her and clutched it tight with both hands as Carl pushed a second golden ring onto her left hand. It got caught on her knuckle, but he twisted it gently until it slipped over the joint. She was wearing my white Chanel dress, the one I had often worn in Paris. It looked like it had been made for her, and she was more beautiful than ever. Her shoulder-length golden hair was curled into thick, flowing waves, half of them pinned up with a clip covered in white pearls.

I should have been happy for her, but all I could feel was how much I missed Allan. I'm sure you must think that I go on and on about him, Jenny. But it's difficult. There are certain memories you just can't forget. They linger and fester, occasionally bursting like a boil and causing pain, such terrible pain.

The Red Address Book
A. ANDERSSON, CARL

As the months went by, it became increasingly clear which sister ruled the house. Agnes, the new wife, took charge, expecting me to agree with her ideas and to do as she said. She was like a child playing grownup. It infuriated me.

One morning, I paced up and down the hallway. The thick wooden planks creaked in two places, and I stepped over them to avoid making noise. It was almost eight, and Carl would soon be leaving for work. When he appeared, I paused and nodded a goodbye. The sounds of the street outside came thundering in as he opened the door and disappeared, but the house soon fell silent again, and I picked up where I had left off. I had bitten the nails on my right hand so low that they stung, but I couldn't stop myself. I stormed into the kitchen.

"I'm not going to stay here any longer. I don't want to be your maid for the rest of my life."

Agnes stared at me as my angry French words flowed. Only the two of us understood this language, so I used it often. I repeated myself until she nodded and tried to hush me. I had already packed my bag, one of the suitcases we had brought from Paris, and changed out of my shirtdress into something more sober. My hair was pinned up and my lips were red. I was ready to face the outside world, to re-establish my place in the hierarchy. As a mannequin, someone who was celebrated. Someone who had been out of the limelight far too long.

"But where are you going to go? Where will you live? Wouldn't it be better if we organized something for you first?"

I snorted at her questions.

"Put down the suitcase. Don't be silly." Agnes was talking quietly. She ran her hand over her dress, a recent gift from Carl. He bought her clothes, made her his own.

"Give it a few more days. Please, stay. Carl knows people, he can help you."

"Carl, Carl, Carl. That's all you ever think about. Do you really think he's the solution to everything? I managed perfectly well in Paris without either you or him. I'll manage in New York too!"

"Carl, Carl, Carl. Did I hear my name? What are you talking about? Is something the matter?" Carl had come back to grab his umbrella, and he wrapped an arm around Agnes and kissed her on the cheek.

"Nothing's the matter," she mumbled.

He raised an eyebrow at me.

"Pas de problème," I said, turning to leave. Agnes ran after me.

"Please, don't abandon me," she begged. "We're sisters. We belong together. You have a home here with us. We need you. At least wait until you've found a job and somewhere to live. Carl can help you, we both can."

She carried the suitcase back to my bed, and I didn't have the energy to protest. Later that evening, I studied my face in the cracked, speckled bathroom mirror. Both the journey and our time in America had left their marks. The once smooth skin around my eyes was now swollen, soft, and dull. I gently raised my eyebrows, pulled them up and up toward my hairline. My eyes shone when I did that, and I looked like I once had. Younger, prettier. The way I should still look. I smiled at my reflection, but the smile I had once been so proud of had lost its former sparkle. I shook my head, and my mouth returned to the usual straight line.

The makeup I had brought with me from Paris was virtually untouched. I unscrewed the lid of the powder jar and dabbed my face with a brush. The red blemishes disappeared, and my freckles were erased. Next, I painted my cheeks; small hints of pink on my cheekbones, becoming larger and larger circles of deep cerise. I couldn't stop myself. I painted thick black lines around my eyes, all the way out to my temples. Drew in my brows as wide as lumps of coal. Covered half my lids beneath them with dark-gray eye shadow. Painted my lips red, outlining them to look double their size. I stared at my grotesque reflection. With tears streaming down my cheeks, I eventually drew a large black cross on the mirror, over my image.

The Red Address Book
P. POWERS, JOHN ROBERT

I stuck it out for a few more months, but that little house started to feel more and more claustrophobic, and once again I wanted to leave. This time, I planned my escape slightly better. When I packed up my things, Carl was already at work and Kristina was asleep. I thought it would be best that way, so my sister and I could have a proper farewell. Agnes cried and gave me all the money she had.

"We'll see each other again soon, I promise," I whispered as we hugged.

I pushed her away and left without turning back; it was too painful to see her tears. I spent the next few nights at a small hotel on Seventh Street. There was barely room to stand; the bed and the small side table took up what little space there was. On my first day there, I sat down to write a letter to Gösta. I wrote honestly about how I felt and what had happened. This time, it only took two weeks for his reply to come, addressed poste restante to the Grand Central Post Office. I was used to going there every day without success, so when the cashier finally handed me a letter, I was so excited that I immediately tore it open. It was written in spidery ink, and I smiled when I saw the handwriting. I had hoped it would contain a ticket back to Stockholm, or at least some money, but it contained only words. He had no money, he wrote; life was hard in Stockholm. The war was affecting everyone. He was managing to survive by swapping his paintings for food and wine.

If I could, dear Doris, I would send a boat to fetch you. A boat that would carry you across the ocean and into Stockholm's beautiful harbor. I would sit in my window with a pair of binoculars, watching the sailors bring her in. And when I caught sight of you, I would run down to the water and stand there, waiting for you with my arms outstretched. That, my darling Doris, would be fantastic. Seeing a dear friend after so many years apart! You are welcome here whenever you like. You know that. My door is always open. The sweet young girl who served me wine at Bastugatan 5, I'll never forget her.

Your Gösta

The letter was decorated with elegant red, purple, and green flowers. They curled up the entire right-hand side of the page, rounding the corner and embracing the text. I carefully ran my index finger over the pretty flowers, a sign of Gösta's fondness for the young maid he had once known. The paint was thick, and I could feel every brushstroke on the coarse paper. Those flowers were more beautiful than any of the strange canvases I had seen him paint in the past.

I still have that letter, Jenny, among all the others in my little tin box. It might even be worth something now, given that he did gain fame in the end, long after his death.

I stood in the post office for quite some time, his letter in one hand and the envelope in the other. I felt as though my last life-line had been severed, and the world around me faded to black and white. Eventually, I slowly folded the sheet of paper and tucked it inside my bra, close to my heart. A strong desire to return to Stockholm as soon as possible replaced my sense of dejection. I ran to the bathroom. Inside, I pinched my cheeks until they flushed and then painted my lips red. Straightened my beige tailored jacket and adjusted the skirt that my hips still hadn't filled out. After that, I headed straight to the John Robert Powers Agency for models. Carl had told me that in New York, beautiful girls found modeling work through this agency. That was how they got mannequin jobs here — not through department stores or fashion houses, as was done in

Paris. My heart was pounding as I placed my hand on the doorknob. I had no idea what a modeling agency was like, but I was willing to find out. My beauty was my only asset.

"Hello," I said quietly, standing at a huge desk behind which a small woman sat. She was wearing a tight black-and-red-checked dress. She looked me up and down, her glasses perched on the tip of her nose.

"I'm here to see John Robert Powers," I stuttered in my hesitant English.

"Do you have an appointment?"

I shook my head, and she gave me a superior smile.

"Miss, this is the John Robert Powers Agency. You can't just walk in here and assume you can see him."

"I just thought that he might want to meet me. I come from Paris, where I worked with some of the big European fashion houses. Chanel, for example. Do you know Chanel?"

"Chanel?" She got up from her seat and pointed to one of the dark-gray chairs along one wall.

"Take a seat. I'll be back in a moment."

I sat there for what seemed like an eternity. Eventually she came back, accompanied by a short man. He was wearing a charcoal-colored suit. I could see a vest beneath it, and a thin golden chain hanging from one pocket. Like the receptionist, he looked me up and down before he opened his mouth.

"So you worked for Chanel?" His eyes flitted upward from my feet. He avoided my eyes.

"Turn around." He emphasized the words by raising a hand and making a spinning motion. I turned 180 degrees and glanced at him over my shoulder.

"It must have been a long time ago," he snorted, turning on his heel and walking away. I stared at the receptionist. What was going on?

"That means you can go now." She nodded toward the door.

"But don't you want me to try on any clothes?"

"Miss, I'm sure you were a pretty model at one point in time, but those days are over. We have room only for young girls here."

She looked almost satisfied. Maybe every girl that Mr. Powers rejected was a personal triumph for her.

I ran my hand over my cheek. It was still soft. Still as smooth as a child's. I cleared my throat.

"Perhaps I could book an appointment? One day when Mr. Powers has more time?"

She shook her head firmly.

"There's no point, I'm afraid. It's better if you look for another kind of job."

15

"What happened to your face?" Jenny leans in closer to the screen. Doris's cheek is covered by a large white bandage.

"Nothing. I fell over and hit myself, but it's nothing to worry about. It's just a scratch."

"But how did that happen? Don't they help you when you get up to walk around?"

"Ah, it was so silly. I overdid it and the nurse couldn't hold me up. I have to try to stay mobile; they'll send me to an old people's home otherwise."

"An old people's home? Who said that?"

"The social worker. I didn't want to say anything to you, but he comes to see me with a form every now and then. He wants me to sign it, so they can send me there voluntarily."

"How does that make you feel?"

"I'd rather die."

"Then we'll have to make sure you don't go. Next time he comes to see you, call me."

"And what will you say then, my dear? That I can live at home? Because I can't. Not right now. In that sense, he's right. I'm not much good for anything at the moment. But I'm not going to give him the satisfaction of admitting that."

"I'll talk to him," Jenny says soothingly. "But how are you passing the time? Do you have anything to read? Should I send you some new books?"

"Thanks, but I still have a few that you sent last time. I liked the Don DeLillo a lot, the one about September 11."

"*Falling Man.* I liked that one too. I'll see if I can send you another . . . Doris! Doris! What is it?"

Doris's face is frozen in pain. She presses her right hand to her chest and waves the other one wildly.

"Doris!" Jenny shouts from the small window on the screen. "Doris, what's happening? Tell me, what's going on?"

There's a faint hissing sound. Doris stares at Jenny with a look of resignation, her face losing even more color. Jenny shouts out, with all the strength she has.

"Nurse, hello! Hello! Nurse!" Then she roars — steady sound coming straight from her mouth. Doris had turned the volume down low on the computer, so that it wouldn't bother the other patients, but the woman in the next bed can hear that something is wrong. She peers over the edge of her bed and sees Doris, apparently asleep. The woman presses the alarm button. Jenny screams and shouts. Eventually, a nurse appears. The woman points to Doris's bed. The nurse lifts the computer from Doris's stomach and places it on the bedside table.

"She's having a heart attack!" Jenny shouts, making the nurse jump.

"My God, you scared me!"

"Check on Doris! She cramped up and was holding her hand to her chest. Then she fainted!"

"What are you saying?" The nurse presses Doris's alarm button, tries to find the pulse in her wrist. When she can't, she starts giving mouth-to-mouth. Between breaths, the nurse shouts for help. Jenny watches it all unfold from her light-green kitchen in California. Three more staff members come running, a doctor and two nurses. The doctor turns on the defibrillator and holds the two paddles over Doris's chest. The shock makes her body lift up and then fall back to the bed. He charges the paddles again and gives her a second shock.

"I have a pulse!" the nurse shouts, her index and middle fingers pressed firmly against Doris's wrist.

"Is she alive?" Jenny shrieks. "Tell me, is she alive?"

The doctor turns around in surprise, raises an eyebrow to the nurses. Jenny hears him mutter: "Why didn't anyone turn the computer off?"

He looks back down at her and nods.

"I'm sorry you had to see that. Are you a relative?"

Jenny nods, panting. "I'm her only relative. How is she?"

"She's old and she's weak. We'll do everything we can to keep her going for as long as possible, but the heart can't handle all that much when you're as old as Doris. Has she had a heart attack before?"

Jenny shakes her head. "Not that I know of. She's always been strong and healthy. Please help her; I can't imagine life without her."

"I understand. Her heart is beating again now. We're going to take her up to intensive care, and she'll spend the night there. Is it OK if we disconnect you now?"

"Can't I go with her?"

"I think it's best if you have a bit of a break." He nods toward Tyra, who is whimpering behind Jenny. She reaches down and lifts the child onto her hip. She hushes Tyra.

"It's fine. I want to stay with Doris for a while, if that's OK."

The doctor shakes his head apologetically.

16

The roar of waves crashing in on the beach is drowned out by the constant stream of cars on the road. The house has a pretty view, but they hadn't given much thought to the traffic when they moved in. No one ever sits on their white porch, looking out to sea.

Not until today.

When Willie gets home from work, Jenny is the first thing he sees. She is sitting, with Tyra on her lap, on the hammock that they strung up many years earlier, back when they were head over heels in love and always wanted to be close. It swings slowly, the chains creaking gently against the hooks.

"Why are you sitting out here, in all the fumes? It's not good for the baby." He smiles at them, but Jenny's face is serious.

"Do you have to call her a baby? She's almost two."

"She's one and a half and has just started to walk."

"She's twenty months, two weeks, and three days. Almost two."

"OK, OK. I'll call her Tyra then." Willie shrugs and opens the door.

"I'm thinking about going to Sweden."

The door swings shut with a thud. Tyra whimpers.

"Huh? Sweden? What's going on?"

"Doris had a heart attack today. She's dying."

"A heart attack? I thought she'd broken her leg."

"It's bad. I have to be with her now. I can't let her die alone. I'll be gone as long as . . . she needs me."

"How's that going to work? Who's going to take care of the kids? We can't manage without you."

"What? Is that all you have to say?"

"I'm sorry about Doris, I really am. I know she means the world to you. But I just don't know how we'll manage."

"I can take Tyra with me. The boys are at school during the day. You'll cope."

Willie takes a deep breath and looks away. Jenny places a hand on his shoulder.

"It'll be fine."

"I know she's important to you, but is she more important than your own family? I've got a job to go to, a job that supports this whole family. I can't be here when the boys get home from school. So who's going to be here for them?"

"There has to be a way. We'll just have to pay someone. She's dying, don't you get that?"

Jenny pulls herself upright and lets Tyra sit at the other end of the hammock. Willie leans against the wall and gently strokes Jenny's cheek with one hand.

"I'm sorry. I'm just stressed. What exactly do you know?"

"We were talking today. Everything was normal to begin with. She was normal. She'd had a fall and there was a bandage on her cheek, but she was joking about it. You know what Doris is like. But then she suddenly started clutching her chest; she couldn't breathe. It was like on TV, like some episode of *Grey's Anatomy*. I screamed, so loud, with everything I had. Eventually they came running with one of those machines with electric paddles."

Willie sits down next to her and takes her hand. "So it was really a heart attack?"

"Yeah. The doctor said she's starting to get weak. The broken bone and the operation must have taken it out of her. They had to do an angioplasty, the nurse told me afterward."

"She could live for a long time yet, love; you don't know. What are you going to do over there? Just sit around, waiting for her to die? I don't think that would be good for you."

He strokes her hand, but Jenny pulls back, pushes him away.

"You don't think it would be good? For *me*? You're only thinking of yourself! It's more comfortable for you if I stay; that's what this is about. But you know what? She's all I have left, my only connection to Sweden. My last link to my mom and my grandma."

Willie almost manages to hide his sigh. "I know today must have been hard, but you can at least wait to see how she's doing? She might recover."

He pulls her close, and her body relaxes. She leans her head against his chest and breathes in his familiar, reassuring scent. His shirt is damp and she undoes a couple of buttons and pushes the fabric to one side so that her cheek is against his bare skin.

"Why do we never sit out here anymore?" she whispers, closing her eyes as the sea breeze blows on her face. A heavy truck thunders past, and they laugh.

"That's why," Willie whispers, kissing her head.

17

"Good morning, Doris." The nurse leans over the bed and smiles gently, sympathetically.

"Where am I? Am I dead?"

"You're alive. You're in intensive care. You had a bit of heart trouble yesterday, a small heart attack."

"I thought I was dead."

"No, no, you aren't dead yet. Your heart is stable again. The doctor managed to clear the blockage. Do you remember going in for an operation?"

Doris nods weakly, uncertainly.

"How are you feeling?"

She smacks her tongue against the roof of her mouth.

"A bit thirsty."

"Would you like some water?"

Doris manages to force a smile.

"Apple juice, if there is any."

"I'll go and get you some. You get some rest now, you'll feel better in no time." The nurse turns away.

"Things aren't looking good for the old hag."

She turns back. "What did you say?"

"Things aren't looking good for the old hag."

The nurse bursts out laughing, but falls silent when she sees Doris's serious face.

"You might not be feeling your best right now, but you're going to be fine. It was just a small heart attack; you were lucky."

"I'm over ninety-six. I've got a limited supply of luck."

"Right, exactly, you're still a long way off a hundred!" The nurse winks and squeezes Doris's hand.

"Death, death, death," she mumbles quietly, once she is left alone. There is a machine by the head of the bed, and she turns and follows its numbers and lines with interest. Her pulse, bouncing up and down, the zigzag pattern of the EKG line, her oxygen levels.

The Red Address Book
A. ~~ALM, AGNES~~ DEAD

Everything came crashing down. Right there, on the street outside the modeling agency. No job. Nowhere to live. No friends. Just a married sister a few blocks away. I remember standing there for quite some time, with my eyes fixed on the heavy traffic on the street in front of me. I couldn't decide which way to go, right or left — but I barely need to tell you which way I really wanted to go, Jenny. Gösta had once made me promise to be true to myself, not to let circumstances take charge of my fate. But there and then, I broke that promise, as I had so many times before. I didn't see that I had any other choice. Slowly, I started making my way back to the house I had recently left.

Carl still wasn't home. Agnes was sewing next to Kristina. They looked up as I stepped through the door. Agnes leapt to her feet.

"You came back! I knew it!" She hugged me tight.

"I'm not staying for long," I mumbled.

"Yes, you're staying. You and Kristina can have the beds upstairs." She nodded toward the stairs. "Carl and I will sleep here, on the pull-out bed."

I shook my head. I couldn't agree to that.

"We've already talked about it. We were hoping you would come back. There's plenty of room for you here. You can help me with the housework."

She hugged me again, and I felt her stomach press against mine.

"It's my turn to help you now. You've helped me so much, and we're going to need you here." She took my hands and placed them on her belly. I raised an eyebrow, and my jaw dropped as the meaning of her words dawned on me.

"You're expecting? Why didn't you say anything sooner! You're having a baby!"

She nodded happily. Her mouth couldn't keep straight any longer; it curled into a smile, accompanied by a giggle.

"Isn't it fantastic!" she cried. "We'll have a little baby in the house!" She held up the piece of fabric she had been embroidering. It was a pale-yellow baby blanket. I felt a jolt in my heart at the thought of the babies Allan and I had once talked of having, but I brushed that away. This was Agnes's baby, Agnes's moment. I beamed at her.

I couldn't do anything but stay. I was so looking forward to the little one's arrival. Carl and Agnes, Kristina and me. An odd family eagerly awaiting a new life. Elise, your mother.

Every morning, Agnes would stand in profile in the kitchen and stroke her stomach. And every morning, it was bigger. We shared her joy at being pregnant, and she let me touch her belly as much as I wanted. There was a child growing inside her, and toward the end of the pregnancy I even saw the outline of a foot when the baby kicked. I tried to grab it, but Agnes brushed away my hand and said I was tickling her.

The days passed more quickly, now that I felt needed. I helped Agnes shop and cook; I cleaned and washed. She became less active and lost weight, her face becoming gaunt. Her stomach was like a balloon on her otherwise slender body. Over and over again, I asked her whether she really felt OK, but she brushed aside my worries and said she was just tired. She was pregnant, after all.

"It's going to be so nice once the baby is here, and I can be myself again." She sighed. She did this more and more often.

One day, when I went downstairs, she was sitting on the sofa in the kitchen, and her lips were a shade of bluish-black. Her skin was mottled, her eyes wide, her breathing strained. I can't write more about it. It's a moment I would rather forget. A moment so much like the last one with my father. Though this time, it wasn't my mother who cried out: it was me.

They managed to deliver little Elise before your grandmother Agnes died. In childbed, as they said at the time; something went dreadfully wrong. Just like that, she was gone. And we were left with a tiny little bundle that never stopped screaming. As if she knew she had been robbed of her mother's love.

I held your mother in my arms every day, almost constantly. Soothed her and tried to learn how to love her. We fed her ordinary cow's milk, heated to body temperature, but it gave her such stomachaches that she cried and cried. I remember that when I laid my hand on that small stomach of hers, I could feel it bubbling away as though something was alive inside. Kristina took over from me sometimes, tried to heal and comfort us both, but she was old and tired.

Carl couldn't bear all the weeping and grief. He started leaving the house earlier and coming home later. Only when he managed to find a wet-nurse, a woman with a baby who was willing to share some of her milk with another child, did calm return to the little house.

Life slowly returned to normal. Elise grew and gave us her first gurgling laugh. I missed Agnes so much, but tried to control my feelings for the sake of the little girl.

One day, I left the house. A short walk, that was all I had planned, to buy meat and vegetables. But my feet carried me to the post office, somewhere I hadn't been in a long time. I was curious to see whether Gösta had written to me. He hadn't, but there was another letter, addressed poste restante to me. From France.

Doris,

Words cannot describe how much I miss you. The war is terrible. More terrible than you could ever imagine. I pray every day that I will survive. That I shall see you again. I have a pic-

ture of you here. In my pocket. You look like the beautiful rose I
met in Paris. The important things seem so obvious here. I keep
your image close to my heart and hope you can feel my love on
the other side of the Atlantic.

 Yours for eternity,
 Allan

There I was. In New York, where he should have been. Where we finally should have been together. But he was in France. I spent the next few weeks in a daze, unable to think of anything but Allan.

Every night, when I put Elise to bed and watched as she slept deeply, she tore me from my thoughts of leaving the country. She was so helpless, so small and sweet. She needed me. And yet I started to stash away some of the money Carl gave me for food.

Eventually I couldn't do it any longer. I packed a bag and just went on my way. I didn't say goodbye to Kristina, though she saw me leave. I didn't leave a note for Carl. Didn't kiss Elise; I never could have managed that. I closed my eyes for a few seconds after shutting the door and then headed straight for the harbor. I was done with America. I was going back to Europe. I needed to be where Allan was. Love drove me toward him.

18

The doctor's eyes are fixed on the stack of papers in the dark-blue plastic document holder.

"Your stats look better." He leafs through the first three sheets, reading chart notes and test results. Eventually he takes off his glasses, pushes them into the chest pocket of his white coat, and looks her in the eye for the first time since he entered the room.

"How are you feeling?"

She shakes her head slightly.

"Tired. Heavy," she whispers.

"Yes, heart trouble does take it out of us. But I don't think you're going to need a bigger operation. You're still strong, and the angioplasty worked well. You'll survive this." He reaches out and pats her on the head, as though she were a child. Doris shakes his hand away.

"Strong? Do I look strong to you right now?" She slowly raises the hand with the IV. A bruise has bloomed beneath the bandage, and her skin strains around the needle when she moves.

"Yes, for your age, definitely. Your stats are good for your age. You just need a little rest, that's all." With that, he turns and leaves.

Not a second too soon.

She shivers, pulls the blanket up to her chin. Her fingers are cold and stiff, and she holds them close to her mouth, breathing on them. The faint stream of warm air heats them. Out in the corridor, she can hear the doctor talking to one of the nurses. He is whispering, but not quietly enough.

"Take her back up to the ward, she doesn't need to stay here."

"But can she really cope with that? Is she stable enough?"

"She's ninety-six. Sadly, she's not going to live for all that much longer, and she definitely wouldn't survive another operation."

Not going to live for all that much longer, wouldn't survive another operation. When the nurse comes in to pack up Doris's things, Doris bites her tongue as a cold wave works its way down her limbs.

"You're going back up to the ward now, that's good news, isn't it? Let me just remove these electrodes." The nurse gently pushes back Doris's shirt and pulls the sticky disks free. The bare skin makes her shiver, which causes a jolt of pain.

"You poor thing, are you cold? Just a minute, I'll get you another blanket." The nurse disappears, but quickly returns with a thick green-and-white-striped blanket, which she spreads across the bed. Doris smiles gratefully.

"I'd like my computer too."

"Did you have a laptop? I haven't seen one; it must still be up on the ward. We'll check when we get up there. You'll have it back soon, don't you worry."

"Thank you. Do you think my great-niece would be able to talk to the doctor? I know she wanted to."

"I'm sure we can arrange that. I'll talk to the doctor on your ward. Right, let's go, are you ready?" The bed jolts as the nurse releases the brake and wheels it out of the room. She swings it into position, and they move slowly down the empty corridor to the elevator. The nurse is chatting away, but Doris isn't listening. The doctor's words are still echoing through her mind, drowning out her own thoughts. Don't be afraid. Don't be afraid. Don't be afraid. Be strong. The beep of the elevator is the last thing she hears.

"Is there anyone we can call, Doris? Any family? Any close friends?" A new nurse is sitting on a chair by her bed. She's back on the ward. A new room, surrounded by new fellow patients. Her black laptop bag is on the bedside table.

"Yes. Jenny, my great-niece. She wanted to talk to the doctor. What time is it?" she asks.

"It's already five in the evening. You've been sleeping since you got back."

"Perfect," she says, pointing to the computer. "Please, could you pass me that? I'll call Jenny. I have a program that I use."

The nurse pulls the laptop out of the bag and hands it to her. Doris brings up Jenny's name on Skype, but the icon shows that she isn't connected, and no one answers when, despite the red symbol, she attempts to call. Strange. It's morning in California, and she's usually online. She hopes that nothing has happened to her. That she doesn't die before she gets to say goodbye to Jenny. She pushes the computer to one side but leaves the Skype window open.

"Let me know if there's anyone else I can call. It might be nice for you to have a friend here?"

Doris nods and allows her head to slump to one side. The pillow feels like cement when she presses her cheek against it, and the blankets are heavy.

"Could you pull back the covers a little?" she whispers, but the nurse has already disappeared. She twists so that the blanket lifts slightly, letting in some air. The computer screen is now right in front of her, and she stares at Jenny's icon, waiting for it to turn green. Eventually, her eyelids droop and she falls asleep.

19

For years Jenny has carried it on a frog keychain made of green metal. DORIS, it says, scrawled in marker on the frog's smooth back. One lonely silver key. On the plane she holds it up, letting Tyra play with it. The little girl hits it with her chubby hands, making it spin. Over and over again. And then she laughs, loudly and gleefully. They have just woken up after several fretful and uncomfortable hours of sleep. From her seat by the window, Jenny can see the dense forests like dark green fields as the plane descends. She lifts up Tyra so that she too can see.

"Look, Tyra, *Sverige!* Sweden. Look." She points downward, but the girl is more interested in the frog. She stretches to reach for it and whines loudly when she can't. The long journey and lack of sleep have made her more irritable than usual. Jenny hands her the frog and then hushes her firmly. Tyra shoves it straight into her mouth.

"Not in your mouth, Tyra, dangerous." The girl yells when Jenny takes the keychain from her, and the passengers in the next row flash them an exasperated look. Jenny rifles through her bag and manages to find a box of jelly beans. She gives them to Tyra one after another and the child settles down, sucking happily on the candy until the plane lands with a thud. They are finally on Swedish soil. As they walk through the arrivals hall, Jenny absorbs the Swedish being spoken around her. She can speak and understand the language, but she almost never hears it.

"Bastugatan 25, please." She makes an effort to mask her American accent when she speaks Swedish to the taxi driver, but she can hear that her pronunciation is far from perfect. Still, what difference does it make? The driver has an accent too.

"Did you have good journey?" he asks, and Jenny nods. Secretly pleased that she can spot his grammatical mistakes. The car drives through a rainy landscape. The windscreen wipers are working flat out, and they screech when the window suddenly gets dry.

She makes small talk to pass the time. "What horrible weather." She forgets the Swedish word for weather and has to say it in English instead. The driver nods in reply, but by the time they reach their destination he has decided to speak only in English. She pays by card and then climbs out onto the street with Tyra in her arms. She glances up at the windows of Doris's apartment and sees that the curtains are drawn. The driver kindly lifts the stroller and her two suitcases from the trunk, but the minute he steps back into the car he tears off, spraying puddle water onto Jenny's trousers.

"Stockholm's just like New York, everyone's in a hurry," she mutters to herself, trying to unfold the stroller while holding Tyra on her hip. The rain makes the little one raise her hands, eagerly trying to catch the drops.

"Keep still, Tyra, still. Mommy needs to unfold the stroller." She lowers her knee against the catch and eventually manages to get the stroller steady. Tyra doesn't protest when she sits her down in it. Jenny buckles her in and tries to push the stroller with her hip as she pulls the two suitcases behind her. It doesn't work. The wheels on the stroller are off kilter, pointing in different directions. She drops the bags and quickly carries the stroller up the stairs into the building. She puts Tyra down, hushes her, runs back out, and grabs the bags. By the time she makes it up to the apartment with the luggage, the stroller, and the baby, Jenny's T-shirt is damp with sweat.

A stale smell hits her as she opens the door. She feels for the light switch in the dark before pulling the stroller inside. Tyra tries to stand up, eager to get to her feet, and coughs loudly with the effort. Jenny holds her palm to the girl's forehead, but it's cool; she's just tired and has a slight cold. She places Tyra on the kitchen floor and then opens all of the curtains and windows. As daylight floods the apartment, she realizes that Tyra is sitting right next to a dark stain on the pale wooden floor. She squats as Tyra gently pats the stain. It must be blood. From the fall. Doris's blood. She quickly grabs Tyra's hand and pulls her up. They go into the living room. It looks just like she remembers it. The dark-purple velvet sofa, the grayish-blue and brown cushions, the teak table from the sixties, a desk against one wall, angels. Doris has been collecting angels for as long as Jenny can remember. She counts them. Eight small porcelain angels in the living room alone. Two of them were gifts from Jenny. She'll take a few of them to the hospital tomorrow, so that Doris has them with her. She picks up the one closest to her, a pretty figurine made from golden ceramic, and holds it to her cheek.

"Oh Doris, you and your angels," she whispers as her eyes well up. She gently places the figure back on the desk. Her eyes land on a stack of paper. She picks up the top sheet and starts to read.

20

A car horn sounds down on the street. It's the taxi Jenny has called. Worried about Doris, she feels that she must go straight to the hospital, that it can't wait until tomorrow. She places the stack of paper back on the desk and strokes it gently with her hand. Doris has written so much. Jenny picks up the top few sheets, folds them in half, and pushes them into her handbag. She has read only a handful of paragraphs so far, and she's eager to read more.

She is soon in the taxi on the way to the hospital, with Tyra in her arms. It's evening now, and darkness has fallen. She yawns, wearily pulls out her phone.

"Hey. I'm here now, everything was fine." Jenny holds the device slightly away from her ear, prepared for the roar from the other side of the Atlantic. Instead, she is met by silence. She hears the rustle of the receiver changing hands. Jack speaks first.

"How could you just leave, Mom? Without telling me? Who's going to make my lunch now? When are you coming home?"

"Doris needs me here. She doesn't have anyone. No friends, no family. No one wants to die alone. And no one should have to."

"But what about us? Don't you care about us? Aren't we important? We don't have anyone to help us either." He shouts at her with the unflinching egocentrism of a teenager.

"Jack, listen to me now!" She raises her voice, something she does only when she's really angry. Meets the taxi driver's eye in the rearview mirror. "I'm sure you can make your own sandwiches for a few weeks. We're talking about sandwiches here, not your life. Try to think about Doris, not just yourself."

Jack has handed the phone to Willie without saying a word.

"How could you just leave like that? With only a note as explanation? Didn't you realize we would be worried? The boys were hysterical. If you're going to be away for weeks, that takes planning. Planning! We need a babysitter to take care of the boys. How were you going to sort that out?"

"We agreed that I was going to come. And I brought Tyra with me, like I promised. It doesn't need to be complicated, Willie. They're big boys. Make them a couple of sandwiches in the morning, put them in the lunchboxes, and make sure the boys take them to school. It's not rocket science."

"And who's going to take care of them when they get home from school? Who's going to help them with their homework? I have to work, you know that. My God, Jenny, you're too impulsive!"

"You're calling this impulsive? Like I'm some dumb teenager? I had to say goodbye to Dossi. Other than you, she's the only family I've got! She took care of me when I was growing up, and now she's dying! What is it that you don't get?"

He snorts, mutters a goodbye, and hangs up. Jenny flashes a strained smile at Tyra, who is looking up at her quietly.

"That was Daddy," she says, pulling her close and kissing her small, round cheeks.

When had things started to go so wrong, she wonders to herself. They had been so tense lately, fighting over money, over chores, and now this. It hadn't always been that way; Jenny remembered a time when all it took to feel happy was a glance at his face. A time when they would stay up all night eating ice cream in bed, talking for hours on end. Oh, how she missed those years.

Finally, they arrive. She follows the signs from the main entrance of the hospital to the elevators and presses the call button. The wait makes her anxious. What if Doris isn't how she remembers her? A ping announces an elevator.

She glances around the strange ward. The smell of disinfectant, the sound of patients' alarms and various machines. A nurse comes to a halt when she spots them.

"Are you looking for someone?"

"Yes, I'm looking for Doris Alm. Is she here?"

"Doris, yes, she's in there." The nurse points to a room. "But you've missed visiting hours, so I'm afraid you can't see her right now."

"I've just flown all the way from San Francisco! We landed a few hours ago. Please, you have to let me see her."

The nurse's eyes dart around, but then she nods and follows Jenny to the room.

"Just be quiet and don't stay too long. The others need to sleep."

Jenny nods. She can make out Doris's outline beneath the covers. She is thin, and smaller than Jenny remembers. Her eyes are closed. Jenny sits down in the visitor's chair and pulls the stroller close; Tyra is sleeping too. Finally she can take out the sheets of paper and read all the words Doris has written to her. She wonders what else she has written about, and finds herself immediately drawn into the story of the address book, of Doris's father, his workshop.

Doris murmurs in her sleep, dragging Jenny back to the present. She stirs, and Jenny stands up and leans over the bed.

"Doris," she whispers, stroking her hair. "Dossi, I'm here now."

Doris opens her eyes, blinks over and over again. Studies her for a long while.

"Jenny," she eventually says. "Oh, Jenny, is that really you?"

"Yes, it's really me. I'm here now, with you. I can look after you now."

The Red Address Book
P. PARKER, MIKE

Mike Parker. It's a long time since his name passed my lips. There are people whose names don't need to be recorded in an address book to linger forever in your mind. And sadly, my story would not be complete without mention of him. He was the one who taught me that certain children born into this world are not the result of love between a man and a woman. He was the one who taught me that love isn't a requirement. That the creation of life isn't necessarily beautiful.

I met him one rainy day, and he left a dark storm in his wake.

No one wanted to travel to Europe during that early summer of 1941. The civilian boats had long since stopped; clay pigeon shooting in the middle of the Atlantic had been replaced by cargo ships carrying missiles and fighter planes. I knew all this. And yet I had still made up my mind not to leave that harbor unless it was on board a ship. Even if I made it only to England or Spain, I would still be closer to Allan. And Gösta. I walked along the pier and looked out at the boats anchored in the harbor. I was barefoot, stepping between rubbish and puddles, gasping in pain whenever the small, sharp stones cut into my soles. My shoes were stashed away in my bag. I didn't want to ruin the last good pair I owned. I had only a small suitcase with me, containing a few items of clothing. My beloved locket hung around my neck. The rest of my belongings were in a trunk in Carl's attic. I hoped I would see them again one day.

"Miss! Miss! Are you looking for someone?" A man came running up behind me, and I flinched in fear. He was slightly shorter than me, but the strength in his shoulders and arms was evident beneath his thin white undershirt. His clothes were flecked with oil, as were his hands and cheeks. He smiled and took off his cap in a polite greeting. Then he reached for my suitcase. I guarded it with both hands. The rain fell gently all around us.

"Let me carry your bag. Are you lost? No passenger ships depart here these days."

"I need to go to Europe. I have to. It's very important," I replied, taking a step back.

"Europe? Why would you want to go there? Don't you know it's at war?"

"It's where I'm from. And now I need to go home. There are people there who need me. And I need them. The only way I'm leaving is on a boat."

"Well, the only way to get over there is to find a job on one of the cargo ships. But you'll have to take off that dress." He nodded to my red skirt. "You got any trousers in that bag?"

I shook my head. I had seen quite a few women in modern long trousers, but it wasn't a type of clothing I had ever owned.

He smiled.

"OK, we can fix that. I might be able to help you. I'm Mike. Mike Parker. There's a boat leaving tomorrow morning. It's full to bursting with weapons for the British army. We need a cook; the man who was meant to be coming is sick. Can you cook, miss?"

I nodded. Lowered my bag to the pier. My fingers had gone numb from its weight and my cramped grip.

"It's hard work, you need to be prepared for that. And I'll have to ask you to cut your hair. You'll never get the job looking like that, like a lady."

I shook my head, my eyes wide. No, not my hair . . .

"You want to go to Europe or not?"

"I have to."

"There's no chance they'll take a woman on any boat leaving this port. That's why we need to cut your hair and dress you like a boy. We'll have to find you pants and a shirt."

I hesitated. But what choice did I have when what I needed was to leave the country? I followed him into a small office among the barracks and pulled on the clothes he tossed to me: brown trousers made from a thick wool fabric of some kind, and a beige shirt with dried patches of sweat beneath the arms. Everything was too big and everything smelled terrible. I rolled up the arms and the legs. I wasn't ready for the first snip when he crept up behind me and chopped off a thick chunk of hair, and I cried out.

"You want to come or not?" He snipped the scissors in the air.

I bit my lip, nodded, and squeezed my eyes shut. He got to work. My beautiful, glossy hair was soon spread across the battered wooden floor.

"It's going to be fine," he said with a grin. I was shaking, anxious and unsure.

He tipped the contents of my suitcase into a jute sack and threw it to me.

"Come back tomorrow at seven. We'll row out to the ship in that." He pointed to one of the small rowboats bobbing by the dock.

"Can I stay here tonight? I don't have anywhere else to go."

"Sure, do what you want." He shrugged and then left me without a goodbye.

A night alone in a harbor involves so many sounds. A mouse running across the floor and then stopping, the wind making the doors and windows rattle, the hiss of a drainpipe beneath the dock. I lay down with the jute sack as a pillow and my red coat, the one I had worn when Agnes and I first stepped off the boat in America, as a blanket. It had been new back then, but now it was tattered and worn. Imagine if I had known then how it would all turn out! The bag beneath my head contained several crumpled remnants of my glamorous life in Paris. I wondered how Gösta was, whether he was safe in his bed in Stockholm. And Allan, was he still alive? I shuddered with worry, but the memory of our love made me forget my fear for a moment. In the distance, I could hear a door banging in the wind. Its rhythm eventually sent me to sleep.

The Red Address Book
P. ~~PARKER, MIKE~~ DEAD

When dawn finally broke, fog lay thick over the harbor. Weak pink-ish rays of light made their way over the surface of the steel-gray water, which split to foaming white against the hull of the boat. Mike rowed with powerful strokes. My eyes were on Manhattan, the Empire State Building's sharp point rising into the sky. Ahead, the American flag hung wearily on the flagpole at the front of the ship. Suddenly, Mike stopped and fixed his eyes on me.

"Keep your head down when you climb on board. Don't look anyone in the eye. I'll tell them you don't speak English. They find out you're a woman and you're off." Mike dropped the oars, stepped over to my side of the boat, and pressed his hands to my breasts. The boat tipped. I gasped and met his stern look with terror.

"Take that shirt off. We need to hide these." I carefully started to undo the buttons, but he hissed that we were in a hurry, pushed my hands away, and tore open the last one. I sat there with my bra and stomach exposed. The damp morning air washed over my body and gave me goose pimples. He rummaged through a first-aid kit and found a roll of bandage. He wound it tightly over the top of my bra so that my breasts were pulled flat against my rib cage. With that, the last trace of my femininity disappeared. He pulled a hat over my cropped hair and then rowed us to the ship.

"Remember what I said. Eyes down. The entire time. You don't know a word of English. No talking to anyone."

I nodded, and when we climbed up the rope ladder hanging against the steel hull of the ship, I tried to move like a man, with my legs wide apart. I had my bag of clothes on my back, the rope cross-ing my chest. It rubbed painfully against my bound breasts. Mike introduced me to the crew and told them there was no point in talking to me; I wouldn't understand a thing they said. Then he showed me the kitchen and left me alone with all of the boxes of food to be unpacked.

In the compact darkness of that first night, I discovered Mike's real motives. He hadn't wanted to help me at all. He held my wrists tight with one hand, pushed them up against the headboard of the bed, and whispered into my ear:

"One word, and you're overboard. I swear. A single peep and you'll be sinking to the bottom of the sea like a rock."

With his other hand, he spread my legs. He spat into his palm and carefully wet my genitals. Rubbed his hand back and forth and then pushed his fingers into me, one to begin with, then two. I felt his nails catch and tear at the delicate skin down there. Then, in one breath, he forced himself inside me. He was big and hard and I had to bite my lip to stop from crying out. Tears of pain, fear, and degradation ran down my cheeks, and my head banged against the headboard in time with his rough thrusts.

That same scene repeated itself practically every night. I lay quietly, unmoving, parted my legs to get it over and done with as quickly as possible. I tried to get used to his panting breaths in my ear, his weathered hands on my body; tried to put up with his tongue licking my firmly closed lips.

During the day, I worked silently in the kitchen. Boiled rice and sliced salted meat. Washed up. The crew came and went. I met their eyes but never dared speak to them. Mike had taken control of me, and I feared what might happen if I tried to get away.

I was cleaning up the kitchen one evening when we were just a few hours from England. Suddenly, I heard noise up on the bridge. The captain was shouting. Men running. And then the shots echoing out across the water. The ship was loaded with weapons and ammunition, and I could hear desperation in the captain's voice as he cried:

"Reverse! Reverse! Turn around! It's the Germans! It's the Germans! We'll explode if we're hit!"

The floors and walls thundered, and I felt the vibrations through my body as the engines went into reverse. I was still in the safety of the kitchen, my refuge, but I knew I would soon have to go up, closer to the deck. When I tried to open the door, I found it locked. Maybe Mike had locked me in, maybe the vibrations had tripped the mechanism, but I had to get out. The shots were growing closer, rattling like fireworks. At one end of the kitchen was a round window facing the messroom. I broke the glass with a pan and then squeezed through it, feet first. The shards of glass tore at my legs and upper arms. The boat was still in reverse, and the engines were straining loudly. I sneaked upstairs and onto the afterdeck. Using my hands to guide me, I found my way to the chest of life jackets. I pulled one over my head and then sat down to wait, pressed up against the cold wall.

It wasn't long before the German ship caught up with us. Our crew turned on the floodlights and shot wildly. The Germans didn't hesitate in retaliating. Several bullets hit the metal directly above my head, and I ducked, terrified that they would ricochet. I was pressed against the floor when one of the hands spotted me. Our eyes met just as he was about to climb over the railing at the far end of the deck, and he waved me over to follow him. I readied myself and ran the few meters to where he was standing, my arms covering my head. I didn't know where he was going, but I followed his lead and quickly climbed down the rope ladder. At the end of it, my foot struck something hard. He grabbed my ankle and pulled my foot down into the bottom of a small lifeboat. Then he pushed us off from the ship, and we slowly drifted away. Bullets whizzed above our heads, and the current carried us closer to the enemy ship. We lay down, our heads beneath the bench and our arms pressed tightly to our ears. The roar of the shots sounded different through the water surrounding the thin hull. Like a faint clucking. In my mind, I went through all of the prayers I had learned in school but never used.

The minutes felt like hours.

Then, suddenly, we heard the dreaded explosion from the ship we had just left. A warm shock wave hit us, and we were both tipped into the water. I heard my savior splashing and gasping for help, but his voice drifted farther and farther away, growing softer and softer, until finally it fell silent. I bobbed in the chilly water, surrounded by pieces of burning wreckage. I watched the huge ship capsize and slowly start to sink, like a blazing torch in the black water. My cork life jacket kept me afloat, and I managed to make my way back to the little lifeboat. It was upside-down now, but I crawled up onto it and straddled it. The Germans had left, and the sea was calm once more. No echoes of shots, no men shouting.

When dawn broke, I was alone, surrounded by charred wreckage and bodies. Some of the men had been shot; others had drowned. I never again saw the man who had saved me.

Mike floated past, a thick layer of dark blood covering his neat beard. He had been shot in the head; it drooped over the edge of his life jacket. His forehead was half submerged in the water.

All I felt was relief.

21

It's late at night, San Francisco time, when they finally make it back to the apartment on Bastugatan. The fatigue is almost paralyzing. Jenny makes some porridge while Tyra sits at her feet, playing with the pans, pulling them out of the cupboard and babbling happily. She's so content down on the floor that Jenny just places the bowl of porridge in front of her and pulls back the rug in case there's a spill.

Jenny opens and closes boxes and cupboards, rifling through Doris's things while Tyra makes a mess with her food. On the kitchen table, a number of items are set out neatly on the blue tablecloth. She picks them up one by one. A magnifying glass covered in dust and grease marks, with a crumpled lace ribbon that has frayed at one end. She studies the remaining items through its dirty lens. The image is blurry. She breathes on the glass and rubs it clean with the corner of the tablecloth. The light-blue fabric wrinkles, and when she tries to smooth it out again, she can only partly do so. She picks up the saltshaker instead. A few yellow grains of rice are visible through the glass. She shakes it and they disappear.

The pillbox contains three days' worth of tablets. Friday, Saturday, Sunday. So Doris must have fallen on a Thursday. Jenny thinks back, tries to remember when they first spoke. It was a school day, so it must have been Friday. She wonders what kind of medicine it is. Whether Doris has had heart problems before. Whether the doctors know about it. Maybe this recent heart attack happened because she hadn't been taking her medicine?

Jenny shoves the pillbox into a pocket in her bag. She'll ask the doctor tomorrow.

Tyra tips her bowl over on the floor and starts crying loudly.

"Should we go to bed, sweetie?" Jenny mumbles. She picks up her daughter, quickly wipes the floor, rubs Tyra's face with a wet wipe, and pushes her pacifier into her mouth.

It doesn't take long before she hears the faint whimpering sound Tyra always makes just before she falls asleep. Jenny climbs into bed, right next to the girl, her nose buried in her neck. She closes her eyes. From the pillow, she can make out the comforting scent of Doris.

It's seven in the evening. Tyra pulls at her hair, pokes Jenny in the eye, and whines. Jenny squints at the glowing hands of her watch and tries to work out what time it is in San Francisco. Ten. The exact time Tyra normally wakes from her morning nap. Dizzy with exhaustion, Jenny tries to lull her back to sleep, but her efforts are in vain. The girl is wide-awake.

The lamp on the table gives off a cloud of dust when she switches it on, and she waves her hand in front of her. The apartment is cold, and she wraps herself in a blanket as she heads into the kitchen, aware that Tyra will soon start crying with hunger. She searches the changing bag for something edible. At the very bottom, she finds a couple of broken crackers and a pouch of puréed fruit, which she opens and hands to Tyra. The girl happily slurps down a little of the fruit, then throws the pouch to one side and turns her attention to the crackers. She places them in one of the pans on the floor. She

bangs the lid a few times before plunging her chubby little hands
into the pan and picking out piece after piece of cracker, which she
then throws back, over her shoulder.

"Cookie, cookie," she laughs, amused.

"You're meant to eat them, love," Jenny says in Swedish, then
with a smile switches to English. "Eat the crackers." She still feels
dizzy. Outside, the sky is dark, and there are no lights on in the
building opposite. Just dark, empty windows whose glass reflects
the yellow glow of the streetlamps. Golden sparks in the night.

The stack of paper Doris has printed out is on the kitchen table.
Jenny picks it up again and leafs through page after page of words.
Rereads the first lines:

So many names pass by us in a lifetime. Have you ever
thought about that, Jenny? All the names that come and go.
That rip our hearts to pieces and make us shed tears. That
become lovers or enemies. I leaf through my address book
sometimes.

The address book. Jenny searches through the items on the
table. Picks up the battered old red-leather book and strokes its yellowed pages. This has to be the one Doris is talking about. She starts
reading. Name after name has been crossed out. After each of them,
Doris has written *DEAD. DEAD, DEAD, DEAD.* Jenny drops the
book as though it has burned her. It's too painful to realize how
lonely Doris must be. If only she lived a little closer. She wonders
how many days Doris has spent alone. How many years. Without
any friends. Without any family. With only her memories for company. The beautiful. The painful. The awful.

And now Doris might soon be one of them. One of the dead
names.

The Red Address Book
J. JONES, PAUL

Many times that night I cursed myself for leaving the safety of America. For what? For a Europe at war. For a dream of meeting Allan again. A naive dream that would never come true. I was sure this was the end, right there in the cold ocean. I lay across the hull of the boat as dawn broke, fantasizing about his face. I felt the cold metal of the locket against my chest, but I couldn't open it. I closed my eyes and tried to bring up a picture of him. Just like that, he was so present that the threatening sea seemed far away. He spoke to me. He laughed, loud and shrill, the way he always did when he told a funny story. Ruining the punch line but making me laugh all the same, his sense of fun was so infectious. He danced all around me, and suddenly he was behind me, then he looked straight ahead and kissed me before disappearing again. Joie de vivre shone bright in his eyes that dark night.

The water was black, the whitecaps glittering like knives in the hazy sunlight. Other than the whistling wind, it was silent. The hull of the lifeboat was warm; my body felt firmly pressed against it. I dug my fingers between the wooden boards to get a better grip, but my strength was deserting me and my arms fell limp to my sides. The thick cork of the life jacket cut into my stomach. Involuntarily I slid ever closer to the water, unable to stop the movement but well aware of what was about to happen. Death was awaiting me, embracing me with a splash as I eventually fell in. The weight of the water pressed against my head as it sank beneath the surface.

I could hear a crackling sound and smell burning wood. The heat streamed toward me, and my cheeks flushed and tightened. I was wrapped in a thick wool blanket, so tight that I couldn't move my arms. I blinked. Was this how it felt to be dead? In the faint glow, my eyes scanned a room. There was a huge walled fireplace in the middle, its chimney rising high above the dark-brown ceiling beams. To the right was a small pantry, and to the left, a hallway and a window. It seemed to be pitch-black outside. I don't know how long I lay there, gazing all around, studying every last detail. The strange tools on hooks in the hall, the ropes, the wads of paper shoved into the cracks in the wooden walls. Where was I? I wasn't afraid. In an odd way, I felt secure in the heat of the fire, and I drifted in and out of sleep. I started to wonder whether I hadn't left the sea after all.

Eventually I woke to the sound of blackout shutters being taken down from the window. Bright sunlight flooded the room. A dog nuzzled my face, licking my cheek with its wet tongue. I snorted to make it go away, shook my head gently.

"Good morning," said a man's voice, and I felt a gentle hand on my shoulder. "Are you awake?"

I blinked over and over again, tried to focus on the person standing in front of me. He was a thin man, older than me, with furrowed cheeks, and he was studying me with curiosity.

"It was a close call. I found you with your head under the water. I didn't think you were alive, but when I lifted you out, you coughed. So many others were dead. There were bodies everywhere. This war . . . it's going to be the death of us all."

"Where am I? I'm not dead?" My throat hurt when I spoke.

"No, but you were probably only a whisker away. You had more luck than the rest of the crew. What's your name?"

"Doris."

He jumped, and an uncomprehending look appeared on his face. "Doris? You're a woman?"

I nodded. Of course, my short hair.

"I wouldn't have been able to get on the ship from America otherwise."

"You had me fooled. Well, man or woman, it makes no difference. You can stay here until you're strong enough to move on."

"Where am I?" I asked again.

"You're in England. In Sancreed. I found you when I was out in my fishing boat."

"Aren't you at war?"

"The war is everywhere" — he lowered his eyes to the floor — "but we don't notice it so much out here in the countryside. They're focused on London. We hear the bombers and black out the lights at night. And we don't have much food. But otherwise, life goes on like normal. I'd gone out to bring in my nets when I found you. I threw the fish back. Didn't want them, not with all those dead souls floating around out there."

The man loosened the blanket so that I could move my arms. I stretched gently. My legs ached, but I could move them. The dog came running back. It was gray and shaggy and it butted me with its nose.

"That's Rox, you'll have to excuse his obtrusiveness. My name is Paul. The house isn't big, but there's a mattress you can sleep on. Simple, but warm and comfortable. Where are you headed? You aren't British, I can hear that."

I paused and thought. Which of my two cities was I heading toward? I didn't know. Stockholm felt like a distant memory, Paris like a utopia that would only disappoint.

"Is Sweden at war?"

Paul shook his head.

"Not as far as I know."

"Then that's where I'm heading. To Stockholm. Do you know how I can get there? Do you know anyone who can help me?"

He smiled sadly and shook his head. I would be there with him for quite some time. I think he knew that even then.

The Red Address Book
J. JONES, PAUL

There was a sleeping loft in the little cottage. A steep ladder next to the fireplace led up to a boarded-up hole in the ceiling, and Paul grabbed a hammer and pulled out the nails. We climbed up together. In the loft, the walls sloped inward to a thick wooden beam, and there was room to stand only in the very center. The floor was covered with junk: piles of old newspapers and books. Boxes of fishing nets, which smelled like seaweed. A big black suitcase. A small homemade rocking horse, which creaked as we moved across the floor. And everything was covered in a thick layer of cobwebs.

Paul apologized, blowing away the dust and spider's webs and causing a thin cloud to spread through the air as he stacked the boxes on top of one another and heaped the books along one wall. I opened the half-moon-shaped window to let in some daylight. Then I scrubbed the floor and the walls with soapy water.

A thin horsehair mattress became my bed. A wool throw my blanket. At night, I would lie awake for hours, listening for planes in the distance. The fear of another explosion tormented me. In my mind, I saw the boat explode over and over again. Saw the bodies flying through the air. The water turned deep red in my feverish dreams. I saw Mike staring up at me with dead eyes. The man who had treated me so badly.

Paul had been right, the war was far removed from the villagers' daily lives, but I wasn't their only unexpected visitor. Several of the neighbors had small pale guests who cried themselves to sleep at night, longing for their mothers and fathers hundreds of miles away. Child evacuees from London. I saw them with their tattered clothes and bare feet as they untangled fishing nets, or scrubbed rugs in such cold water that their hands became chapped and red, or carried heavy objects on their weak backs. In exchange for somewhere to sleep, they were expected to perform manual labor.

I was put to work too. Paul taught me how to gut the fish that he caught. Using a sharp knife, I made a quick incision just above the gills on fish after fish from the boxes he placed in front of me. I stood at the end of the jetty, next to a rickety table made from weathered old wood, cutting off their heads and pulling out their innards, which I threw to the gulls. My fingertips were soon torn to shreds and dry from the sharp scales. But Paul just grinned when I complained.

"They'll harden up soon enough. You just need to get your city fingers used to a bit of hard work."

I was covered in fish blood. It made me feel sick, a constant reminder of death. But I held my tongue.

One night, we were in the cottage, eating our evening meal by the light of a single candle. Paul rarely spoke at the dinner table. He was kind, but not especially talkative. But now, he suddenly looked at me.

"You're the only one of us getting fat from this food." He held up his spoon and allowed the watery broth to run back into his bowl. It splashed onto the table and made the candle hiss.

"What do you mean?"

"You're getting fat. Haven't you noticed? Are you stashing food somewhere I don't know about?"

"Of course not!" I ran my hand over my stomach. He was right. I had put on weight. My stomach was as taut as a sail in the wind.

"You're not up the duff, are you?"

I slowly shook my head.

"Because we hardly need another mouth to feed."

That night, my hands stroked a rounded belly that wouldn't flatten, even when I lay on my back. I had been so stupid. My nausea

22

Page by page, the stack of paper moves from one side of Jenny to the other. Tyra is lying next to her in bed, in a deep sleep, her thumb in her mouth. Every now and then, she makes a smacking sound as her suck reflex takes over. Jenny carefully pulls out the thumb and replaces it with a pacifier, but the girl immediately spits it out and raises her hand to her mouth again. Jenny sighs and turns her attention to the text. So many words, so many memories she'd never heard about. When she finally falls asleep, it's with the lamp turned on and a half-read sheet of paper on her chest.

The hospital is huge and gray. A lump of concrete in the suburbs, with sea-green and rust-red details. On the roof, the huge white letters seem to float freely: *Danderyds sjukhus.* She pushes Tyra toward the entrance, past a glass booth in which gown-clad patients huddle, smoking and shivering. Inside, she sees more patients, all of them dressed in white, some with a drip snaking down to a hand. Each has pasty winter skin. San Francisco feels distant in terms of both space and time. The house, the sea, the traffic. Jack and his surly teenage moods, David, Willie. The washing, cleaning, and cooking. Now it's just her and Tyra. One stroller to keep track of, one child. A sensation of freedom spreads through her body, and she takes a deep breath and heads down the corridor.

"She's a little brighter now, you'll be able to talk to her. But she still needs her rest, so please try not to stay too long. And no flowers, I'm afraid," the nurse says, shaking her head at the bouquet Jenny is holding. "Allergies." Jenny reluctantly puts the flowers down and, with a sigh, pushes the stroller toward Doris's room. She pauses when she catches sight of her in bed. She is so small and thin, she almost seems to be disappearing. Her white hair is like a halo around her pallid face. Her lips are tinged with blue. Jenny leaves the stroller and runs forward to embrace her gently.

"Oh, my dear," Doris whispers in a rattling voice, patting her on the back. A IV line is inserted into one of the thick veins on the back of her hand.

"And who do we have here?" In the stroller, Tyra is sitting wide-eyed, her mouth half-open.

"Ah yes, she's awake this time."

Jenny lifts Tyra from the stroller and sits down on the edge of the bed, with the child in her lap. She speaks to the girl in a mixture of Swedish and English. "This is Auntie Doris, Tyra. Auntie from the computer, you know? Say hello."

"Itsy-bitsy spider climbed up the waterspout," Doris sings. Jenny bounces her leg up and down, making Tyra jump. Her sleepy face soon cracks into a smile. She laughs loudly as Jenny swings her legs from side to side.

"She's just like you," Doris says, reaching out for the chubby little legs. "You had fat thighs when you were her age too." She winks and grins.

"Nice to see you still have your sense of humor."

"Yes, the old woman's not dead yet."

"Ugh, don't say that. You can't die, Dossi, you just can't."

"But I have to, my love. It's my time, I've had my fill. Can't you see how decrepit I am?"

"Please don't talk like that . . ." Jenny squeezes her eyes shut. "I did some reading yesterday. Those pages you wrote for me. I cried when I saw them, everything you wanted to say. Everything that happened to you. There's so much I didn't know."

"How far did you get?"

"Oh, I was so tired, I fell asleep in the middle of Paris. You must have been so scared on that train. You were so young. Like Jack today. It's unbelievable."

"Yes, of course I was scared. I can still remember it now. It's strange. As you get older, your memory of recent things fades, but your memories of childhood become so vivid, it's as though they just happened. I can even remember how it smelled that day when the train pulled into the station."

"You can? How did it smell?"

"Thick smoke from wood-fired ovens, freshly baked bread, almond blossom and musk from all the rich gentlemen on the platform."

"Musk, what's that?"

"A scent that used to be common. It smells nice, but very strong."

"Do you remember how you felt when you first got to Paris?"

"I was so young. When you're young, everything is about the here and now. And in the worst cases, maybe a bit of then. But my mother had long since let me down, so I didn't miss her all that much. The one thing I did miss was the sound of her voice in the evenings when she thought we were sleeping. She sang so beautifully. But I was probably quite comfortable with Madame. At least that's how I remember it."

"Which songs did she hum? The same ones you sang to me when I was a child?"

"Yes, I probably sang some of them for you. She liked hymns, "Children of the Heavenly Father" in particular. And "Day by Day." But she just hummed, like I said; she never sang the words."

"That sounds so nice. Wait, I can play them for you." She pulls out her phone, presses play, and holds up the YouTube video for Doris, who squints at the small screen. A children's choir singing "Children of the Heavenly Father" in their bright young voices. They can't quite reach the high notes.

"That was exactly how it sounded when my mother sang; like a terrified child, she could never manage the high notes. She always had to start again from the beginning." Doris laughs.

"I always liked it when you sang for me, when I sat on your knee and you bounced me this way and that. What was that song?"

"The priest's little crow . . ." Doris sings the opening line of the old Swedish nursery rhyme and then hums the rest.

"That was it, yes! Oh, we have to sing it for Tyra." Doris smiles and holds out her hand, places it on Tyra's chubby leg. Then they sing together. Jenny stumbles over the words, mumbles and mutters, but they come back to her as she listens to Doris's rattling voice. She wraps an arm around Tyra and swings her gently forward and back. The metal railing at the edge of the bed is digging into her legs, but it's too much fun to stop. Tyra chuckles. "She slipped this way, she slipped that way . . ."

"Everything was always so good when you came to stay with us. Dossi, I've missed you so much!"

With tears in her eyes, Jenny turns to Doris. She is lying with her eyes closed, her mouth half-open. Jenny quickly reaches toward her, feels the warm breath streaming out. Dossi is just sleeping.

23

She's ashamed of what she is doing, but she can't stop herself. Every box, every shelf, every wardrobe, every nook and cranny. She searches everywhere. Finds photographs, jewelry, souvenirs, foreign coins, receipts, notes on loose sheets of paper. Studies them carefully. Places them in piles, sorts them by geographical location. So much that she never knew about.

On a chair she spots a gray patterned cardigan, which smells faintly of lavender. Jenny wraps it around herself and sits down on the edge of the bed. Tyra is on her back, fast asleep, with her hands raised above her head. She is wearing only a diaper, and her round little stomach rises and falls as she breathes. Her mouth is half open and her breathing rattles gently. Her cold hasn't let go; the cool Swedish air is always difficult.

"Sweet baby," she whispers, kissing Tyra on the forehead. She breathes in the scent of baby-soft skin as she covers her daughter with a blanket.

Jenny is tired and would prefer to go to sleep herself, but Doris's things have piqued her curiosity. She sinks back down onto the cold floor. Reads old receipts, a few of them handwritten in elaborate script. One, from La Coupole, is tucked inside a well-thumbed envelope; on one corner is a heart drawn in faded black ink. A bottle of champagne and oysters. Luxurious. She googles the restaurant on her phone and quickly finds that it still exists, in Montparnasse. She'll visit it one day, and experience what Doris experienced. She wonders who Doris went with and why there is a heart on the envelope.

She opens a battered wooden box. Inside are a few French coins and a checked silk handkerchief. A huge silver locket catches the light. Jenny gently opens it. She has seen it before, so she knows what to expect. A black-and-white face peers up at her. She squints to get a better look at the small image, but it has faded, and the features look almost flat. The man in the picture has short, dark hair, combed to one side. Doris hadn't answered when Jenny asked who he was. She gently pulls the picture loose. There isn't a name on the back.

Doris's words are in a pile on the bed. It's almost midnight, but Jenny wants to know more. She takes another sheet from the pile and continues. Hears Doris's voice in her head as she reads.

24

After hugging Doris the next morning, the first thing Jenny does is pull the locket from her bag and let it hang from her hand.

"Who is this?"

Doris smiles secretively, shuts her eyes tight, but doesn't reply.

"Come on, answer me. I've asked you before, but you have to tell me now. Who is he?"

"Ah, just someone from the past."

"It's Allan, isn't it? Tell me it's Allan, because I know it is."

Doris shakes her head, but her smile and the glimmer in her eye give her away.

"He's handsome."

"Of course he is, what else would he be?" Doris holds out her hand and tries to catch the locket.

"Swimming in the Seine. Oh, it must have been so romantic."

"Let's see." Doris opens the locket with trembling fingers and squints at the image. "I can't see a thing these days."

Jenny has brought Doris's magnifying glass from the apartment. She reaches for it on the bedside table.

Doris laughs. "Imagine if Allan knew that seventy or so years later, I'd be lying here yearning for him through a magnifying glass. That would've made him happy!"

Jenny smiles. "Dossi, what happened to him?"

Doris shakes her head.

"What happened? I don't know. I have no idea."

"Is he dead?"

"I don't know. He disappeared. We met in Paris and fell in love. He left me, but then he sent a letter from the United States, asking me to follow him there. I got the letter a whole year too late, so by the time I arrived in New York he was already married to someone else. He had assumed I didn't want to come. We still loved each other, and we cried when we realized it was all a misunderstanding. Then he left for France, to fight in the war. His mother was French; he was both French and American. He wrote me a letter from there, saying that he loved me and wanted to live with me, that he had been stupid. He probably never made it home, though; otherwise I would have heard from him after the war. He probably suffered the same fate as the bridge we swam beneath. Blown to pieces by the Germans. There was nothing left. Just rubble."

Jenny is silent for a long moment.

"But . . . but where were you after the war? Did he know where you were? Maybe he tried to find you?"

"Love always finds a way, Jenny dear, if it's meant to be. It's fate that guides us, I've always believed that. He probably died, he must have, but oddly enough it hasn't ever felt that way. He's always been by my side. In a strange way, I've often felt his presence."

"But what if he didn't, what if he's still alive? If he still loves you? Aren't you curious about what he would be like, what he would look like?"

"Bald and wrinkly, I suppose." Doris's quick answer makes Jenny laugh. Tyra, who was asleep in her stroller, jumps, and her blue eyes snap open.

"Hi, sweetie!" Jenny places her hand on the girl's forehead. "Go back to sleep."

She gently rocks the stroller back and forth, hoping the child will quickly doze off again.

"If he's still alive, we have to find him."

"Oof, don't be daft. I'm barely even alive. No one is still alive. Everyone's dead."

"Everyone is not dead! Of course he could still be alive. You were the same age, weren't you? You're still alive!"

"Barely."

"Come on, don't give me that, you're still alive. And you still have your sense of humor. Don't forget that you were healthy and living at home just a few weeks ago."

"Forget all that, forget Allan. It was too long ago. Everyone has a love they never get over, Jenny. It's normal."

"What do you mean, 'Everyone has a love they never get over'? What does that mean?"

"Don't you? Someone you find yourself thinking about now and again?"

"Me?"

"Yes, you." Doris gives her a knowing look, and Jenny's cheeks flush. "An unfinished love, one that never got a proper ending. Everyone does. Someone who dug deep into your heart and stayed there."

"And who, as the years pass, seems much better than he ever was?"

"Of course. That's part of it. There's nothing as perfect as lost love." Doris's eyes glitter. Jenny sits in silence for a moment. The redness flares up on her cheeks again.

"You're right. Marcus."

Doris laughs, and Jenny raises a finger to her mouth to hush her, glances over to the stroller.

"Marcus, yes."

"Do you remember him?"

"Yes, of course. Marcus. The pretty boy with the self-tan lines on his forehead."

Jenny raises an eyebrow in surprise.

"Self-tan lines? He didn't have those, did he?"

"Oh yes, he did. But you were too in love to see them. He also went crawling about in the woods to give his jeans the perfect amount of wear, do you remember that?"

"Oh my God, right!" Jenny is bent double with suppressed laughter. "But he was handsome. And funny. He made me laugh. And dance."

"Dance?"

"Yeah, he always said I should let loose more. It was fun."

The two women smile in mutual understanding.

"Sometimes I keep myself amused by playing 'what if,'" Doris says.

Jenny gives her a questioning look.

"You know, what if . . . What if you had chosen Marcus as your life partner? What would your kids have looked like then? Where would you have lived? Would you have stayed together?"

"Uh, those are horrible thoughts. Then I wouldn't have met Willie, and wouldn't have had the kids. Marcus and I definitely would've broken up. He would never be able to take care of children. Even Willie can barely manage that, and he's normal. Marcus was too obsessed with finding the perfect jeans. I can't even imagine him with a slimy patch of kid sick on his shirt."

"Do you know what he's up to these days?"

"Nope, no idea. Haven't heard a peep from him. I tried to find him on Facebook recently, but he didn't seem to be there."

"Maybe he's dead too?"

Jenny looks at Doris. "You don't know Allan is dead."

"I haven't heard a single word from him since the Second World War. Do you know how long ago that was? The odds aren't too good, if you ask me." Doris snorts and fumbles for the locket. Her fingers shake as she parts the two sides and uses the magnifying glass to study the smiling man. A tear fills her eye, runs down her cheek.

"They're so wonderful, those lost loves," she mumbles. Jenny squeezes her hand.

The Red Address Book
J. JONES, PAUL

Month followed month, and I was full of disgust for the new life growing inside me. The life that had been planted there by evil. It was consuming my body, this life that I didn't want as a part of me, though it was, all the same. Every day it reminded me of the evil. Would my child look like him? Would it be evil too? Would I ever be able to love it? At night, when its movements grew intense, I would hit myself hard in the stomach to make them stop. Once, I caught its foot in my hand and held it there. It hurt my skin, and I wondered whether it hurt the child too.

Paul and I never talked about the baby or what would happen when it arrived. He was a recluse, and he continued to live like one.

There was no money for clothes, but Paul let me borrow his when mine grew too small. Toward the end, I wrapped my legs and stomach in a wool blanket, which I tied above my breasts with a length of old fishing line. There was no money for food either. We ate fish and turnips. Or bread baked from water and flour, bulked out with finely ground bark from the trees in the garden. I spent my days as if in a trance. From the cottage to the beach. From the beach to the dining table. From the dining table to the loft.

As my stomach grew, my daily tasks became more and more difficult to carry out. My back ached, and my stomach got in the way when I reached down for the fish in the box. I bent my knees as much as I could, clutching at the slimy fish, which constantly slipped through my fingers. Rox rarely left my side, but I usually didn't have the energy to care about the poor dog.

The United States felt increasingly distant, Paris like a vague dream, Stockholm too. I kept track of my days with Paul by drawing lines on the chamber-pot cabinet next to my bed. As the months passed, the number of marks increased. Line after line. I don't really know why I did this because I never counted them up, didn't want to know how long I had left. Still, I couldn't help but notice the march of time. The heat was replaced by a damp coolness. The sun by incessant rain. The blooming green fields by thick mud.

We were sitting at the dinner table one evening when a jolt of pain suddenly carved its way through my body. I gasped for air, feeling equal parts pain and fear.

I looked over to Paul, who was slurping his watery fish soup across from me. "What are we going to do when it comes?"

He looked up. His face was covered by a thick white beard; small crumbs of food often got caught in it.

"It's time, you mean?" he muttered, looking somewhere over my shoulder.

"I don't know. I think so. What do we do?"

"Let your body handle it as best it can. I've birthed a lot of calves; I'll have to help out. Go and lie down." He nodded toward the ladder up to the loft.

Calves. I stared at him but then slumped forward onto the table as yet another jolt of pain shot through my body. It radiated down my legs and up into the base of my spine, and I clung to the table. I started to feel sick, felt the soup bubbling in my stomach.

"I won't make it up there, I can't, it's not possible," I panted in terror.

Paul nodded, got to his feet, and fetched a blanket, which he spread out in front of the fire.

Evening turned into night, which turned into day and night once again. I sweated, groaned, screamed, vomited, but no child wanted to come out. Eventually, the pain vanished and everything fell silent. Paul, who had been sitting next to me in a rocking chair the entire time, frowned. He looked blurry to me, as if he was off in the distance. Then, suddenly, he was right by my side. His face was distorted, like the reflection in a polished thermos: his nose stuck out and his cheeks were sucked in.

"Doris! Hello, hello?" I couldn't reply, couldn't utter a single word.

At that, he opened the door and ran straight out into the dark night. Cold air came flooding in, and I remember how good it felt as my sweaty, aching body cooled down.

That's where my memories end.

When I next woke, I was in bed up in the loft. The room was quiet and dark around me. My stomach was calm, but with a tight wound running downward from my navel. I stroked the bandage and felt the stitches beneath it. There was a candle burning on the bedside table, and Paul was sitting on a stool to one side of the bed. Only Paul. No baby in his arms.

"Hello." He looked at me in a way he never had before. It took me a while to realize that he looked afraid. "I thought you were going to die."

"I'm alive?"

He nodded. "Would you like some water?"

"What happened?"

Paul shook his head, his eyes sad and his mouth a thin line. I placed both hands on my stomach and closed my eyes. My body was mine again. And the life in there, the one that had come to me in the worst circumstances possible, was one I would never have to see. I breathed a sigh of relief, my body relaxed, and I sank back against the rough horsehair mattress.

"I ran to get the doctor, but there was nothing he could do. It was too late."

"He saved me."

"Yes, he saved you. What do you want to do with the baby?"

"I don't want to see it."

"Do you want to know what it was?"

I shook my head. "What I had inside me, it wasn't a child. I've never had a child."

But when Paul eventually got up to climb down the ladder, the trembling started. It began in my tender stomach and spread outward, into my arms and legs. It was as though my body was driving out the evil. Paul left me alone. He understood.

25

The nurse hesitates when she spots Jenny and the stroller. "She's sleeping."

"Has she been asleep long?"

"Almost all morning. She seems very tired today."

"What does that mean?"

The young woman shakes her head regretfully. "She's very weak; it's hard to say how long she has left."

"Can we sit with her?"

"Of course, but try to let her rest. She was upset about something yesterday. She spent a long time crying after you left."

"Do you think that's strange? Isn't she allowed to cry? She's dying, of course she's going to cry. I would too."

The nurse gives her a strained smile and then disappears without a word. Jenny sighs. Of course people are expected to die without any tears. In this country, at least. Struggle through life, be like everyone else, and then die without shedding a single tear. But deep down, she suspects she knows the real reason for Doris's tears. Dejected, she fishes her phone from her handbag.

"Hello?" A sleepy voice on the other side of the Atlantic.

"Hi, it's me."

"Jenny, do you know what time it is?"

"I know. I'm sorry. I just wanted to hear your voice. You don't have Tyra waking you up every night right now, so can you handle me waking you up just this once? I miss you, sorry for leaving so suddenly."

"Of course, sweetie. I miss you too. What is it? Has something happened?"

"She's going to die."

"We've known that a long time, babe. She's old. That's how life works."

"It's morning here, but she's fast asleep. The nurse said she was tired, and she cried a lot yesterday."

"Maybe they're tears over things she regrets?"

"Or people she misses . . ."

"Yeah, or maybe it's both. Is she happy to have you and Tyra there?"

"Yes, I think so."

They fall silent for a moment. Jenny hears him yawn. Summons her courage.

"Willie, can you help me with something? I need to track down a man called Allan Smith, Allan with two *l*'s. He was probably born around the same time as Doris, around 1920, and he might live somewhere in or near New York. Or in France. His mother was French and his father was American. That's all I know."

Willie doesn't say anything for quite some time; he doesn't even yawn. When he eventually speaks, his reaction is exactly what Jenny has been expecting.

"Sorry, what did you say? Who? Allan Smith?"

"Yeah. That's his name."

"You've got to be kidding. An Allan Smith from 1920, how am I supposed to find him? Do you know how many people there are with that name, even with the double *l*? There must be hundreds!"

Jenny smirks, but she is careful not to let it show in her voice.

"What about your friend Stan, he works for the police in New York. I thought maybe you could give him a call and ask him to check. If Allan lives anywhere near New York, that should work. Tell Stan it's important."

"Important in comparison to what . . . murders in Manhattan?"

"Stop. No, of course not. But it's important to us, to me."

"Are you even sure he's still alive?"

"No, not exactly sure . . ." She ignores Willie's snort, despite its being so loud that it definitely isn't meant to be ignored. "But I think he might be. He was very important to Doris, which makes this important to me. Really important. Please, just check it out. For me."

"So you want me to track down a man who's almost one hundred, who might be alive, and might live in or near New York?"

"Exactly. I think that was everything."

"I don't understand you. Can't you just come home? We miss you here, we need you."

"I'll come back as soon as I can — sooner, if you help me with this. But right now, Dossi needs me here more than you need me there. And we both need to find out what happened to Allan Smith."

"OK, but do you have any more information about him? An old address? A picture? What did he do?"

"He was an architect, I think. At least before the war."

"Before the war? Which war are we talking about here? Not the Second World War, surely? Please tell me she's heard from him since the Second World War."

"Not much, no."

"Jenny . . . not much or not at all?"

"Not at all."

"Do you know how poor the odds are of finding him?"

"Yes, but . . ."

"Stan's going to laugh so hard he cries! Am I supposed to just call him up and ask him to look for a man who disappeared during the Second World War?"

"You don't understand, he didn't disappear. She just hasn't heard from him. He probably came home, had a couple of kids, lived a long and happy life, and now he's just taking it easy in a rocking chair on a porch somewhere, waiting for death. Just like Doris. And thinking of her like she's thinking of him."

She listens to Willie's breathing. When he speaks again, he sounds resigned. "Allan Smith, you said."

"Allan Smith. Yes. Two *l*'s."

"I'll do my best. But don't get your hopes up."

"I love you."

"I love you too. Clearly!" His warm laugh makes her long for home.

"How are the boys?"

"Yeah, don't worry. There's always fast food. God bless America."

"I'll come home as soon as I can. I love you."

"Come soon. Nothing works when you're not here. And I love you. Say hi to Dossi."

Jenny peers into the room where Doris is lying, sees her stirring beneath the covers. "She's waking up now, I have to go." She whispers goodbye to her love back home and walks toward the painful wait for death.

The Red Address Book
J. ~~JONES, PAUL~~ DEAD

I lay there for days, possibly even weeks. Allowed the time to pass while I stared up at the ceiling and experienced all the hormonal changes: my breasts straining with milk, my womb slowly contracting. But eventually, I got bored. I didn't go straight down to Paul; I began by exploring the loft, everything hidden away in its boxes and cupboards. The chamber-pot cabinet was locked, but I decided to break it open one day. I found a bowl full to the brim with garish toy cars. The inside panels of the cupboard were covered in faint lines of red chalk, looping forward and back, up and down, a tangle of markings only a very small person could have left behind. The cars were heavily dented and their paint was peeling. I turned each one over in my hands, set them out in a row on the floor, and pictured the races that had taken place on the rough wooden floorboards. Where was this child now? I rifled through the trunks. In one, I found a number of dresses, folded up and tied with coarse green fishing line. I wondered whose they were. What had happened to the woman who had worn them, and to the child?

Curiosity eventually sent me back downstairs. My belly strained as I descended the ladder. It was still big, and my back ached, just as it had during the last few weeks of pregnancy. Paul smiled when he saw me, even said that he had missed me. He made me sit down at the table, heated up some soup, and handed me a piece of dry bread. But when I asked who the cars belonged to, his mouth tightened and he shook his head. He didn't want to tell me. Maybe he couldn't. Who knows what sorrows a person bears? I didn't ask again, and started fantasizing about the woman and child instead, gave them names and pictured how they looked. In an old exercise book, I wrote short stories about their characteristics and adventures. When I started talking to them at night, I realized it was time for me to move on.

I wrote to Gösta, a cry for help. His reply arrived at the post office two weeks later. He had been worried for some time, he wrote, and wondered why he hadn't heard from me. Now I could finally go to live with him. In the envelope, he had included a name and address. A friend of a friend had been given a painting in exchange for bringing me home on a cargo ship. I left Paul's cottage a few nights later. I saw his bearded chin tremble, saw him bite his lip. In that moment, I think I truly came to know Paul. During our two years together, he had rarely looked me straight in the eye. Right then, I finally understood why. Saying goodbye would be painful.

Paul and I exchanged letters for years. I never stopped caring about him. Paul, the recluse, living in his temple of memories. When he eventually passed away, I traveled to England to bury him alongside the urn containing the ashes of Rox, his beloved dog, who had died a few years earlier. Only three people turned up for Paul's funeral. The priest, his closest neighbor, and me.

The Red Address Book
N. NILSSON, GÖSTA

Our reunion was exactly as Gösta had imagined in his letters. The sailors cast their ropes ashore; the dockworkers grabbed them and wound them around the bollards on the pier. The iron gangway was rolled into position on the uneven pavement. A light rain was falling, and Gösta was standing there on the dock, beneath a big black umbrella. I walked toward him. I was no longer a pretty young woman, not at all the person he held dear in his memory. I didn't have a single intact piece of clothing, nor a good pair of shoes. My hair was lank, and the years had taken their toll on my skin, leaving it rough. Still, he held out his arms to me, and I fell into them without a moment's hesitation.

"Oh, Doris! You're here, finally!" he whispered, refusing to let go.

"Yes, it's certainly been a while, darling Gösta," I replied, sniffling.

He laughed. Took a step back, held my shoulders in his hands.

"Let me see you."

I dried my tears and with a sense of uncertainty met his eye. That was enough to breathe life back into our friendship. Suddenly, I was that little thirteen-year-old again, and he was the unhappy artist.

"You have wrinkles." He laughed, his finger stroking the skin around my eye.

"And you're an old man." I laughed back, placing my hand on his round stomach. He smiled.

"I need a better housekeeper."

"And I need a job."

"So what do you say?"

I was still clutching my duffel bag, which contained a few mementos from England.

"Shall we do it? When can you begin?"

I looked up and smiled.

"How does right now sound?"

"Right now is good."

He held out his arms to me, and we hugged, this time to seal an affectionate business deal. Then we walked together, up the hills of Södermalm, to Bastugatan. When I saw Madame's building farther down the street, my stomach lurched. I approached it cautiously, pausing outside to read the names on the door.

"A young family lives there now. Four kids they've got, crashing about and yelling, bothering Göran in the apartment below. It's driving him mad, he says."

I nodded but didn't reply, reached for the handle I had turned so often. To think that my hand had been here, to think that the very first time . . .

"Come on, let's go home now and get some food in you." Gösta placed his hand on my shoulder. I nodded.

The hallway smelled of turpentine and dust. Paintings were stacked against the walls in long lines. Paint was splattered on the pine floor, and the living room furniture was covered in white sheets. Flies swirled among the piles of dirty plates in the kitchen.

"You do need a housekeeper."

"I told you."

"Well, now you have one."

"You know what that involves. I'm not always in the best of moods."

"I know."

"And I need complete discretion with regards to . . ."

"I'll stay out of your private life."

"Good."

"Do we have any money?"

"Not much."

"Where can I sleep?"

He showed me to the maid's quarters. A small room with a bed, a desk, and a walk-in closet. There were women's magazines, traces of a female presence. I turned and gave him a questioning look.

"They always quit when they find out . . ."

He never used the word *homosexual*. It wasn't something we talked about. Whenever his nocturnal guests came over, I would push cotton balls into my ears to avoid hearing them. During the day he was just Gösta, my friend. I went about my business, he went about his, and we would eat together in the evening. If he was in a good mood, we would talk for a while. Sometimes about art. Sometimes about politics. Our relationship was never that of employer and maid. To him, I was just Doris, the friend he had been missing for many years who had finally returned.

One night I showed him the short stories I had written in Paul's cottage, about the woman and child. He read them carefully, occasionally going over the same page twice.

He sounded surprised when he eventually spoke. "Did you write all this?"

"Yes. Is it bad?"

"Doris, you're talented. You have the gift of words — I've always said that. You need to make the most of it."

Gösta bought me an exercise book, and I began writing in it every day. Short stories suited me best, as I never had the energy to properly structure anything longer. My stories became a way for us to put more food on the table. I sold them to women's magazines; they would buy anything so long as it was about love. That was what sold. Passion. Romance. Happy endings. We sat there on Gösta's dark-purple velvet sofa, laughing at the banalities I came up with. We, who had been marked by life, laughed at those who believed in happy endings.

26

"Could you give me a little water?" Doris reaches toward the table for her glass. Jenny holds it as Doris places her hand on her wrist to raise the glass to her lips.

"Do you want anything other than water? Coca-Cola? Soda? Juice?"

"Wine?" Doris's eyes crinkle mischievously.

"Wine? You want wine?"

Doris nods. Jenny smiles.

"Well, of course you can have wine. White or red?"

"Rosé. Cold."

"OK, leave it to me. It'll take a while, but you can rest in the meantime."

"And strawberries."

"And strawberries. Anything else? Chocolate?"

Doris nods and attempts to smile, but her mouth can't manage it. Only her upper lip slides above her teeth, transforming the smile into a grimace. Her breathing is labored, every breath rattling in her chest. She seems much wearier than she was yesterday. Jenny leans forward and rests her cheek against Doris's.

"I'll be back soon," she whispers, thinking: Don't die while I'm gone. Please, don't die.

She half-runs through the slush and the Nordic darkness, toward the brown exterior of Mörby centrum mall. Tyra giggles and points to the wheels and the water being sprayed up as they rush through the puddles. Jenny can feel it soaking through her leather boots. A dark, wavy tidemark has appeared on them; the soles are too thin to handle winter in Sweden. They'll never be right again; she forgot to treat the leather.

In the supermarket, she finds out that you still can't buy alcohol there — it's available only at Systembolaget, the state-run liquor store. She swears and hurries over there. She has deep feelings for Sweden, the place where her grandmother and great-grandmother grew up, and tends to put the country on a pedestal. But she has clearly not spent enough time there to smoothly negotiate the basics of everyday life. She sighs and sits down at the information counter in Systembolaget. After five minutes, a man in a checked green shirt comes over.

"Hi! Can I help you with anything?"

"Hi, yes, I need two bottles of rosé, something nice," she says. He nods and leads her over to a shelf of rosés. Reels off suggestion after suggestion, asks what kind of food she'll serve it with.

"Just chocolate and strawberries," she says wearily.

"Aha, in that case, maybe you'd prefer something sparkling? Or maybe —"

She interrupts him. "No, just an ordinary rosé wine. Choose whichever you would pick yourself." She feels like screaming: just give me a fucking rosé! But she manages to control herself and nods politely when he holds out two bottles. Once he leaves, she glances down at a different bottle, one with a nicer label, and discreetly swaps them.

"Do you sell wineglasses?" she asks the woman at the checkout as she hands over her American passport.

The woman shakes her head. "Try the supermarket, I'm sure they have plastic ones."

Jenny sighs and heads back there.

The stroller gets caught in the slush three times on the way back to the hospital, and by the time Jenny pushes it onto the ward, she is so warm that her cheeks are flushed. Tyra is sleeping. She peels off her coat and hangs it over the stroller handle, making the bottles in the bag clink against each other. Doris is awake, and at that sound, her mouth curls into a more convincing smile. Her face no longer looks quite so gray.

"Oof, walking is hot work." Jenny grabs a newspaper and fans herself with it. "You're looking brighter!"

"M o r p h i n e," Doris says slowly, then laughs. "They give it to me whenever the pain gets to be too much."

Jenny frowns. "You're in pain? Where?"

"Here and there. Everywhere. In my hip, my leg, my stomach. In a new way. Almost like it's radiating from within. Like my entire skeleton is full of thousands of sharp pins."

"Oh, Dossi, that sounds awful! I wish there was something I could do!"

"There is." Doris smirks knowingly.

"You want some? Is it really OK, considering you've been given morphine?"

Doris nods and Jenny grabs the purple bag from the space beneath the seat of the stroller. She places both bottles on the table and crumples the empty bag.

"It makes no difference, I'm going to die anyway."

"Nope. I don't want to hear a word about that." Jenny bites her lip.

"My darling, I'm never going to leave this bed. You know that, don't you? You do understand?"

Jenny nods dully and sits down right next to Doris, who slides even closer. She grimaces slightly when she moves her leg.

"Does it still hurt, even with the morphine?"

"Only when I move. But let's talk about something else now. I'm so sick of suffering. Tell me about Willie. And David and Jack. And the house."

"Happy to. But first, it's time for a toast." She pours the pink liquid into two plastic cups, the closest thing to a glass she could find at the supermarket. Then she presses the button to raise the head end of the bed. Doris slips down slightly, and Jenny lifts her head by putting her hand behind her neck, and gently tips the cup to her mouth. Doris noisily slurps down a few drops.

"Like a summer's evening in Provence," she whispers, closing her eyes.

"Provence? Have you been there?"

"Many times. I often used to go when I lived in Paris. There were parties there, at the vineyards."

Jenny hands her a huge red strawberry. "Was it pretty?"

Doris sighs. "Wonderful."

"I read about your adventures in Paris last night. Did you really write all that for me?"

"Yes, I didn't want to die with everything in my head. The knowledge that all my memories would be lost with me was too painful."

"How was Provence back then? And the parties? Who else was there?"

"Oh, it was exciting. Many of the greats. Authors, artists, designers. Everyone wore clothes more beautiful than you could imagine. There were different fabrics back then. They had luster, quality. We were in the middle of the countryside, but everyone was dressed like they were going to the Nobel Prize ceremony. High heels, strings of pearls, and huge diamonds. Rustling silk dresses."

Jenny sighs. "And you were a live mannequin! What do you know! That's why you were never impressed by the simple fact that I was working, when I was younger. But why did you never talk about your own work, Dossi? I can't remember that you ever mentioned it."

"No, it's possible I didn't. But I've written about it for you now, so you'll know everything. Usch, it was such a vanishingly short period in a very long life. You know how it is. Talking about it once you're older just leads to surprised faces. Who would believe that an old biddy was once a model? And besides, I ended up back where I began. A simple housekeeper. No more, no less."

"Tell me more, I want to hear everything. What did you wear at those parties?"

"It was always something out of the ordinary, those magnificent creations. That was why I was there. To show off the dresses. Dazzle society."

"Gosh, how exciting! Doris, I wish I had known all this. I've always admired you for your beauty, so I'm really not surprised, and I don't think anyone else would be either. When I was young, I always wished I would grow up to look like you, do you remember that?"

Doris smiles, pats her gently on the cheek. Then takes a deep breath.

"Yes, life was easier before the war. And it's always easier to be young and beautiful. You get a lot of things for free."

"I recognize that." Jenny laughs loudly and pulls at the skin on her neck. "How did this happen? When did I become middle-aged and wrinkly?"

"Pssh, nonsense. I won't hear you talk about yourself like that.

You're still young and beautiful. And you have half your life ahead of you, at least."

Jenny looks at Doris. "Do you have any pictures from back then?"

"Just a few; I didn't manage to take many with me from Paris. Those I do have are in a couple of tin boxes in the wardrobe."

"They are?"

"Yes, they should be, under my clothes somewhere. Battered, rusty old tin boxes that I luckily managed to get back from New York. They've been halfway around the world, and it shows. One of them was a chocolate box that Allan gave me, so I never wanted to throw it away. It's thanks to him that I enjoy saving memories in tin boxes."

"I'll look for them tonight. How exciting! If I find any pictures, I'll bring them in tomorrow so you can tell me all about every single person in them. Would you like another strawberry?"

Tyra whimpers and waves her arms in the air. Her whining soon turns into a full-blown tantrum. Jenny picks her up and holds her little body tight against her own, kisses her on the cheek, and bounces her up and down to comfort her.

"She's probably hungry; I'll take her down to the cafeteria. We'll be back soon. You get some rest, so you can tell me more about Paris later."

Doris nods, but her eyelids have started to droop before Jenny even manages to turn away. She studies her for a moment. Doris is wrapped in one of the hospital's pale-yellow blankets, and she is as thin as a bird. Her hair is flat and sparse, the skin of her scalp glowing bare and white between the strands. The beauty that followed her through life has gone. Jenny resists the impulse to hug her again and quickly heads down to the cafeteria. Don't die, please don't die while I'm gone, she thinks again.

The Red Address Book
N. NILSSON, GÖSTA

He was a perfectionist through and through, and possessed an intensity verging on the manic. I had never seen anything like it, and never did again. When he painted, he might spend weeks on a single canvas. And he was unreachable during that time. Didn't eat much, didn't talk. Directed all of his energy into fields of color and building his compositions. It was a love affair, a passion that took over his body and his consciousness. He couldn't do anything about it, he said; it was just a matter of following his senses and letting the picture take shape.

"It's not me doing the painting. I'm always surprised when I see the finished piece. The pictures just come to me, as though someone else had taken over," he explained whenever I asked him about it.

I often watched him from a distance. It fascinated me how, even as the critics shot him down, he managed to retain his creative energy. Some claimed to understand him, and kept him from starving by buying his paintings. People with lots of money and a burning interest in art.

That apartment on Bastugatan had an interior that bore signs of our dreams of Paris. The walls of the studio were covered with pictures of our beloved city. Some Gösta had painted himself, some were cut from papers; some were postcards that I had sent to him. We talked often about the city we both longed for, and he still wanted to return there. We fantasized about going back together one day.

When the war came to an end in 1945, we both went down to Kungsgatan to celebrate with everyone else. It was unlike Gösta to be out among the crowds, but he didn't want to miss the moment. He walked with the French flag in his hand, I with the Swedish. The euphoria was tangible — people celebrated the end of the conflict by laughing, singing, shouting, and throwing confetti.

"Doris, do you know what this means? We can go now, we can finally go." Gösta laughed louder than I had ever heard him laugh before as he waved the Tricolor. Usually so bitter and suspicious about the future, he at last seemed hopeful.

"Inspiration, my dear, I need to find inspiration again. It's there, not here." His eyes grew wild at the thought of seeing his artist friends in Montmartre once more.

But we never had enough money. Nor the courage to do what comes more naturally to youth — simply pull up sticks and leave. Paris remained a dream. Like all lost loves, that city grew ever more precious in our minds. In a way, I'm glad Gösta never managed to return. The disappointment of meeting the reality of Paris, after idealizing it for so long, might have been too much for him to bear. A painful discovery — his inspiration wasn't so strongly connected with one particular place after all. It was within him, and it was his job to find it and put it to use, however slow and difficult that process was. And to do this over and over again.

The city hung over us like a constant shadow of the past, when everything had seemed so much better. In truth, it still hangs there today. In the furniture, the French books, the paintings. Paris is the city that captured our souls.

When Gösta was in a good mood, I often spoke French with him. He understood only the odd word, so I tried to teach him more. He loved it.

"We'll go one day, Doris. You and I," he repeated, even after he must have realized it would never happen.

I always nodded and smiled.

"Yes, one day, Gösta. One day."

27

Jenny shovels in the baby food, stew and potatoes this time, from the colorfully labeled glass jar. Organic. The sauce smears around Tyra's mouth, and between chews Jenny scrapes it away with the spoon. The little one chomps away noisily, reaches for the spoon, and grasps at the air. Jenny shakes her head and pushes Tyra's hand back.

"We need to hurry. Fast, fast. Eat quickly," she says in a baby voice, making airplane sounds as she brings the spoon toward the girl's mouth. Tyra opens wide for the plane, but then snaps her mouth shut and starts grabbing for the spoon and protesting loudly. In the cafeteria the people at the next table glare as the whimpering becomes a piercing scream. Jenny gives up and hands the spoon to Tyra. She immediately quiets down and hits the spoon against the plate, making the sauce splatter. The neighbors glare again. Just give up, at least she's not crying, Jenny thinks, wiping the table with a napkin to clean up the worst of the mess.

"Mommy will be back in a minute." She gets up and runs over to the counter, where she buys a sandwich. Constantly glancing over to the girl in the high chair. Before she makes it back to the table, she has taken two bites of the dry bread. She pauses and allows the taste of Swedish ham to fill her mouth. A memory rears up. The sandwiches Doris used to make for her to take to school — the first real sandwiches she ever had in her lunchbox. Before that, it had always been crackers or cookies, maybe an apple or two.

Jenny can remember exactly where she was the first time they met. She had been sitting in the corner of the red sofa, staring at the flickering TV. A blanket was tightly wrapped around her. She was four. Doris had knocked on the door, unannounced, and stepped into a home full of chaos. Jenny's mother lay asleep on the kitchen rug, drool running from the corner of her mouth. Her skirt didn't reach even halfway down her thighs, and her tights were torn just beneath the knee. Little Jenny had seen her fall. A trickle of dried blood revealed that she had somehow cut herself.

Jenny shudders. The memory of fear. The memory of how she had recoiled when the strange old lady who spoke English with an accent entered the room. She had thought Doris was someone from social services who had come to take her away; her mother had often threatened Jenny with this possibility. She covered half of her face with the blanket, and her breath dampened the fabric. When Doris caught sight of Elise, she turned her on her side and phoned for an ambulance. She had stroked Elise's forehead while they waited for help to arrive. As Elise was carried out into the cold night by two muscular paramedics, Doris sat down next to Jenny on the sofa. Her hair was damp with sweat at her temples, and her heart was beating so hard that Jenny could feel her pulse. Doris was crying, and somehow those tears made her seem less dangerous. Jenny's teeth were chattering; she stared straight ahead, shivering. She couldn't stop trembling. Doris gently cupped a warm hand under her chin and used the other to stroke her back. Hushed her and said *there there, there there, shh* for so long, her words became a melody filling the silent room. They sat like that for hours. Doris didn't attempt to talk to her. Not then. Jenny fell asleep in her lap that evening, with Doris's warm hand on her cheek.

A thud tears Jenny from her thoughts. Tyra has thrown the glass jar onto the floor, and she has food all over her face and T-shirt. Jenny pulls off the girl's top, wipes her face with the clean side, shoves the top into the changing bag, and pulls out a fresh one. Tyra has already managed to press her sticky hands to her round belly. With a pleased grin, she studies the pattern of purée and claps her hands again, making sure the mess spreads over even more of her skin.

"Oh, no, Tyra. We need to be quick, hurry, hurry." She rubs a wet wipe over the girl's stomach, throat, face, and hands, and then transfers her, half-naked, to the stroller. She puts the clean top to one side. Leaving a scene of chaos on the table, Jenny quickly pushes the stroller away. She needs to get back to Doris. She needs to hear everything before Doris dies. She half-runs down the corridor, barreling through the door while pushing the stroller.

"How did you know to turn up right then?"

Doris jolts awake and rubs her eyes. Tyra sneezes and moans loudly. Jenny wrestles her into the clean top, her eyes fixed on Doris.

"Who was it that called you? When you saved Mom's life, the first time I met you. How could you have known?"

"It was . . ." She clears her throat, can't say the words. Jenny picks up the glass of water from the bedside table and helps her drink.

"She called," Doris continues.

"Mom?"

"Yes, I hadn't seen her in several years, not since you were a baby. She wrote sometimes, and I phoned her every now and then. It was expensive to phone in those days, and she rarely answered."

"But what did she say when she called? What made you travel to the United States?"

"Darling . . ."

"Tell me. You can tell me anything. She's dead. I want to know the truth."

"She said she was going to give you away."

"Give me away? To who?"

"To anyone. She said she was going to drive to one of the rich neighborhoods in New Jersey and leave you on a sidewalk. That anything would be better than a life with her."

"She was probably right. As I remember it, it was the drugs, not her, that ruled my life. Almost anything would be better than that."

"I came straightaway, caught a plane from Stockholm that same evening."

"What if . . ."

"Yes, what if . . ."

"What if she'd died right there and then? I could have had a different life."

"Yes, I think that's precisely what she was trying to do. Elise didn't want to live any longer, she couldn't cope."

"It was thanks to you that she survived."

"It's all about timing." Doris squeezes Jenny's hand gently to show her that she's joking, right in the middle of this dark memory.

"I'm going to play 'what if' all evening."

"What if I'd never gotten to meet you?"

"No, I can't imagine that, not even as a game. You had to be part of my life, Doris. I don't know if I can cope without you." She bursts into tears. "You saved my life!"

"You'll cope, Jenny. You're strong. You always have been."

"I wasn't strong that day, when you had to hold my chin to stop my teeth from chattering."

"You were four at the time, my love. But yes, you were strong even then. And brave. You were. You lived your first few years in complete chaos, and yet you managed to survive and become the person you are today. Can't you see that?"

"What am I today, though? A frumpy mother of three who doesn't have a career."

"Why do you say that? Why do you see yourself as frumpy?

You're more beautiful than most people. And smarter. You know that. You've been a model too. And you've also been to college."

"I've got a face that's like a blank page. And a tall, slim body. Is that beauty? No. That's someone who can adapt to the changing requirements of her surroundings. Who can please. That's all fashion is about. Plus, I never graduated. I met Willie. And became a mother."

"Stop putting yourself down. It's never too late." Doris gives her a stern look.

"Who says it's never too late? You said yourself that it's easier to be young and beautiful."

"You are beautiful. You're talented. So. That's enough. Focus on something else. Start cultivating your talents rather than going through life thinking that you aren't good enough. Start writing again. Work on yourself. In the end, that's all that really matters. You're never any more than your soul."

Jenny snorts. "Write. You've always gone on about that."

"When will you realize that you're talented? You won competitions in college. Have you forgotten about that?"

"Yeah, I might have won a few competitions. But what am I meant to write about? I have nothing to write about. Nothing. My life is flat. Perfect, maybe, in other people's eyes, but flat. No passion. No adventures. Willie and I are like two friends who run the business that is our family. No more, no less."

"So come up with something, then."

"Come up with something?"

"Yes, make the life you want to live. And write . . ." — she pauses here, gasping for air, and then continues at a whisper — "everything down. Don't miss this chance. Don't waste your memories. And for God's sake, don't waste your talent!"

"Did *you*?"

"Yes."

"Do you regret it?"

"Yes."

Suddenly, Doris jumps and her chin slumps against her chest. Her mouth twists, and she squeezes her eyes tight. Jenny shouts for help and a nurse comes running. She presses the alarm button and three women dressed in white are soon stooped over Doris.

Jenny tries to peer between their shoulders. "What's going on? Is she OK?"

Doris's expression is back to normal; her mouth has relaxed. But her skin has turned a shade of bluish-purple.

"We need to take her back down to intensive care." A nurse pushes Jenny to one side and releases the brake on the bed.

"Can I come?"

Another nurse, dark-haired and short, shakes her head.

"She needs rest. We'll keep you informed."

"But I want to be there if, when, if she . . ."

"We'll make sure you're there. She seems stable now, but her heart is a little unsteady. It's normal. You know, so close to the end."

She touches Jenny's shoulder and then turns to join the others, who have already begun rolling the bed down the corridor. Jenny remains where she is, watching them. She can't see Doris over the end of the wood-and-steel bed. She clenches her fists and wraps her arms around herself.

28

She finds the tin boxes of photographs at the very back of the wardrobe. One with a thick layer of tape wrapped around it, one without. She cuts the tape with a kitchen knife and then opens both tins and spreads out the images in an arc across the kitchen table. Mixes memories from Paris with memories from New York. There, right in the middle of the pile, she spots herself. A small, curly-haired girl dancing so that her skirt floats out around her. She smiles and puts it to one side; she'll save it to show Willie later. One of the few pictures from her childhood. Many photographs are older. In one, Doris is leaning against a wall, with a hand on her hat. Her head is turned in profile, and she is gazing toward the Eiffel Tower. She is wearing a dark pleated skirt and what seems to be a matching blouse, with a white collar and fabric buttons. Her soft curls frame her face. Another is a close-up shot. Doris's eyebrows are thin and sharp, painted in darkly. Her skin is powdered white and her lips glisten with lipstick. Her lashes are long and her gaze lingering, as though she is dreaming of something far away. Jenny picks up the black-and-white image and studies it more closely. Doris's skin is completely smooth, without a single trace of wrinkles or sun damage. Her nose is dainty and straight, her eyes big, her cheeks rounded like a teen-ager's. She looks so young and so unbelievably beautiful.

Jenny scans the pictures. It's like visiting a different era. The words Doris has written take on new weight, now that she can see how things actually looked. She picks up an image of Doris wearing strappy heels and a dress with a bell skirt and a wide lapel over the chest. A round hat, like a wool beanie, hugs her head. She is posing with one hand slightly away from her body. Her chin is raised, and her face has a determined look. Her eyes are turned away from the camera.

It's nothing like the fashion photography of the eighties, when Jenny herself posed for the camera. Back then, you had to pout your lips, or even part them. Your eyes had to "make love to the camera," you were told, and plunging necklines showed off your breasts, rubbed with oil to make them glisten. Using enormous fans, the photographers tried to make it look as if a model's hair was blow-ing in the wind, but the results were never particularly good: loose strands blew into your face, into your eyes, or straight up above your head. If there was one thing that infuriated stylists in the eighties, it was those fans. Jenny smiles at the memory. One day, she'll show the kids the pictures stashed away in the attic. They're still inside the modeling portfolio she had to carry around. The one she showed to photographers and advertising agencies whenever she was look-ing for work. Willie has seen the pictures, but the kids haven't; they don't know anything about that part of her life. It's best if she tells them herself. So they don't experience what she did. Doris should have told her long ago.

The phone rings, and she throws herself at it to stop the noise from waking Tyra.

"Hi, Willie!"

"I'm just going to say this once, OK? Please come home!"

Jenny is taken aback by the sudden outburst. She goes to the kitchen, shuts the bedroom door behind her, leaving a slight gap so she can hear Tyra in case she needs her.

"What's going on?"

"Jenny, I'll lose my job if this continues."

"Continues? If what continues? Tell me what's going on."

"Chaos. Chaos is what's going on."

"Have the boys been fighting?"

"That's putting it mildly. They fight constantly. I can't do my job *and* take care of them *and* look after the house. It just doesn't work. I don't know how you manage!"

"Calm down! Please, calm down, it's not that bad. We can fix this, you just need to get some help."

"How long does she have left?"

Jenny feels something break inside; now *she* is the one who can't do this anymore.

"How long? Wait, just let me ask the grim reaper, he's standing right here breathing down my neck. How the hell should I know? But thanks for finally asking how she's doing. Not well, is the answer. She doesn't have long. And I'm not having much fun here either, in case you're interested. I love her. She's the only grandmother I ever had. No, more than that; she's like my mother. She saved my life once, and I'm not going to let her die alone. The fact you can even ask me something like that . . ."

Willie doesn't say anything for quite some time. When he does speak again, his voice sounds embarrassed, apologetic.

"I'm sorry, baby. Sorry. I went way too far. But I'm completely desperate over here. I'm serious, how do you make it through the day? It's awful."

"I make it through because I love you all. It's no simpler or more complicated than that."

She can practically hear him smiling. Waits for him to say something.

"What was the name of that girl we used as a babysitter recently?"

"The one who lives on Parkway Drive? Sophie."

"Do you think she could help out, make lunch for the boys, be here in the afternoon when they get home from school?"

"Maybe. Call her and ask. I can send you her number."

"Thanks. Have I told you that you do a fantastic job?"

"No. It's actually the first time you've ever said that."

"Sorry. I'm incredibly selfish."

"Incredibly."

"But you like me anyway?"

She pauses for a second, holds back her answer.

"Yeah. Sometimes. You have your good sides."

"I miss you."

"I don't miss you. Not when you're being like this. You have to realize that it's important for me to be here. And that it's difficult enough as it is."

"Sorry. I really mean that."

"OK."

"Sorry, sorry, sorry."

"I'll think about it. How did it go with Allan?"

"What? Who?"

"Allan Smith. Two *l*'s. You were going to check with Stan. No, don't tell me you forgot! We have to find him!"

"Shit! It's been so chaotic here, Jenny, I completely forgot."

"How could you forget? It's so important! So important for me and for Doris."

"Sorry again! I'm a terrible person. I'll call him right now. Right now! I love you, speak soon!"

The Red Address Book
A. ANDERSSON, ELISE

A little red dress with a full skirt. Light curls that frizzed at the temples. Arms waving in the air. You always did love to dance, Jenny. Round and round my legs. I tried to catch you, and you laughed. Then I grabbed one hand, pulled you close, and we laughed together. I blew raspberries on your stomach. Your warm, soft stomach . . . You pulled on my ears, kneaded my earlobes between your finger and thumb. It hurt when you did that, but I never wanted to tell you to stop. Didn't want to push you away, now that you had come so close.

Those moments we had, they were the best of my life. I never got to experience the joys of motherhood. Maybe it was just as well. But I had you. I got to be part of your life. I got to give you unconditional love. I got to be there when your mother wasn't enough. I'm so happy about that. That I was able to help you. To me, it was a gift, and even today, I'm ashamed that I occasionally felt relieved when she disappeared. I got to pack your lunchbox, take you to school, kiss you goodbye. I got to help you with your homework. I got to take you to the zoo, sing about all the animals, and eat ice cream.

You never wanted to eat meat after our visits to the zoo. You would sit there in your chair, pressing your lips together whenever I tried to give you ham or chicken or fish.

"The chicken is alive and it's happy," you said firmly. "I want it to live. All animals should live!"

And so we ate rice and potatoes for a few weeks, until, as children often do, you forgot about the animals and started eating meat again. You had a good heart even as a child, dear Jenny. You were friends with everyone. Even your mother, who let you down time and time again. Elise wasn't there. Elise didn't understand your needs. She didn't have an easy life, nor did you. No one in her life had it easy.

She used to send you presents from rehab. Huge toys that we had to pick up from the post office. Play tents, doll's houses, teddy bears bigger than you. Do you remember that? You used to look forward to the deliveries. More than you looked forward to seeing her again. We played with those toys for hours. It was just you and me then. You and me and our games. We both felt secure in that.

29

At the very bottom of the tin boxes, Jenny finds a number of letters. Thin envelopes bearing Doris's address and American stamps. She looks at the dates and the handwriting. Immediately drops the letters. Lets them sail to the floor.

Hot jets of water in the shower warm her, but she can't stop shaking. She sits down in the corner, curled up, with the showerhead between her knees. She can see her reflection in the polished metal. Can see her eyes — they look so tired, surrounded by crow's feet. She should get some sleep, should lie down next to Tyra. But then, with Doris's pink dressing gown wrapped tight around her body, she sits down and stares at the letters. Was it here that her mother wrote that she wanted to get rid of her?

Eventually, she plucks up the courage. Snatches the letters from their envelopes.

Hi, Doris, I need money. Can you send more?

One after one. The letters contain no greetings, no questions about how Doris is.

The books you sent arrived. Thanks. Schoolbooks are good, but I need money too. We need money for food and some new clothes for the little one. Thanks for understanding.

Jenny sorts the envelopes by postmark date. Puts them in order. To begin with, they are all about money. But then the tone changes.

Doris. I can't cope, having her at home. Do you want to know how I got pregnant with her? I never told you that. I was high as a kite. The usual, heroin. I don't even know what he looked like. Just that he came from somewhere and fucked me all night. I was black and blue. What kid would want to come into this world like that? She was high when she was born. Screamed and screamed and screamed. Please, come back and help me.

Jenny reads on.

She won't sleep since you left. She cries herself to sleep. Every night. I'm not going to keep her. I'll give her to the first person I see tomorrow. I've never wanted her.

"Hello? Hello?"

Jenny is sitting with the phone in her hand, staring at Willie's image on the screen.

"Jenny? Jenny, is that you? Did something happen? Is Doris dead?"

"She never loved me."

"Who? Doris? Of course she did. Of course she did, baby!"

"Mom."

"What do you mean? What happened? What did Doris say?"

"She didn't say anything. I found some letters. Letters in which my mom wrote that she hated me. That I was high on heroin when I was born."

"But you knew that already, didn't you?"

"She was raped. That's how I was made. I wish I'd never opened the letters."

"Did you know they were from her before you opened them?"

"I recognized the handwriting. I couldn't help myself." She loses control and starts to shout. "Fucking shitty childhood!"

"You're an adult now, you have a good life. You have me. And the kids. They love their mother. And I love you, more than anything else, though I know I've been awful lately."

She sniffs, rubs her eyes. Runs a hand through her hair. "Yes, I have you. And the kids."

"And you've had Doris all your life. Imagine if she hadn't been there."

"Mom probably would've given me away to who knows who."

"Doris came when your mom needed to go into rehab. I'm sure that was when she wrote those letters, while she was high. Phone calls were expensive back then. I'm sure she wrote them and put them in the mail without thinking. Doris shouldn't have saved them. You had good times too."

"What the hell would you know about it?"

"Don't swear. I'm trying to comfort you. And I know. You told me."

"What if I just made that up? To seem normal."

"Did you?"

"Maybe, a little. I don't remember."

"Throw those letters away. It's ancient history. It doesn't matter now. Try to get some sleep, if you can."

"Of course it matters! My entire life, I've been living in hope."

"What do you mean?"

"That she did love me after all."

"She did. She wasn't herself when she wrote that stuff. And you are loved. I love you. I love you more than anything else. The kids love you. You mean so much to so many people. Never forget that. It wasn't your fault."

"It wasn't my fault."

"No, it wasn't your fault. It's never a child's fault if their parents aren't enough. It was the drugs."

"And the rape."

"That wasn't your doing. You were meant to come into this world. To be the strong and beautiful person that you are. With a laugh that makes time stop whenever I hear it. And to be my wife, and our kids' wonderful mother."

The tears are streaming down her cheeks again. "Doris is going to die soon."

"I know it's hard. I'm sorry I only thought about myself when I said you should come home."

"So you don't think I should come home?"

"No. I miss you, I love you, I need you, but I understand now. I wish I was there to kiss you good night."

"And hold me."

"Yeah, and hold you. Try to get some sleep now. Things are going to get better. I love you. More than anything."

Jenny hangs up and continues to stare at the envelopes. She doesn't want to, shouldn't, but she can't help herself. She reads the words over and over again. Words from a mother who wasn't there. Who wasn't really a mother.

30

It isn't the pain or the nausea. Not the grief or the longing for her family back home. It's the memories, seemingly long forgotten, that keep bubbling up. One by one, they visit her. Everything she has repressed. They keep her awake in the quiet, dark Stockholm night. Eventually there are so many thoughts swimming in her head that she leaves Tyra and goes to sit at the kitchen table, wrapped in a blanket, her bare knees drawn up beneath her chin. Doris's stack of paper is in front of her, the story of a life. She starts to read, searching for good memories. But she can't focus; the letters on the page merge. She suddenly can't understand the Swedish words.

All of her worst memories are in English. All of her worst memories are from America. Swedish stands for safety. Doris means love. She came when she was needed, stayed as long as necessary. For months, if she had to. Even when Elise was released from rehab. Doris represented normalcy, and to a child who had never experienced that, who had only caught glimpses of it from her friends' lives, normal was the most beautiful thing a person could be. Sandwiches in a lunchbox, reminders about her gym clothes and homework, signed forms to hand back to the teacher, two braids in her long hair, clean clothes, and warm food on real plates.

Unlike life with her mother. When she went to school in worn-out shoes. She remembers one pair with an enormous hole in one sole. She dragged that foot behind her so that her friends wouldn't see the dirt on her sock and laugh at her. Because of this, Jenny developed a particular way of walking, a loping gait that, even today, sometimes returns.

The hardest nights were those when Doris announced that Elise was coming home. Jenny became extremely anxious. Doris always promised to stay a while longer, and she kept her word. Doris didn't break a commitment. Wonderful, comforting Dossi.

Jenny goes back to bed and lies down against Tyra's soft, warm baby's body. She strokes the little girl's pale hair and dries her own tears on the pillow. Jenny can't breathe through her nose; it's blocked and swollen. I need some nose drops, she thinks, getting up to go to the bathroom. She looks through Doris's things. Finds hairspray, setting lotion, hair conditioner. Doris's hair was always important to her, she knows that; she used to give it at least one hundred strokes with the brush every day. When Jenny first met her, Doris's hair had still been long and thick, with just a few stray grays like silver threads among the blond. She had let it age naturally, had never dyed her hair. Now, it's white and very thin, cut in a short style Jenny is sure she must hate. She has completely forgotten about the nose drops, and picks up the setting lotion, rollers, and conditioner. She puts them in the changing bag.

Doris shouldn't have to die ugly. She has always been the most beautiful person on earth. Jenny scans her makeup. Finds eye shadow, a rusty-red blush, and some powder. Lipstick. She immediately feels more invigorated, and starts looking through the dresses in the wardrobe. Doris can't die in a white hospital gown, which keeps slipping open to reveal her wrinkled skin. But the sack-like everyday dresses in the wardrobe won't do either. There are too many dark-colored items competing for space on the hangers, and not enough color. She'll have to buy a new dress. A modern, happy one. Yellow or green or pink. Pretty and comfortable.

Dress.

She writes the word on a note and places it on top of the changing bag.

It's four in the morning when she finally climbs back into bed. The streetlamps send narrow beams of light through the cracks between the blind and the window. She closes her eyes, transported back to the New York of her youth. It's no longer Tyra next to her, keeping her sad company. It's Doris. Hushing her and loving her. Stroking her hair when she's afraid. Making her feel safe and getting her to doze off. She quietly hums the tune Doris always sang to her.

Summertime, and the livin' is easy. Fish are jumpin' and the cotton is high . . .

Unloved. She sighs deeply.

No. Loved. Doris was there. Doris is the one who matters. She hums on, now more quietly, and drifts off, exhausted, to sleep.

The Red Address Book
A. ANDERSSON, ELISE

Every time she came home from rehab, her cheeks were rosy and her hair was neat, with a new style and color. She came loaded with gifts, toys, clothes, and teddy bears, but you never even looked at her. You hid behind my legs, held my thighs tight. She couldn't get through to you then, and she never would. The distance between you two just grew. As you got older, you had a door you could close and friends you wanted to play with. But she did try, and I hope you remember the good times. When she cooked a three-course meal in the middle of the week and invited your closest friends over for dinner. Or when she sat up all night sewing your Halloween costume, an orange crab with stuffed claws. You were so proud as you walked around the neighborhood with your little bucket of candy, though you could barely walk. The costume was so heavy, you lost your balance and fell several times. Imagine if I had a picture of that, or a film; I'm sure your kids would like to see it.

Elise was unlike anyone else in my family. Not like my mother, not like your grandmother Agnes. Maybe her fragility came from her father's mother. Kristina was anxious by nature. I never quite understood that side of Elise. I told her to pull herself together. I often got angry with her. Particularly when she was carried away with one of her stupid ideas, like turning to prostitution to make more money, or giving you up for adoption. She said these things only to get more money or get me to stay. And it usually worked, because I stayed. Of course I did. For your sake. Do you remember that summer when she decided to shave off her hair, to liberate herself? She did it, despite our protests. During another period she walked around the house naked, so that you would grow up a free soul. Yes, my word, she had plenty of strange ideas!

But then she might suddenly meet a man, and she would entirely adapt herself to him. If he was a musician, she would become obsessed with music; if he was a lawyer, she would suddenly start dressing smartly, wearing tailored dresses. She believed in God, she was a Buddhist, or an atheist, or whatever else felt right at the moment.

Do you remember everything I'm telling you, Jenny? You were there; you saw it all. We didn't know her. Not you. Not me. She probably didn't even know herself.

31

"Look what I have." Jenny gives Doris a loving smile and starts to pull things out of the changing bag. "Are you ready for your beauty treatment?"

Doris gently shakes her head. "You're a madwoman," she whispers.

"My great-aunt's not going to die with a flat head of hair," Jenny jokes, but she bites her lip when she sees the panic in Doris's eyes. "Sorry, I didn't mean . . . no . . . that was a stupid joke. Really stupid."

"Is it really flat? I haven't seen a mirror since I fell."

Jenny laughs when she realizes that the panic in Doris's eyes has nothing to do with death.

"No, not completely flat . . . but it could be better. Let me work my magic."

She gently combs the thin, white strands. A few fall out and get caught in the red teeth of the comb.

"Does it hurt?"

Doris shakes her head. "It's nice, keep going."

Jenny gently lifts Doris's head so that she can reach the back, placing her hand behind the neck and slowly pulling the comb through her hair. Next, she twists it onto the rollers, one lock at a time. She needs only seven. Doris's hair is so thin and sparse. She sprays setting lotion onto the rollers and covers Doris's head with a red-and-white-checked tea towel. An elaborate *A* is embroidered on it, in a slightly lighter shade of red.

"It was my mother's, that tea towel. Imagine the quality! I got that and some furniture from an old neighbor when I came back from England," Doris explains.

"From England? When did you go there?"

"You'll have to keep reading." Doris yawns and rests her head against the pillow.

"It's fantastic, everything you've written. I've been reading a bit every night. There's so much I never knew."

"I want to give you my memories. So they don't just disappear."

"You remember so much, so many details."

"It's just a case of closing your eyes and thinking back. When time is all you have, your thoughts become quite deep."

"I wonder what I'll remember. My life hasn't been as exciting as yours. Nowhere near."

"It's never exciting when you're in the middle of it. It's just diffi-cult. The nuance becomes visible only much later."

Doris sighs. "I'm so tired," she continues at a whisper. "I think I need to rest for a while."

"Do you want anything?"

"Chocolate, a little bit of milk chocolate would be nice."

Jenny sorts through the changing bag, remembering a piece she furtively ate while Tyra was sleeping, but all she can find is the empty wrapper and a few sticky crumbs. She turns back to Doris, who has fallen asleep. Jenny quickly holds a finger in front of Doris's mouth. A faint puff of warm air. She relaxes.

"Come on, Tyra, let's go shopping." She lifts the girl from the stroller and lets her walk. She plays with her, tickles her stomach, and gets a bubbling laugh in return. The contrast between this new life, so full of the joy of discovery, and the old life in the hospital bed, is liberating. She can laugh with Tyra, despite the sorrow in her heart. She picks her up and swings her from side to side.

"The priest's little crow . . ." She sings loudly, making the nurses smile as they pass by. Tyra laughs and wraps her chubby little arms around Jenny's neck.

"Mommy!" she shrieks, burying her face in her mother's neck. Jenny can feel the cold nose against her skin. She accidentally elbows Tyra, who starts to shout.

"Mommy, Mommy," she shouts, waving her arms. As though she has just dropped her most valuable possession. She wants to be back against her mother's neck. Where it is warm and safe. Jenny quickly pulls her close, hugs her tight, and strokes her back.

"Mommy's here, baby, Mommy's here," she whispers, kissing her on the head. Tyra seems to miss her even though she is right by her side. She wonders how her other two kids are, whether they also miss their mom.

With Tyra clinging to her neck, Jenny walks the last few meters to the kiosk and the chocolate.

When they get back, Jenny gently strokes Doris's cheek with two fingers. She is still deep in sleep. Tyra hits Doris's hand, and Jenny is about to stop her from doing so again when Doris's eyes snap open.

"Is that you, Elise?" she whispers. She seems to have trouble focusing.

"It's Jenny, not Elise. How are you feeling? Are you dizzy?" She turns her head to look for a nurse. "Just hold on, I'll get someone."

She puts Tyra into the stroller and runs out into the corridor. There's no one there. At the nurses' station, she spots three nurses, each holding a cup of coffee. She runs to them.

"Something's wrong. Her eyes, they're rolling around."

She can hear Tyra crying loudly and runs ahead of the nurses. When she gets back to the room, she sees Doris, despite how weak she is, trying to comfort the little girl. She is struggling to sing a song, but the notes are all wrong, which makes Tyra scream louder.

"Mommy!" Tyra's face is blotchy with tears. Jenny picks her up. Doris whispers, desperation filling her faint voice:

"I'm sorry, I tried..."

Jenny wants to hug them both. Keep the old one alive and transfer courage and strength to the little one. The nurses examine Doris, and Jenny watches them from a distance: the blood-pressure monitor being pumped up, the oxygen monitor on Doris's index finger, the stethoscope on her chest.

"She's weak. It was probably just a dizzy spell." The nurses pack up their instruments and leave the room.

Probably just a dizzy spell. Probably *just*. Jenny finds herself getting riled up at their words.

"Should we take those rollers out now?" she asks, gesturing toward Doris's head.

Doris nods.

"So you'll look extra nice."

Doris smiles weakly. Jenny allows her own tears to well up and roll toward her nose. She gently loosens the rollers, one by one.

"I've heard that salt water's good for the hair," Doris says in a rattling whisper.

Jenny smiles.

"I'm really going to miss you. I love you so much."

"I love you too, my most darling child. And you." She nods toward Tyra, who is calmer now, and busy throwing everything from the stroller onto the floor. Jenny lifts her up to the edge of the bed so that Doris can talk to her, but Tyra protests and wants to get back down. She jumps into thin air, and she is safe, because her mother's hands are there to catch her.

Doris says, "Put the little one down, Jenny. Watching an old lady die isn't much fun."

Back on the floor, Tyra grabs hold of a picture book. She throws it against the side of the bed with such force that part of the cover comes loose. Jenny doesn't bother telling her off. So long as the girl is quiet and happy, everything is fine. She combs and sprays Doris's hair. The thin strands gain volume and now cover the bare areas of her scalp. Jenny studies the result with satisfaction and then turns her attention to Doris's face. She carefully powders the wrinkled cheeks, buffs rusty-red blush onto the skin in a circular motion, paints the lips. The makeup brings life to the old woman's face. Jenny takes a picture and shows it to Doris, who nods happily.

"Eyes too," she whispers.

Jenny bends down and gently applies a little light-pink eye shadow. Doris's eyelids droop over her eyes, leaving only half of her iris visible. The color catches in the creases and looks uneven, but it doesn't matter.

"I bought you a dress. A comfy one; you can sleep in it too, if you like."

She pulls the Gina Tricot bag from the compartment beneath the stroller and holds up the dress. It's all one color, deep pink, and made of jersey. The arms are long and the neck rounded, and the fabric is pleated over the chest.

"Pretty color," Doris whispers, lifting her fingers to feel the quality.

"Yeah, I remembered how much you like pink. You always bought me pink dresses. Mom hated that color."

"Hippy." Doris gives a labored cough after that single word.

"Yup. It's true. She was a real hippy. I don't know where she got it from, but her approach to life came close to killing her several times." Jenny sighs. "I suppose it did, in the end."

"Drugs are the devil," Doris whispers.

Jenny doesn't reply. She helps Doris with the dress, one step at a time. "What do you know about my dad?" she then asks.

Doris quickly looks up and shakes her head.

"Nothing?"

"No."

"Nothing at all?"

"We've talked about this, my dear."

"I know you know more than you're letting on. I found Mom's letters. They were in the box with the photographs. She hated me."

Doris shakes her head.

"No, my love, don't think that. She didn't. She was on drugs, she wanted money. She sent those letters, without thinking, during one of her bad spells; she could never afford to call me. I don't know why I kept them. Stupid."

"She was raped."

Doris doesn't reply. She closes her eyes.

"You loved me, I know that. I feel that."

"Elise loved you."

"When? While she was injecting heroin into her veins? Or while she was lying on the kitchen floor, vomiting and leaving it for me to clean up? Or when she wanted to give me away to a stranger?"

"That was when she was high." Doris's voice is weak.

"She always promised she would stop."

"She tried. But she couldn't."

"Was that why you loved me? Because I didn't have a mother?"

Doris opens her eyes; they're glossy and have started drifting again. Jenny rushes forward.

"Sorry, we don't need to talk about it. I love you. You've been everything to me."

"I always came when you needed me," Doris whispers, and Jenny nods. Kisses her forehead. "And I loved you because I loved you."

"Don't talk any more now, Dossi, get some rest. I'll stay here and hold your hand."

"Where is Gösta? Has he had his coffee?"

"You're confused, Doris. Gösta is dead. He died before I was born. You remember that, don't you?"

Her memories catch up with her, and she nods. "Everyone's dead."

"No, everyone is not dead. Not at all."

"Everyone who means anything. Everyone but you."

Jenny slowly strokes Doris's arm, the deep-pink fabric of the new dress.

"Don't be scared," she whispers, but she doesn't get a reply. Doris has fallen asleep again. With each labored breath, her chest rises and her lungs rattle.

A nurse comes in and raises the rails at the sides of the bed.

"I think it's best if Doris gets some sleep now. You and the little lady too," she says, waving at Tyra.

Jenny dries her tears. "I don't want to leave Doris. Maybe I should sleep here?"

The nurse shakes her head.

"You go. We're good at knowing when the end is near. She'll make it through the night, and if things do get any worse, we'll call."

"But you have to promise me to call right away, at the slightest change. The very slightest!"

The nurse nods patiently. "I promise."

Jenny reluctantly leaves the ward and heads toward the elevator. Tyra is impatient in the stroller; she wants to get up and walk. Those long hours of sitting still in Doris's room have put her in a bad mood. Jenny lifts her from the stroller and lets her walk by her side. Clutching the side of the stroller tight in her chubby hand, she staggers forward. Jenny scrolls through her phone. Ten missed calls, all from Willie. Then a text message: *You're not going to believe it. Allan Smith is alive. Call me!*

32

"He's alive? Really?"

"He's alive. If it's the same Allan Smith."

"Get over there!"

"Are you crazy? I can't just go to New York. Who'll look after the boys?"

"Take them with you! Go!"

"Jenny, I'm starting to think you've completely lost your mind."

"You have to go. Doris has been alone her entire life. Her entire life. Other than the years with the gay artist she worked for. She's had one love in her life. One true love. And that was Allan Smith. She hasn't seen him since the Second World War. Do you understand? She has to see him before she dies. Go! Take the computer with you, so we can Skype. Call me when you're there."

"But we don't even know if it's the same Allan Smith. What if it's a completely different man?"

"How old is he?"

"Born in 1919."

"That sounds right."

"He lives on Long Island. Widower for the past twenty years."

"Could be right. Allan was married."

"According to Stan's email, he lived in France from 1940 to 1976. He took over a factory and made a fortune manufacturing bags."

"Doris told me he went to France during the war."

"His mother was French; he has two surnames in his passport. Allan Lesseur Smith."

"It has to be him, his mother was French. Go!"

"Jenny, you're crazy. The boys are at school. I can't just drop everything and leave."

"To hell with school!" She can barely control her voice. "What difference does it make if they miss a few days? This is more important than anything else right now. Doris doesn't have long to live, and she needs to see him one last time. We might be talking about hours here. Go! If you can't do it for any other reason, do it for me. I'm begging you!"

"For your sake, then, just for your sake I'll do it."

"Swing by the school and pick up the boys, then take the first flight to New York. If Mrs. Berg kicks up a fuss, tell her a close relative is sick. It's an excused absence, if I remember correctly."

"An excused absence?"

"Yeah, you know, there are rules about when kids are allowed to be absent from school. Some circumstances are excused, others aren't. But forget that now, just go. And don't forget David's asthma medicine."

"And what do I do when I get there?"

"Talk to him. Make sure he's the right Allan, and see if he remembers Doris. Then call me right away."

"But listen, what good will it do for her now to find out he's alive? That he's been alive all these years? She'll die unhappy. Isn't it better for her to believe that he passed away years ago?"

"It's not going to help, no matter what you say. Go now! I'm going to hang up on you."

"OK, I'm going, even though I still don't really understand. Just don't get your hopes up; it could be a different Allan."

"Yes, I know, but you don't need to understand right now. All I'm asking is for you to go. It's the right choice, trust me. I'm hanging up now. Sorry, but I really have to."

She ends the call before he has time to reply, switches the phone to silent, and drops it into her bag. Tyra is on the hallway floor, rifling through the things stored beneath the stroller. She has spread them out in a semicircle. A banana, a book, a couple of clean diapers, some poop-stained tights, rice cakes. Jenny quickly gathers everything and nods to some passers-by. Tyra staggers off down the corridor, and she hurries to catch her. The girl struggles as Jenny tries to put her into the stroller and pull on her coat and hat; she whimpers and cries.

"We're going home now. Home to eat. Shh."

But there is no silencing the scream; Tyra gasps for air between bouts of tears. Jenny leaves her to it. She has too much on her mind. She pushes the stroller quickly and hopes that the movement will calm the little one and quell that pang of shame that mothers feel when a child has a tantrum in public.

The Red Address Book
S. SMITH, ALLAN

They say that people never get over their first real love. That it builds a nest deep in their body memory. That's where Allan still lives. He may be a fallen soldier or a deceased retiree, but he still lives within me. Deep inside my wrinkled body. And when I go to my grave, I'll take him with me, hoping I'll find him up there in heaven. If I'd known where to find him here on earth, I would have followed him all my life. I'm convinced of that.

He said that his heart was French, his body American, and his mind a jumbled mix. That he was more Frenchman than American. His spoken French had a few rounded American vowels, and I used to laugh at his pronunciation as I danced through Paris by his side. That laugh took hold of my heart and became a symbol of happiness — a happiness I sadly never got to experience again. He carried within him a unique combination of acuity and playfulness. He was as thoughtful as he was lighthearted, as lively as he was serious.

He had studied to become an architect, so whenever I saw pictures of new buildings in magazines, I always read the texts carefully, searching for his name. I still do. It's silly. Nowadays I might be able to find him with the help of the Internet, but when I was younger, such a search would have been much harder. Maybe I didn't make enough of an effort. But I sent letters, masses of letters poste restante, despite having no idea where in the world he lived. I sent them to post offices in Manhattan, in Paris. He never replied. Instead, he became something of a ghost. I spoke to it at night. This memory in my locket. My one true love.

Gösta bought us a sofa in exchange for two of his paintings. A big, soft sofa with dark-purple velvet covers. We often sat in it in the evening, sharing a bottle of red wine and all our hopes and dreams. They were sprawling and many. They made us laugh and cry.

Gösta often asked me about men. He was both frank and uninhibited, so he asked plenty of intimate questions. He was the only one who knew about Allan, but he didn't understand me, thought I was crazy. He did everything he could to stop me from loving Allan from afar. To make me open my eyes to others. Men or women. It made no difference to Gösta.

"It's the person, Doris. The gender is not what's important. Attraction arises when related souls meet and recognize each other. Love doesn't care about gender, nor should people," he used to say.

The greatest comfort in life comes from freely expressing one's opinion and being met with nothing but love in return, even when opinions diverge. That was why it felt good to live with someone as tolerant as Gösta. We had everything. Only passion was missing. Once, he did actually try to kiss me. It made us both burst out laughing.

"No, that wasn't good," he said, grimacing. That was as close to romance as we came.

I didn't spend my entire life alone. Gösta was my family. And you, Jenny, you are my family. My everyday life was good and comfortable, it really was. Sadly, Allan remained out of reach, but I had a good life.

Often, while sitting here at home, I think of him. More and more, the older I get. I can't understand how a person can work his way into a person's life like Allan did. I would so dearly like to know where he went. Did he die there on the battlefield, or did he grow old? And if he grew old, what did he look like? Did his hair turn white or gray? Was he fat or thin? Did he ever get to construct those buildings he once dreamed of? Did he think of me? Did he feel passion with the woman he married, as he did with me? Did he love her the way he loved me?

A constant stream of questions flows through my mind. It will be that way until I die. Perhaps he and I will meet one day, in heaven. Perhaps I'll finally be able to relax in his arms. The dream of seeing him again makes believing in God worthwhile. Here's what I'd say to him:

Hello, God. It's my turn now. My turn to love and be loved.

33

So many sheets of paper in the pile. So many words. Maybe there are even more on the computer, the one on the bedside table in the hospital. Jenny leafs through the pages, chooses sections about the same person. Reads about Elaine and Agnes in order, about Mike and Gösta. Entire lives summed up in a few short lines.

So many memories. So many people now dead. What secrets did they take to the grave? She goes to fetch the address book and flips through it, curious about those not mentioned in Doris's stories. Who was Kerstin Larsson? On a notepad she finds next to the bed, she writes down the name in large letters. She'll ask tomorrow. How Kerstin died. What importance she had in Doris's life.

She follows the lines with her index finger. Her own name is there too. One of the few without an unsteady line drawn through it. But the address is wrong; it's her old house. Her student apartment, where she lived during that brief spell of trying to get an education. Before Willie. Before the kids. Was she happier then? She shivers, wraps herself in Doris's knitted cardigan. Maybe. She crosses out the address and carefully writes in the new one. Where her family lives, where happiness should live. Where it might be found.

It was Doris who paid for the creative writing course that she took. Six months of exercising her imagination and reading aloud in groups. Doing the writing itself was wonderful, but the readings were awful. She didn't handle criticism well. And then, suddenly, there was Willie. Strong, handsome, and safe. He made her forget all her dark thoughts, and they had so much fun together: surfing, cycling, playing tennis. And so she gave up, dropped out, and found a job as a waitress in a restaurant. What would have happened if he had never shown up, if she hadn't stopped writing? Doris still nags her about it. Asks her how it's going, as though it was obvious that she would be carrying on with it. The truth is, she hasn't written much at all since then.

Another truth: writing lies dormant within her, like a vague dream she can't quite catch hold of. She knows she can do it. She has the talent. Deep down, she knows that. But she is where she is. First of all, who would take care of the kids? Who would cook their meals and clean the house? And second, it's too daunting. Only one percent of all manuscripts submitted to publishers become books. One measly percent. The odds are against her. Why should her manuscript be the lucky one? What if she isn't talented enough? What if she fails?

Jenny brushes those thoughts away and pulls out her phone, scrolls to Willie's name among her most recent calls.

"Hey, love. How is it going, have you left yet?"

"No, we haven't left yet."

She sighs. "Please, Willie . . ."

"I'm going. I have a ticket for tomorrow morning. David is staying at Dylan's, and Jack can look after himself until I get back."

"Thank you." Relief in her voice, the tears welling up. "Oh, Willie, thank you!"

"I hope it's worth it." His voice is tense, blunt.

"What do you mean by that?"

"I understand what you're doing, but not why you want to subject her to it."

"But ... what don't you understand? She's dying. He was the love of her life. What is it that you don't understand? It's obvious, isn't it? Or have you never been in love?"

"My God, Jenny, don't be so dramatic. Of course I have. I love you, I hope you know that."

"OK."

"Good. Don't be sad. I'm helping you find Allan, I fly tomorrow."

"OK."

"I love you. I have to go now."

"OK. Bye."

She ends the call, wipes away a stubborn tear. Breathes in. Breathes out.

She racks her brain. It's fifteen years since they met. Back then, when they first fell in love, they would spend all day in bed. Make love ten times a day, until their skin was raw. That was love, wasn't it? But it had been so long now. She thinks about it. Maybe only once since Tyra was born. She's a mess down there now, after three kids, so maybe it isn't a good idea after all? It wouldn't be very nice for either of them.

She frowns.

Only once since Tyra was born?

That can't be true.

She crawls into bed and lies close to Tyra, right up against her. The way she used to lie next to Willie. Up close, with her nose to his neck. Tyra smells both sweet and sour. The hair at the nape of her neck is damp and curly. Like Willie's curls. He's a part of her.

She phones him back.

"Yeah?" he says brusquely.

"I love you too."

"I know. Of course, what we have is true love. I've never said any different."

"And we're still in love, aren't we?"

"Yes, of course we are."

"Good."

"Get some sleep now. Rest."

"OK. I will."

"I'll call you as soon as I know if it's the right Allan."

"Thanks!"

"I'm doing this for your sake. I'd do anything for you. Remember that."

"That's love."

"Yeah, that's what I'm saying."

34

A strong smell of urine hits her as she opens the door to Doris's room. Doris is lying on her side in bed, and the nurses are busy changing the sheets.

"They dropped the bag," Doris mouths, wrinkling her nose, bothered by the stench.

"You spilled pee in her bed?" Jenny hisses at the nurses.

"Yes, there was . . . it was an accident. We're just cleaning up."

"Isn't she going to have a shower?"

Doris's hair is flat again. Her pink dress is a damp heap on the floor. While she waits for the standard white hospital gown, her body is covered by a towel, which is far too small.

"According to the schedule, she's due for a shower tomorrow."

"But she's covered in piss!"

"We'll clean her up with wet wipes. If she has a shower, it takes more staff."

"I don't give a damn what it takes! If you spill urine on a patient, you'll just have to ignore the schedule!"

In embarrassed silence, the nurses start to clean Doris. Then one of them stops.

"Sorry. You're absolutely right, of course she should have a shower. Do you think you could help us?"

Jenny nods and pushes Tyra, who is sleeping in her stroller, over to the wall. Together, Jenny and the nurses lift Doris into a shower chair and then push her into the bathroom. Her head hangs; she doesn't have the energy to hold it upright. Jenny carefully washes her with soap.

"We'll fix your hair again."

"The old lady won't die ugly," Doris whispers.

"No, the old lady won't die ugly. I promise. Though you've never been ugly. You're the most beautiful person I know."

"Now you're lying." Doris sounds out of breath. When they lift her back into bed, she falls asleep right away. Jenny places a hand on her forehead.

"How is she?"

"Her pulse is weak. Her heart is still fighting, but it might not be able to manage for much longer. We're probably talking days now."

Jenny leans forward and rests her cheek against Doris's. The way she used to as a child while they sat on the sofa in New York. Suddenly, she's that little girl again. Rootless, insecure. And Doris is her life jacket, keeping her head above the surface.

"Please, you can't leave me," she whispers, kissing her forehead. Doris sleeps on, one rattling breath at a time. Tyra wakes up and starts whimpering. Jenny lifts her and holds her, but the girl squirms and Jenny lowers her to the floor. Jenny partly lies down on the bed next to Doris. Close, close. Deep breaths.

"You need to keep an eye on your daughter." A nurse comes into the room with Tyra in her arms. "Hospitals are full of dangerous things."

Jenny nods, flashes the nurse an apologetic look. Takes the girl and hands her a bag of candy. Tyra smacks her lips happily. Jenny puts her back into the stroller and fastens the belt around her.

"Sit there awhile, please. Sit there. I have to . . ."

"Is she causing trouble?" Doris whispers, barely audible.

"Hello, are you awake? How are you feeling? You fell asleep after your shower."

"I'm very tired."

"We don't need to talk if you don't feel up to it."

"I want to tell you. Everything I didn't have time to write down. And answer your questions."

"Oh, there are so many, I don't know where to begin. You've written so little about your years with Gösta."

"Twenty years."

"Yeah, you lived together for so long. Did he take care of you? Was he kind? Did you love him?"

"Yes, like a father."

"You must have been so sad when he died."

"Yes." Doris nods and closes her eyes. "It was almost like losing an arm."

"What happened, how did he die?"

"He just got old. He died a long time ago, in the sixties."

"When I was born?"

"Just before. When someone beloved dies, another is born."

"And you inherited all of his things?"

"Yes. His apartment, a bit of furniture, and his paintings. I sold the big ones over the years; they slowly became worth a lot of money. That's what I lived on all the years after his death. And I continued to write pieces for women's magazines here and there. Some of that money went to your mom."

"Those paintings sell for millions today."

"Just think, if Gösta had known."

"He would have been happy. Proud."

"I don't know, it was never money that motivated him. But he could have gone back to Paris if the paintings had started to sell sooner. We could have gone together."

"Would you have wanted that?"

"Yes."

"He probably knows he found success. Maybe he's an angel up there, and you'll get to see him soon." She picks up one of Doris's porcelain angels from the bedside table and holds it out to her.

"He was so afraid of dying. Back then, in those days, they said that homosexuals didn't get into heaven. He believed it."

"Was he religious?"

"Not publicly. But in private. Like all of us."

"If heaven exists, Gösta will be there waiting for you."

"We can have a party." Doris gasps for air as she tries to laugh.

"You're so wonderful. It's so good to hear your laugh. It keeps me going. It's always there, inside me. I can call it up whenever I need it."

"Marshmallow war."

"Yes, you remember!" Jenny laughs at the memory. "In the kitchen, with that table we didn't have room for. You, me, and Mom. We laughed so much. And ate. My stomach ached all evening."

"A bit of silliness does you good."

Jenny nods and strokes Doris's hair with her palm. The strands are as soft as a baby's.

"Let's make your hair nice again."

Doris falls asleep as Jenny winds her hair onto the rollers. Her breathing is heavy. Tyra has finished her candy but Jenny ignores her restlessness. She continues to comb and roll. Only when a nurse draws her attention to the crying child does she finally lift her into her arms.

35

The phone is ringing.

Jenny fumbles for it in the darkness. Tyra murmurs in her sleep.

"Hello?" she whispers sleepily, afraid that the call is from the hospital.

"Jenny, get online so we can Skype!"

"What?"

"I'm sitting here with Allan. He *is* the right one. He's old and sick, just like Doris. But he remembers her. He started to cry when I told him she was still alive."

Jenny sits bolt upright, her heart pounding and her ears ringing. Allan!

"You found him!"

"Yes! Are you with Doris? If not, go now!"

"It's the middle of the night, but I'll head over."

"Take a cab, hurry."

"OK, I'll call when we get there."

She leaps out of bed and runs to the bathroom. Splashes some cold water on her face, pulls on yesterday's clothes, and calls a taxi. Drops her laptop into the changing bag and wraps a blanket around Tyra. The girl mumbles as she is lifted into the stroller, but she doesn't wake. Not even while bouncing down the stairs on its back wheels. The taxi is waiting outside. She transfers Tyra into the car as the driver folds up the stroller and puts it in the trunk. They drive through the Stockholm night without speaking. Old love songs are playing on the radio. "Purple Rain" — she knows the words by heart and smiles at the memories. There was a time when she and Willie still slow-danced in the kitchen, and he would hum the song in her ear. Close together, his erection pressing against her. Before the kids, before everyday life. When she gets home, she'll play it for him. And they'll dance.

"Is the little one sick?" The driver speaks up as he turns off the main road.

"No, we're visiting someone. Could you just pull up by the main entrance?"

He nods and brakes gently. By the time she climbs out of the car with Tyra in her arms, he has already taken the stroller out and unfolded it. He nods to her.

"Hope everything is OK."

She thanks him quickly, but she is too stressed to smile.

When Jenny runs into the room, Doris is awake, her eyes clear and her face not quite so pale as it was earlier. Thankfully, Jenny didn't encounter any nurses on the way in.

"You're awake!" Jenny whispers so as not to wake the other patients.

"Yes." Doris gives her a broad smile.

"I have a surprise for you. We need to get you into your dress and move you into the corridor." She releases the brake and rolls the bed toward the door. A nurse appears, her eyes wild.

"What do you think you're doing?"

Jenny shushes her and continues to move the bed. The nurse follows, obviously agitated.

"What are you doing? You can't just . . . Do you know what time it is?"

"Just let us stay here for a bit. It's important. And no, it really can't wait. I know the others are sleeping; this way, we won't wake them."

She pushes the bed into a corner of the day room and flashes the nurse a rushed smile. The nurse shakes her head and turns on her heel without a word. Jenny pulls the dress out of the changing bag. It's still slightly damp from Jenny's hand-washing.

"What are we doing, Jenny? Are we going to a party?"

Jenny laughs. "It's a surprise, I told you. But yes, you could say that."

She gently combs through Doris's hair and powders her cheeks with a little blush.

"Lipstick too." Doris purses her lips.

Jenny mixes pink and beige until she finds a shade she knows Doris will like, and then she paints the lipstick onto the dry, thin lips. She sits on the edge of the bed with the laptop on her knee. She can't hold back any longer.

"Dossi, he's alive!"

"What? Who's alive? What are you talking about?"

"We have, or Willie has . . . we've found Allan."

Doris startles, and stares at Jenny. "Allan!" She sounds terrified.

"He wants to see you, to talk to you on Skype. Willie is with him now. I just need to call them." She opens the silver lid of the laptop.

"No! He can't see me like this." Doris's eyes dart nervously, her cheeks flushing. Apparently the blusher was unnecessary.

"He's old too, and dying. This is your last chance. You have to be brave and take it."

"But what if . . ."

"What if what?"

"What if he isn't how I remember him? What if I'm disappointed? Or what if he is?"

"There's only one way to find out. Take the risk. I'm going to call them now."

Doris pulls the blanket up to her chin. Jenny pulls it back down.

"You look beautiful. Trust me."

She clicks Willie's name and the program calls him. He answers immediately.

"Jenny, Doris, hello." Willie grins and waves. The dark circles beneath his eyes reveal how little sleep he has had lately. "Are you ready?"

Jenny nods. Willie turns the computer screen to face a man sitting in a dark-brown armchair. Doris gazes at the screen. His hands are clasped in his lap. His feet rest on a footstool, and a red blanket covers his legs. His face is furrowed, his cheeks sunken. His jacket hangs unevenly on his thin shoulders. Just like it used to in Paris. His shirt is buttoned to the top, and the skin of his neck hangs loosely over the collar. He smiles and waves a gnarled hand, squints toward the screen. Willie leans forward.

"Turn on the camera, Jenny," he says, placing the laptop on the old man's knee.

Jenny glances up at Doris. She is staring straight into Allan's eyes, her mouth half-open. When Jenny asks if she is ready, she nods eagerly.

Allan gives a start when he catches sight of the slender woman in the hospital bed.

"Oh, Doris," he gasps, his voice sorrowful. He reaches out with a trembling hand, as if to touch her.

They sit in silence for a while. Jenny nods impatiently off-screen and gestures to Doris, to talk. Allan breaks the silence.

"I never forgot you, Doris." Tears are rolling down his cheeks.

Doris reaches for the locket Jenny has hung around her neck. She tries to open it, but her fingers are too weak. Jenny helps her, and Doris holds the picture out to Allan. He squints to see and then laughs loudly.

"Paris," he mumbles.

"Those few months were the best of my life." Doris whispers these words to him, and her eyes well up. "I never forgot you either."

"You're still so incredibly beautiful."

"The best months of my life. You —" Her voice breaks. Her eyes lose focus and roll. Jenny places a hand on her wrist to check the pulse. It's weak.

"I searched for you," she manages to whisper.

"I searched for you too. I wrote."

"What happened? Where were you?"

"I stayed in Paris after the war. For years."

Doris wipes her eyes. "And your wife?"

"She died in childbirth. The child too. I eventually remarried, after many years. I looked everywhere for you, I traveled to New York, I wrote letters. Eventually, there was nowhere left to look. Where did you go, where have you been all these years?"

"I left New York for you, traveled to Europe. I was planning to come to Paris, but France was still at war when I arrived, times were difficult. Eventually, I ended up in Sweden, in Stockholm."

"I never stopped thinking about you. About our dinners, our walks . . . the car trip to Provence."

Doris is silent, smiling fondly at the memories. Jenny sees the joy on the old woman's face. Her eyes have suddenly come to life. Doris blows an unsteady kiss to Allan and continues:

"That night beneath the stars, do you remember it? That wonderful night!"

"When I kidnapped you from the fashion show."

"Ah, you really didn't. You waited patiently until I was finished; you were asleep on the grass outside the castle. Do you remember? I woke you with a kiss."

"I remember. I remember every single step I took with you. It was the time of my life."

Doris's voice weakens again, sounding sad. "You broke my heart in New York. Why did you do that, if you loved me so much?"

"I had no other choice, my love. You were the reason I went to Europe."

"What do you mean? You said you were going because of the war. You left me behind!"

"I ran. I couldn't look my wife in the eye once I knew you were in the same city. I couldn't stop thinking of you. Leaving you both was my way of escaping."

They look at each other in silence. In the background, they hear Willie clear his throat. Jenny leans forward to see whether he is on-screen, but it's still just Allan. She pulls out her phone and sends a single red heart to Willie.

"And you're still alive. I can't believe it." Doris lifts her fingers to the screen. He raises his hand to meet them.

"Oh, my love," he mumbles.

"You're so far away, why are you so far away?" Doris sniffs. "I wish I could be in your arms one last time. That you could hold me. Kiss me."

"I can't believe you've had my picture in your locket all these years. If only I'd known . . . We could have . . . We should have . . . Oh, Doris . . . All the children we were going to have. The life we were going to live together." His head slumps into his hands, but he forces it up again. Tries to smile through his tears, his fingers still covering his face. "We'll meet in heaven, my love. I'll take care of you there. I love you, Doris. I've loved you every day since I first saw you. It's always been us, in my heart it's always been us."

Allan's words echo down the deserted corridor. Doris's head is resting on the pillow, and she is struggling to keep her eyes open. She tries to talk, but makes half-stifled sounds.

Behind the screen, Jenny dries her tears. She leans over to the computer camera.

"Hello, Allan. I'm sorry, she's so weak, I don't think she can manage much more."

"I can manage." Doris finds her voice.

"You sleep, my love. I'll stay here and watch you sleep. You're still so beautiful. Just as beautiful as I remember. The most beautiful."

"And you're the same as ever, full of big words." Doris smiles wearily.

"When it comes to you, there are no words big enough. Nothing could be more beautiful than you. Never has been."

"I've always loved you, Allan. Always. Every hour, every day, every year. It's always been us."

"And I've always loved you. And always will."

Doris sighs, and as she drifts off to sleep, the smile remains on her lips. Allan watches her in silence. Tears are running down his cheeks. He no longer wipes them away.

Jenny comes back into the picture. "I'm sure you'll be able to talk again tomorrow."

"No, no, please, don't turn it off. I'm begging you. I need to look at her a little while longer."

Jenny smiles, tries to remain composed. "I'll leave the computer on; you can turn it off yourself whenever you like. I understand. I understand."

36

She studies Doris and glances at Allan on the screen. He is sitting in his chair with his eyes closed; he'll soon be asleep too. Her phone buzzes in her pocket. Her heart swells when she sees Willie's face on the screen.

"I understand," he says warmly. "I really do understand now."

"Yeah . . . love. I wanted to give Doris this, I didn't want to let her die with an unhappy love in her heart."

"I know, I understand. And listen, I love you. You're fantastic; you always understand this kind of thing. I'm so grateful I didn't lose you. That I get to live my life with you. Sorry I'm such an idiot sometimes."

"Glad you can admit it."

"What, that I'm an idiot or that I love you?"

"Both." She laughs.

"I wish you were here now, so I could hold you. For a long time. I know this must be so hard for you. I'm sorry, again. I didn't mean to be so insensitive."

"I know. I wish you were here too. That you could say goodbye to her."

Doris moans and Jenny whispers, "I have to go, I love you, bye." Allan seems to be sleeping, and she closes the lid of the computer to avoid waking him. Then she sits on the edge of the bed, placing her hand on Doris's forehead. The skin is cool, but it also feels damp. Doris's eyes open and start to wander; it seems she can't focus. Jenny rushes off to fetch the nurse.

"Allan," Doris shouts. "Allan!"

A nurse comes running, pulls down the neck of Doris's dress, and listens to her heart.

"Her heart doesn't sound good. I'll call for a doctor."

"We rang an old friend of hers. Maybe I shouldn't have done it, not right now, in the middle of the night."

Jenny is crying. She's shaking.

"She's going to go no matter what you do, sweetie. She's old." The nurse steps over to Jenny, puts an arm around her, and strokes her back to comfort her.

"Doris! Doris, please wake up! Please, talk to me . . ."

Doris struggles, but just one eye opens. She meets Jenny's gaze. Her lips are pale blue.

"I . . . wish you . . . enough . . . ," she whispers, sounding exhausted, then closes her eye.

"Enough sun to light up your days, enough rain that you appreciate the sun. Enough joy to strengthen your soul, enough pain that you can appreciate life's small moments of happiness, enough meetings that you can . . . say a farewell . . ." With trembling lips, she fills in the words she has heard Doris say so often.

The rattling breaths alter. A deep clearing of the throat makes Jenny and the nurse jump. Doris's eyelids snap open and she stares at Jenny with clear eyes.

Then she is gone.

37

With tears streaming down her cheeks, Jenny takes out a pen and draws a thin, shaky line through the name on the inside of the cover. Doris Alm. Next to it, she writes the word Doris herself had written so many times. DEAD. She writes it twice, three times, four times. Eventually, she fills the entire cover.

On the table before her are Doris's belongings from the hospital. A few pieces of jewelry. The locket. The pink dress. The clothes she was wearing when she was admitted, an old dark-blue tunic and gray wool trousers, which have been cut open. A handbag containing her purse and cell phone, which is still turned on. Her laptop. What should she do with it all? She can't throw anything away. The apartment has to stay as it is. For a while, at least. She glances around and runs her hand over the rough surface of the table, the same table Doris has always had. Nothing has changed in this apartment.

Suddenly, she remembers what Doris wrote about the letters. There must be more boxes than the two she has found so far. She runs to the bedroom and gets down onto all fours by the bed. There, in the back corner, she can see a rusty tin box. She pulls it out and blows away the thick dust, opens it, and gasps. So many letters. She'll read them tonight.

In the kitchen, Tyra is banging pots and pans, laughing at the noise. Jenny leaves her to it, sitting with her back to her, so the child doesn't have to see her mother crying. The poor girl hasn't had much attention over these past couple of days, but she won't remember. Luckily, she's too small to understand.

Jenny is tired. A night and a day have passed without sleep, and now that evening is approaching, her skin feels tight, her eyes tired. She rubs her face, rests her head in her hands. The small child within her has lost its one source of comfort. She doesn't want to be a mother. Doesn't want to be an adult. Just wants to lie in the fetal position and cry until she runs out of tears, until Doris comes back and holds her. She can feel sniffles turning into sobs that she can't hold back.

"Mommy sad." Tyra pats her firmly on the leg and pulls at her top. Jenny picks her up and holds her tight. The girl's chunky arms wrap around her neck.

"Mmm, Mommy misses Dossi so much, baby," she whispers, kissing her on the cheek.

"Hoppital," Tyra says, wanting to get back on the floor. She runs over to her stroller, but Jenny shakes her head.

"No, not now, Tyra, play with this for a while." She holds out her phone. "We won't be going there anymore," she whispers to herself.

She opens the lid of Doris's laptop, presses the power button, and watches the icons appear on the desktop. There are two folders. One is called *Jenny,* the other *Notes.* She clicks on *Jenny* and goes through the documents. She has already read most of them; they're the printed pages she's been reading, but inside that folder is another one, called *Dead.* The word makes her shudder. She pauses for a moment and then clicks on it. There are two documents inside. One is Doris's will. It's short. She has written that eve-rything goes to Jenny, and that she has stuck a printed and attested copy beneath the desk. Doris wants red roses on her coffin, and she wants jazz rather than hymns. And then there is a short message:

> *Don't be afraid of life, Jenny. Live. Help yourself. Laugh. Life isn't here to entertain you; you have to entertain life. Seize op-portunities whenever they come along, and make something good out of them.*
>
> *I love you most of all and have always, never forget that. My darling Jenny.*

Then, a little lower down:

> *P.S. Write! It's your talent. Talents should be used.*

Jenny smiles through her tears. In truth, writing was Doris's tal-ent, she knows that now, having read through her memories. Writ-ing was Doris's dream. But it was also Jenny's. She finally admits that to herself. She opens the second document and slowly starts to read. Word after word. Doris's last echo.

The Red Address Book
N. ~~NILSSON, GÖSTA~~ DEAD

Almost everyone is dead now. Everyone whose life I have mentioned to you. Everyone who ever meant anything. Gösta passed away in bed, with me sitting by his side. I held his hand in mine. It was warm, and then it grew colder and colder. I didn't let go until I knew that all the life had run out of him, leaving only a shell behind. It was old age that killed him. He was the second great love of my life. A platonic love. A friend I could lean on. The man who saw the child in me while I lived with Dominique, and who continued to see the child in me even as my hair turned white.

I'm going to tell you Gösta's secret now. I promised him I wouldn't say a thing while he was still living, and I kept my word. But I don't want to take any secrets to the grave, so I'll pass them on to you for safekeeping.

My apartment has a hidden room. It's two meters by two meters, behind the closet in the maid's room. You can get into it by moving the skirting board at the very back.

There, Gösta hid his paintings of Paris, his very own treasure-trove. They remain there to this day. Beautiful paintings of the place he held most dear. Paris was Gösta's city.

Those paintings are now yours. If you want to put them on show for the world to see, do it in a museum in Paris. That would have made him proud.

The Red Address Book
A. ~~ANDERSSON, ELISE~~ DEAD

Now for the very last chapter. Your mother. Her fate has haunted you for as long as you can remember. Nothing I can write will change your image of a mother who tried, time and time again, but always failed. Nothing I can write will rewind the tape and make the needle she stuck into her arm drop to the ground and break.

But I can unburden my heart. Tell you what I have never dared say out loud. What has tortured me all these years. I hope I'm dead when you read this. And if I'm not, I beg you to let this story stand and become the only version. I won't be able to answer if you ask me any questions, wanting to know more.

It was my fault. I abandoned Elise when she needed me most. Not once, but several times. It began when I walked out of that house and left a crying baby with her sickly, elderly grandmother. When I left for France. For Allan. Elise was crying when I left, but I just closed the door behind me, preoccupied with myself and my hopes for future happiness. You've always seen me as someone who gets involved, who cares, and who helps. But that wasn't the case back then. All I could think about was my own situation, my own future. And with my mind full of those thoughts, my future became more important than Elise's. Every time Carl, your uncle, wrote and pleaded for me to come back, I threw his letters in the wastebasket. I sent her presents on her birthday, but that was all. An expensive teddy bear or a pretty dress, as if gifts could make up for my absence.

The drugs were never the real problem. It was her start in life. It made her insecure. And that insecurity made her susceptible to drugs; they helped her flee from her fears. If it hadn't been for that, she would have been a better mother.

I often tried to talk to her. Tried to make her leave the past behind. To see the goodness in life. But she just shook her head. She once told me that she felt happy only when she was high. That the drugs made her float above her problems, which vanished beneath her.

When Carl called to say that you had been born, I returned to New York for my first visit. Gösta had recently died, and I was alone. It was love at first sight. I sat with your foot in my hand and just looked at you. Then I returned when you were one, when you were four, five, six, and every year after that until you started college.

I lost a child once. A child I didn't want, who I never even thought of as a child. But emptiness followed that loss, just the same. You filled it. You became my everything, and it was so easy to love you. You gave me a chance to compensate for everything, and I promised myself that I would let nothing bad happen to you. That you would get the support you needed to live your life. Because it is hard, Jenny. Life is hard.

Promise me that you won't blame your dead mother anymore. I'm sure that Elise loved you. Forgive her. I should have been there for her the way I was for you. But I couldn't. It was my fault. Forgive me.

Epilogue

They are sitting on the floor in Jenny's kitchen, sorting the envelopes by postmark date. They slice open the ones that are sealed. Mary, Allan's great-niece, is sitting next to Jenny. She had called to say that Allan was dead. He died less than forty-eight hours after Doris. And Mary too had found letters.

The envelopes have two things in common. All have the words *Address Unknown* stamped over the name, and all have been returned to the sender.

7 November 1944
Poste restante Allan Smith, Paris

Darling Allan,

Worries about how you are eat away at me. Not a day passes without thinking of you. I search for your face in the news reports, study soldier after soldier. I hope you managed to leave Paris unscathed and that you are back in New York. I am in Sweden now, in Stockholm.

Your Doris

20 May 1945
Poste restante Doris Alm, New York

*Doris, I am alive. The war is finally over, and I think of you
every day. Where are you? I wonder how life is for you and
your sister, whether you are well? Write to me. I will stay here,
in Paris. If you are reading this, come back.*
    Your Allan

30 August 1945
Poste restante Doris Alm, New York

Dear Doris,
    *It is my great hope that you will one day set foot in the
Grand Central Post Office and read my words. I can feel that
you are alive, you are there in my thoughts. I want to be reunited with you. I am still in Paris.*
    Your Allan

15 June 1946
Poste restante Allan Smith, New York

*Sometimes I wonder whether you exist only in my dreams. I
think of you at least once a day. Please, dear Allan, give me a
sign. Just one line. I am still in Stockholm. I love you.*
    Your Doris

On it goes: 1946, 1947, 1950, 1953, 1955, 1960, 1970 . . . Short
messages bouncing back and forth, passing the other by. If only . . .
what if . . .
    Jenny and Mary smile at each other.
    "Incredible. They loved each other their entire lives."

Love rests beneath every headstone. So much love.
Glances that throw an entire life out of balance.
Entwined hands on a park bench.
A parent's gaze at a newborn child.
A friendship so strong that no passion is required.
Two bodies, coming together as one, time and time again.
Love.
It's just one word, but it holds so much.
In the end, all that matters is love.

Did you love enough?